IT'S A COLD GAME II:

By
William Travis III ©2024

But I'm All In

WT3 Publishing LLC.

3400 Cottage Way

Suite G2

Sacramento Ca 95825

Visit our website at: WT3publishing.com

Instagram: @williamtravisthe3

X: @williamtravist3

ISBN: 978-969-589-237-4

eISBN: 978-969-589-238-1

Prologue

— • • • —

Texas Hold 'em Back

The Whole Cards

We often hear the famous adage, 'I am just playing the cards I was dealt.' But have you ever taken the time to consider who the dealer is or why you are constantly receiving a losing hand? Well, that answer varies depending on your geographic location, race, and social status. For instance, if you are a descendant of enslaved people, then for centuries, the dealer has purposely skipped your lineage when it was time to deal. Could you imagine playing a poker game where every time it was your turn to receive a card, the dealer bypassed you only to distribute your card to your opponent? Then, once you fight for your right to be dealt into the game, the dealer blatantly deals your cards from a loaded deck. Sadly, this allegory reflects the experience of the over 40+ million

African Americans living in the United States. Why? Because after slavery was abolished, the enslaved people were then left with nowhere safe to eat, sleep, or shit. Therefore, many became sharecroppers to purchase land from the slavers, who were incapable of doing the labor themselves. The slavers often loaned the property at a price they knew the sharecroppers couldn't afford to repay in three lifetimes. This practice created a system to impose generational debt, denying African Americans the opportunity to build generational wealth.

The Flop

Through perseverance and determination, African Americans lifted themselves by their bootstraps and created successful business practices. However, in 1921, the U.S. government sanctioned the massacre of a prosperous working-class black community in Tulsa, Oklahoma. The residents were attacked and slaughtered by a mob of citizens, while their businesses were fire-bombed by airplanes and cocktails. This single event led to the loss of billions in generational wealth due to stolen opportunities for property acquisition and long-term investments. Since the intent was to perpetually harm an entire lineage of African American people, this remains one of the most egregious forms of structural violence in American history.

The River

In 1929, The Great Depression began. On October 29, 1929, Black Tuesday marked the turn of events. There was widespread unemployment, and the stock market crashed. As a result, the financial markets and banks collapsed. After the crash of 1929, the government dealt financial bailouts to many affected citizens while excluding African Americans. These bailouts gave rise to widespread home loans and housing programs like Section 8, which systematically disenfranchised African Americans. Furthermore, most African Americans were excluded from receiving these financial bailouts. The practice of redlining, which prevented African Americans from receiving home loans based on their race, was prevalent across the United States. This practice was specifically designed to prevent black residents from owning their homes. As a result, instead of gaining an asset to pass down, African Americans were forced to rent homes, indirectly paying the mortgages of their white landlords. This allowed their counterparts to have their mortgages paid while retaining the ability to invest their earnings elsewhere.

The Turn

It came with a twist once the African Americans finally gained access to the same governmental assistance as their counterparts. Because Section 8 and Housing Authority apartments were densely populated with low-income families, these communities were easily targeted. The government funneled cocaine, heroin, and other addictive substances into these areas with impunity. They mass-incarcerated African American men while leaving African American women dependent on government assistance. Sadly, since the men weren't depleting quickly enough, high-capacity firearms were funneled in from overseas. This well-designed plan created the need to protect one's drugs from those desperate enough to kill for it. To make matters worse, law enforcement was directed to arrest anyone in possession of such drugs to ensure mass incarceration. The combination of poverty, drug abuse, and years of structural violence eventually gave rise to gang culture and a widespread loss of self-worth.

The Fold

Considering the current state of Black America, many of its citizens have decided to fold their hands instead of truly playing the cards they were dealt. Playing the cards you are dealt means fighting adversity without victimizing others. Playing the cards you are dealt means you prevail, even with all the cards stacked against you. Playing the cards means you oppose the system of oppression by assisting those who are also oppressed out of their state of oppression. Playing the cards you are dealt means you parent your children to the best of your ability, regardless of whether the pregnancy was planned, especially since unprotected sex is logically the first step in planning a pregnancy. Playing the cards you are dealt means you avoid incarceration, understanding the emotional, financial, and psychological strain it places on your family. Playing the cards you are dealt means you support your spouse and try with everything in your power to avoid adding stress to their already complicated life. Playing the cards means you are present in your child's development into adulthood because nothing in American history gave you a reason to trust the system. Playing the cards you are dealt means you realize less than three percent of college athletes make it into the league; therefore, you inspire your child to pursue a career that serves and uplifts the oppressed. This includes professions such as doctors, lawyers, scientists, or politicians. Playing the cards means you realize a celebrity is not a capable leader because their obligation lies with shareholders, not the oppressed. Who cares if an athlete has a sports camp when the children A to return to tumultuous living conditions at home? Playing the cards you are dealt means you fight for your opportunity to serve on the jury panel since that is where the modern-day lynching occurs. If you have ceased fighting for the rights of the oppressed, then you have undoubtedly folded your hand. The only question is, who is the dealer?

CHAPTER ONE

Banks desperately banged on Johnny's screen door until he heard the innocent giggles of his daughters.

Alisha called out, "Daddy's here!"

"Alisha?" Banks replied.

Oddly, there was no response. He put his left ear to the screen door and covered his right ear to drown out the children playing in the next-door neighbor's yard. There was nothing but complete silence on the other side of the door. He then stepped back and realized his mind was playing tricks on him. He realized that hearing his daughter's voice was just a figment of his imagination.

"Banks! Banks! What's wrong?" asked Lil' Chris from the sidewalk.

Snapping out of his trance, Banks replied, "Nothing! They're not here. And the next time I tell you to stay in the car, you'd better listen. Now, let's go!"

"Let's go where?" Lil' Chris asked as they got back into the car.

"To Erica's house. I'm praying they're there. Now put your seat belt on, and be quiet so I can try to piece this shit together."

Banks drove down Havenscourt, turning right onto East 14th Street. He made a quick left, then a right, pulling into the 65th Village housing project.

Banks left his car running while he bounced out and ran into Erica's apartment complex. He hadn't been to Erica's apartment since the last time he snuck over to avoid being seen by her badass kids. He was certain they would've told Tonya if they had seen him there, so he had to creep. He never would've dreamed that his late-night lustful escapades could have led to such a tragic ending. What made matters worse was knowing he was reaping what he had sown. He pounded on her door with a closed fist. He wanted to ensure anyone inside knew he was there. Finally, after hearing him repeatedly knock for four minutes, Erica's nosy-ass neighbor, Zakia, stepped out of her apartment.

Zakia said, "This the first time I've seen you in the light of day. I thought you were a damn vampire, witcha fine self. Erica isn't here, though. She rushed up out of here in a hurry. She said she was headed up to Highland Hospital—something about Tonya being in some kind of accident or somethin'."

"Was she by herself?" Banks asked, hoping she said no.

"Nuh-uh. She had four little delinquents with her. Why, DeMarcus—he's yours, huh?"

"What? Nah, man."

"Shoot, the timeline fit."

"What? Anyways, did she have a set of twins with her?"

"As a matter of fact, she did. But them Tonya kids. Why are you worried about them? Ooooh, I get it. I heard them talking about how their daddy just got out of jail. So that's why you stopped the late-night creeping for so long. Now that's some real soap opera shit right there. You got kids by Erica and her cousin Tonya. Ta'Ronda ain't gon' believe this one here."

Banks said, "Hey, whatever, lady," and pulled out a one-hundred-dollar bill.

"You got a phone?" he asked.

Motivated by the money, she replied, "I sure do," before pulling one from her robe pocket and handing it to him.

He accepted the phone, dialed his number, and saved it in her phone.

He showed her his number and said, "This my number. Have Erica call me if she shows back up a'ight?"

Zakia quickly snatched the one-hundred dollar bill from Banks' hand before tucking it into her bra.

"Don't trip, I gotchu, baby daddy," she replied in an attempt at being sexy.

What she didn't know was she was fifteen years too late. But that was the irony when it came to dope fiends. They never realized that the crack diminished all sex appeal. Yet, despite missing teeth and all, they still believed they had it.

Banks was weaving through traffic on the 580 freeway like he was racing against time. Getting pulled over was the least of his worries. Meanwhile, Lil' Chris gripped onto his seat belt with protruding eyes. He was paralyzed by the adrenaline rush caused by Banks' menacing driving. Yet he chose not to complain since he didn't know Banks enough to test his patience. The only thing he knew about him was that he had just gotten out of prison. And that was where all of the killers and people who didn't play that shit went. Lil' Chris was relieved when Banks merged into the slow lane because it meant they were about to exit the freeway onto Fourteenth Avenue. To Lil' Chris, it felt like it took them forever to get there. Nonetheless, they had finally arrived at Highland Hospital. It was through the grace of God, they made it in one piece. Banks hurried and ushered Lil' Chris out of the car after he double parked and flicked on his hazard lights. Banks approached the hospital with only one thing on his mind: finding his daughters, wherever they may be. They entered the hospital through the emergency room's entrance. Then, they headed through a set of double doors that led to a corridor connecting the emergency room to the waiting room.

Banks heard Alisha cry aloud, "Daddy," and clear this time. He knew his mind wasn't playing tricks when he whipped his head around and spotted her sprinting from the vending machine. She jumped up, wrapping her arms and legs around him, suspending herself off the ground.

"Daddy!" Falisha yelled.

Banks quickly turned his head toward the loud tapping sound Falisha's shoes made as she approached him. She was smiling, filled with utter excitement. Seeing them brought a level of joy he had never felt before. Everything and everyone else in the room had temporarily disappeared. It was only him and his two precious angels, reunited at last. When Falisha reached them, she aggressively nudged Alisha, causing her to let him go.

"Move so I can hug him too," Falisha demanded.

Banks knelt and kissed them back and forth to equally show his affection.

"Are y'all alright?" he asked.

Concerned with their well-being, he examined their faces to see if they had any fresh marks or bruises.

"We're okay, Daddy," Alisha replied.

"But mommy's hurt really bad," Falisha added.

"How bad?" Banks asked, feeling regretful.

"Bad enough," said Erica as she approached Banks from his blindside.

Banks stood up and locked eyes with her as the tension built between them. Banks wondered if Erica had thrown him under the bus to save face with Tonya. Or simply because she was jealous of what they had at the time. I mean, why else would they still be cool after everything that was said and done? He knew he didn't snitch on himself. So it had to have been her loose-lipped ass.

Banks said, "Ay, y'all girls go on over there and eat y'all snacks. I need to talk to Erica for a hot second. It won't take long, I promise. A'ight?"

They both put their heads down and sadly returned to where they were previously seated.

"What's wrong with Lil' Chris?" Erica asked softly.

Banks replied, "Look, I haven't told the girls yet, but my mama and CJ were shot early this morning. Unfortunately, CJ didn't make it. I don't know any of the details yet, either. But one of the cops said they rushed my mother up here. I need to find her so I can find out what the hell happened."

"I do remember hearing them saying something about a female with multiple gunshot wounds needing to be prepped for surgery. I think they wanted to use the same surgeon that worked on Tonya because I kept hearing them paging Dr. Yu all morning."

"Surgeon? What kind of accident was Tonya in?"

"You might not believe this, but she got blown up."

"Blown up?" Banks repeated, acting surprised.

He could've won an Oscar for his performance. Knowing he was the one who caused the damn explosion in the first place.

Erica said, "Yeah, man. It was because of that crazy-ass nigga she was fucking wit. She got caught up in the crossfire of some of his bullshit. Somebody blew up his car trying to kill him. She just happened to be with his ass when it exploded. Now she's all fucked up."

Banks asked, "So what are her chances of survival lookin' like?"

"We'll, she's recovering. They said she was severely burned, but she is in stable condition now. The doctor said they had to remove glass particles from her face to avoid any possible infections."

"So I take it she won't be trying out for any beauty pageants anytime soon, huh?"

"What?" Erica replied with her nose scrunched up at him.

It was clear that she did not appreciate his distasteful platitude.

He said, "Nothing. So this Johnny dude, he dead?"

"As a doorknob. They said he was burned to a crisp. You didn't have anything to do with this, did you? 'Cause she told me y'all had words."

"Hell nah, I didn't have anything to do with that. So don't be repeating no crazy shit like that to nobody else, especially to no law enforcement. Ya hear me?"

"I know. I ain't stupid."

"Now, you keep saying they told you. Who are they?"

"The homicide detectives. They left me a card and told me to contact them if I remembered anything. Wanna see?"

"Hell nah. I ain't got shit to say to them. The baby daddy is always the first suspect. But I do need you to watch the kids while I go find out what hospital room my mom's in."

"Okay, I could do that for you."

"A'ight, I gotta make a few phone calls first, though."

He then pulled out his cell phone and began dialing as he walked away.

CHAPTER TWO

• • •

Face pulled up at the spot on 106th and Walnut, where he was supposed to meet Sincere after the drop-off. He had called Sincere's phone multiple times on the way over, trying to figure out why Sincere had deviated from their original plan. A plan that Sincere had explicitly come up with himself. They had agreed to meet at the trap house on 106th, but for some reason, Sincere kept it lit instead of exiting the freeway behind him. He was getting fed up with Sincere's pattern of not sticking to the script while making it clear he felt obligated to. He tried to call Sincere's phone one last time for good measure, but he received his voicemail like the previous few attempts.

Donnie yelled, "Ay, Face! Check it out, blood," from behind a black spiked metal gate.

Face held up a finger in response, indicating he would be there in a second. He rolled up the windows, cut the engine, and grabbed his .40-caliber pistol from the glove compartment. Next, he opened the door, stood up, and hid his pistol in his lower back for quick access. After closing the door, he adjusted his shades and straightened his shirt before heading for the black gate. Out of respect for Face, Donnie held the gate open until he safely entered the yard. He then monitored the street with his hand on his pistol in case Sav's goons were creeping.

Donnie said, "Wassup, blood? You heard the news yet?"

Face replied, "What news?"

"Walk wit me. Ay, y'all fools, keep watch while we talk business, a'ight?"

"A'ight," one of the two gunners standing on the porch replied.

"Wassup wit y'all killas?" Face asked as he walked up the stairs.

"Shit, just holdin' it down," replied the other gunner.

Face briefly glanced down and saw an AR-15 leaning against the wooden couch they sat on.

Face said, "Good. I wish all my soldiers were this disciplined. If they were, Sav's bitch ass would've been six feet under by now."

"Oh, don't trip. We're gonna fire his ass up if he slides through here wit that fuck shit," said Donnie.

"Off top," one of his soldiers replied.

As soon as they entered the trap house, Face smelled the pungent aroma of dog food—AKA heroin—lingering in the air. There were four youngstas posted in the living room bagging up dope. Face said "Wassup" to the youngster standing at the front of the window, holding a Mack-11. He knew he couldn't have been any older than eighteen years of age. When they reached the kitchen, two big booty hoodrats from 102nd were smoking a blunt of Jupiter and sipping on some Hennessy XO. Their names were Venus and Reina. They were known in the hood for boosting and sliding hot credit cards at high-end department stores. But every now and then, they would slide up under some ballers and get them to trick their money off for some ass.

Donnie said, "Ay, y'all get up out of here. We gotta talk business."

"Okay," Reina replied before hurrying out of their way.

Reina whispered to Venus on their way out, "That's Face."

Once the hoodrats left the kitchen, Face gave Donnie a quizzical look, waiting for an explanation.

"What was that all about?" Face asked.

"Oh, them bitches? I've learned over the years that keeping some in-house pussy keeps my soldiers on point. It's like they got something to prove or somethin'."

"Well shit, if that's the key to making your quota every day, be my guest. Now, what did you need to holla at me about?"

"Oh yeah! That boy Reiko—he's dead, blood."

"What? Where you hear that shit at?"

"Man, that shit was all over the news. The spokesman said the cops responded to reports of shots fired. When they arrived at the scene, the house was engulfed in flames. They say they recovered a body, but they haven't identified it yet."

"So, how do you know it's Reiko then?" Face asked argumentatively. "It could be anybody."

"Well, who else could it be? That fool lived alone."

"I know. But that fool was supposed to have been out of town handling some business for me. Have you heard anything from Cell-Bo or Tyson in the last few days?"

"Nah, I ain't heard shit from Cell-Bo, and I don't fuck wit that shady-ass nigga Tyson. I almost smoked him on Two-Four and Mead leaving Jimmy's one night. He was on some drunk shit."

"What about Sincere? Have you heard anything from him? He was supposed to meet me over here."

"Nuh-uh, he don't too much hang out around these parts now that the heat done turned up."

"What's that supposed to mean?"

"Nothin'. It's just the streets talkin' like Sav got Sincere scared to show his face in the hood now. I mean, if Sav was hittin' your trap houses, would you be ducked off in a mansion wit some hoes? Or slidin' through every block in The Town until you found him?"

"Muthafucka, these are my trap houses. And we're working an angle to dead that nigga. Slidin' through every block in The Town ain't gon' do shit but get us arrested. We're already under investigation."

Face thought about informing Donnie about his recent encounter with Detective Jones but decided the less he knew, the better, since niggas tend to gossip like hoes.

Face said, "You just worry about running the spot. Leave all the complex shit to us. I don't want you to have a brain aneurysm or anything. In the meantime, where's that trap at?"

Donnie gave Face a blank look as if contemplating his response, then clapped his hands together.

He said, "I like that, I like that."

Face sensed Donnie's discontent and immediately took offense to his deflective response. He assumed it meant the rumor was, they weren't handling their business the way they should've been.

Face replied, "You like that? Now see, that's the problem with y'all generation. Y'all are so caught up in rap videos that y'all done lost sight of reality. Standing on them corners don't make you no real nigga. Ain't no love on no street corner. Most of them dudes are just codependents, depending on each other to get high. Half of them only bond because they have a mutual need to support their habits. They commit crimes together and then tell on each other once they get caught because they weren't really family from the get-go. Now see, your real family are the ones you sit down and break bread with. But you new age cats gotta show y'all faces on the block, 'cause y'all don't trust y'all so-called homies around ya bitch. At least not enough to invite 'em into your home—or y'all are too worried about them doubling back to rob your shit. Tell me this, how many of your potnas have you invited to the house you just bought?"

"Shit just you, Sincere, and Bando. You know I stay low key."

"Exactly! You just made my point for me. How does allowing people you claim to love into your sanctuary not fall in line with laying low? Not unless you feel revealing your location to them is a threat to your safety and security. They ain't your enemies, right?"

Donnie looked at Face with newfound respect after being enlightened by his explanation of why they operated the way they did.

Face said, "Everybody wanna holla this mob shit. Taking on made-men nicknames, like they really live that mob shit. They don't even know that the Sicilians didn't even respect us. They say we are too loud and too damn flashy. Which I can't disagree with. Dudes get a few dollars and swear they're in a Too Short music video. But the thing they dislike most is our disloyalty to family. La Cosa Nostra was built on family. That's why even the coldest of the made men had a wife and kids. I mean, how could you trust somebody to sit behind you with a loaded gun while daily he is denying his flesh and blood? You can't. Yet fools are still running around the hood like they're factors 'cause they're making money. Yet they're denying their own damn kids. I ain't saying every hustla is like that, but the ones that are, are fucking up the game. Anybody could make money. What separates the real from the fake is what they do with the money once they've acquired it. You got cats like LeBron James making millions, but he's also giving back to the community every chance he gets. In my eyes, that makes him realer than most cats from the hood. It takes a real man to stand up and handle his responsibility no matter what, especially against all odds. I mean, really do what he has to do to take care of his family. Even if that means working a square-ass nine-to-five job. 'Cause going to prison don't do shit but add to the burden our families already carry. At the end of the day, this organized crime shit is just another avenue to feed your family. And don't forget, everybody has two families. The one you're born into and the one you choose. Just because y'all got the same blood flowing through y'all veins don't make y'all family."

"That was some real shit, blood. You really put shit into perspective," Donnie replied.

"I've got a lot of love for you, bruh. I just want you to see the game for what it really is. Don't get caught up in all the hype. We've lasted this long because we see through all of the bullshit these niggas sellin', for real. Now go get that trap before Sincere gets here."

"A'ight, I'll be right back."

As soon as Donnie left the kitchen, Face redialed Sincere's number, hoping he would finally pick up. Unfortunately, Sincere still wasn't answering his calls.

Face heard Donnie yell, "Fuck!" at the top of his lungs, making him pull out his pistol in a hurry. He then ran into the master bedroom, where Donnie was hanging halfway out of the window, waving his gun back and forth.

Face yelled, "Donnie!" confused about the entire situation.

Donnie slowly pulled his head back inside the window, reluctant to explain what happened.

"Wassup, blood? What the fuck you doin'?" asked Face.

Donnie turned around and said, "Man! Them punk-ass bitches ran off with the trap, bruh."

"Nigga, you playin'."

Two soldiers posted inside the living room ran into the hallway and stood behind Face, trying to figure out what was happening.

Donnie said, "Reina and Venus just ran off with the trap. Them hoes hit the back gate."

"What?" One of them asked like he hadn't heard everything Donnie just said.

Donnie said, "Muthafucka, you heard me. Don't just stand there—go after them bitches!"

Face stepped back out of the doorway so they could slide past him. Next, they hurried over to the window and climbed out one after another. Once they got outside, both of Donnie's pit bulls started barking like crazy, reacting to the adrenaline.

Donnie shouted, "Shut the fuck up! Y'all wasn't barking when them bitches stole my shit."

Face said, "So much for keeping your boys on point, huh."

Donnie replied, "Look, bruh. I don't know what got into them hoes, but Reina's daddy stays on 102nd. She can't get too far."

"How much was in the bag?" Face asked angrily.

"Forty-seven bands."

"You mean to tell me, those hoes did all that for forty-seven bands? Somethin' ain't right. Sincere ain't picking up his damn phone, Reiko might be dead, and now this shit."

Face looked down at Donnie's Rolex and asked, "Why didn't you put the money inside the safe?"

"I did have it in there, but after you called and said to be ready, I bagged it up to be ready for transport."

Suddenly, a light bulb went on inside Face's head.

"When I called, were those bitches within earshot of our conversation?" Face asked worriedly.

Donnie paused for a brief second, contemplating his response.

"Yeah, Venus was. Why, what's up?" he replied.

Face said, "Fuck! Strap up," then ran toward the front of the house.

But before he could even reach the front of the house, he heard a barrage of gunfire erupt outside. As bullets tore through the house, he ducked into the bathroom to avoid being hit. After hearing what sounded like return fire, he eventually poked his head out and was surprised to see the youngster standing at the front window returning fire from his Mack-11. Sadly, his stand didn't last long. Face knew he was hit when he heard him cry out in agony before falling backward and crashing through the glass coffee table sitting in the middle of the room. Face desperately stuck his arm out of the bathroom and fired blindly at the front door. He planned to force his assassins to retreat, giving himself enough time to escape.

Until "Click!"

He had emptied his clip. Now, he had to mentally prepare himself to make a run for the back door.

"Ay, Donnie, you hit?" Face yelled.

"No, I'm good," Donnie replied as he walked past, clutching his automatic shotgun and wearing a Kevlar vest.

"Boom! Boom! Boom! Boom!"

Donnie blasted huge chunks out of the door as he approached, fearlessly unloading his shotgun. Suddenly, he heard the tires screeching from the hit team fleeing the scene. Donnie opened what was left of the front door and scanned the front yard, ready to kill anything moving. He stepped onto the front porch, where he saw both of his point men laid out, bleeding in puddles of their blood. Face slowly walked up behind Donnie while also surveying the crime scene.

"C'mon, we gotta get outta here, blood," Face stated urgently.

They both ran toward Face's car as fast as they could to minimize the amount of people that could identify them. While Donnie was getting into the passenger seat, he noticed someone who appeared to be dead lying next to an AK-47 on the sidewalk. The body was contorted in front of the neighbor's driveway. He knew it wasn't one of his boys because he didn't recognize him, and all their bodies were accounted for. Therefore, Donnie hopped inside the car and slid his shotgun onto the back seat.

"Did you see that? We got one of them bitch-ass niggas, blood," Donnie said proudly.

"Yeah, I seen 'em," Face replied as he started the car.

"Good thing that was a poorly executed hit 'cause they almost had us. What are we gonna do now? 'Cause my DNA all over that muthafucka."

"Shit, mine is too. But with all that DNA in there, unless they got an eyewitness, we'll just be persons of interest."

"After that shit, Venus and Reina should be the least of our worries."

"Nah, them hoes made the call. They stole the money thinking we wouldn't be alive long enough to do shit about it. How long have they been lingering around here again?"

"Shit, for a couple of months now. They been servin' like one of the soldiers, except with the extra benefit of getting some head every now and again. I didn't see any harm in it. But you know, in hindsight—"

"Normally, it wouldn't be, but this nigga Sincere got all kinds of shit brewing. He got us getting shot at. Now I can't even get in contact wit him. Did that fool laying on the sidewalk look like an LA nigga to you?"

Donnie shot Face a puzzled look before responding.

"An LA nigga? I mean, he didn't have any Chucks on or anything. Why did you ask that?" Donnie replied.

"Nothin'. We've gotta split up though, we hot."

"I know. Just drop me off at my brutha's house in Sobrante Park so I can get rid of these thangs."

"A'ight bet, that's just right around the corner."

About ten minutes later, they arrived at Donnie's brother's house, where they could still hear the police sirens loud and clear. Only now, the ghetto bird had predictably joined the party. It was a good thing his brother wasn't home, which allowed Face to park along the side of the house and avoid being seen by the neighbors. Donnie hurried out of the car and slipped through the side door into the garage. A few minutes later, he returned carrying a Hefty garbage bag and a pair of gardener gloves.

After climbing into the back seat, he said, "Here, hand me yo thang."

Face paused briefly, feeling like Donnie was trying to keep some insurance.

"Why? Whatchu finna do wit it?" he replied.

"Bleach 'em, break 'em down, and dispose of 'em. Unless you'd rather take your chances riding around with it."

Face reached into his center console and pulled out a white towel. Then, using the inside of his shirt, he gripped the gun and wiped away his fingerprints with the towel. Once he finished, he used the towel to hand his gun over to Donnie.

Donnie accepted it and said, "Damn, blood, if I didn't know any better, I'd think you didn't trust me."

"I don't trust nobody with my life. But you got an interest in makin' sure that evidence disappears. Ya feel me?"

"Yeah, I feel you. But the estuary will do just fine. Consider it done."

"Whatever, just make sho they don't end up in an evidence locker."

"A'ight, blood. Be safe. I'll call you in a couple hours."

"Oh, ay! Make sure you grab a burner phone, too. Them hoes had your number. And destroy that fucking SIM card."

"Oh shit!"

Donnie instantly pulled out his phone and snapped the SIM card in two.

Donnie said, "I know your number by heart. I'll hit you when it's done."

"A'ight, bruh. We're gonna figure this shit out. In the meantime, keep your head on a swivel."

"No doubt. In a minute."

"In a minute."

Face backed out of the driveway slowly before turning up the street. That was one of the few times he regretted having a nice whip, as it made everyone on the block take a mental picture of him. It felt like the whole hood was outside, watching him drive in slow motion. But in reality, nobody was even out there. His phone rang. *Finally*, he thought, hoping it was Sincere calling to fix the mess he'd made. Instead, he looked down and saw the name 'BANKS' on the screen. He knew getting pulled over for talking while driving was the last thing he needed. It was an unnecessary risk, even if the cops were busy responding to their recent shootout.

He pressed talk, then clicked the speakerphone button before attaching it to his hands-free device.

On the sixth ring, he finally answered, "Hello."

After hearing Banks say, "Come up to Highland—Mama got shot," everything else sounded like gibberish.

"Wait, what?" Face asked, feeling completely devastated.

Banks barked, "Nigga, you heard me. Now get your ass up here," before hanging up the phone.

CHAPTER THREE

· · ·

Angela was inside one of Sav's guest bedrooms, curled up sleeplessly on the bed. Even though she was tired from all of the tossing and turning she had done all night due to the nightmares, she refused to close her eyes. It seemed like every time she tried to, she would have a flashback. The memory of being trapped inside that trunk with Cell-Bo's dead body haunted her. She glanced over at the computer, thinking about checking her Facebook account. She wondered if anything had been posted on social media regarding her graphic abduction. For instance, those sick fucks could have taken a video of her incapacitated body and posted it online. Part of her hated her brother for being the reason she was subjected to such brutality. However, she was also grateful that he came to her rescue when he did.

Suddenly, there was a series of knocks at the door.

Angela finally shouted, "Come in!" after the third succession of knocking.

The door opened slowly, and a beautiful chocolate sista rockin' the Halle Berry hairstyle walked in. The 'Halle Berry' is a short, stylish haircut designed to accentuate a woman's facial features. Her name was Domonique, and she'd been Sav's fiancée for the past four years. Even though she knew deep down inside that he never planned on marrying her ass. Nevertheless, they canceled each other out because she was cool with all the perks being his main bitch entailed, and so was her gold-digging ass mother. She always reminded Domonique that if the streets were ever to catch up with Sav, everything he owned would be left to their three-year-old son, Lil' D, anyway. Therefore, since she was Lil' D's legal guardian by default, she would have complete control over how his money was spent.

Lil' D ran past Domonique and climbed on the bed, using the bedpost to pull himself up. He was unaware that Angela was broken, and the last thing she wanted was to be bothered by him.

He shouted, "Hi, Auntie Angie!" in a loud squeaky childish voice.

"Hey, little monster," Angela replied, forcing a smile.

Once Lil' D climbed onto the bed and jumped into Angela's lap, she gave him a big bear hug like she always did when she came over. She hid her true emotions since she knew it wasn't his fault that tragedy had struck her. After all, he was the most innocent person she'd ever known. Meanwhile, Domonique stood in the doorway, saddened by the pain written on Angela's face. She tried her best to keep it together in front of Lil' D.

Domonique said, "I hope you're hungry, 'cause I made you a bomb-ass breakfast. And here's some chamomile tea to help you with your anxiety."

Angela replied, "Thank you. You can set it down right there on the dresser. I'll eat it in a minute."

They both knew Angela didn't really plan on eating the pity platter. Domonique figured she was being polite and decided to play along despite her situation. She stared at Angela like she was trying to find the best way to get her to open up about what had happened during her abduction.

Domonique set the food tray down and said, "Okay, Lil' D. You said hi to your auntie Angie. Now I need you to go in there with your cousin and play so me and Angie can talk. Okay, baby?"

"Okay, mama," Lil' D replied before kissing Angela goodbye.

He then climbed out of the bed and ran out of the room, oblivious to the pain his auntie suffered from.

Domonique said, "Your brother thought it would be a good idea if we talked, woman to woman, about what happened. At least it'll give you a chance to get it off your chest, rather than holding it in, allowing it to fester."

Angela replied, "I don't know why. I told him everything I could remember about what happened, and it wasn't much. Those motherfuckers drugged me, remember? Everything's all fuzzy."

"Not about that, sis. He wants me to take you to see a doctor. He said when he found you, there were clear signs of vaginal bleeding like you had been raped. Now, I can understand you not wanting to relive that traumatic experience, but you need to get checked out. There could be some permanent damage. Or, you could've contracted something viral."

"I know that. But I'm not ready to have some stranger prodding around inside me. Swabbing me like I'm some kind of lab rat. If there is something permanent, the damage has already been done. What good is seeing a doctor about it now, anyway? And if I've contracted something, I can just as easily see a doctor after my symptoms develop. But most importantly, if I do a rape kit, and that dead man's DNA is in the database, I'll probably be arrested for his murder. And I'm not willing to go down that road."

"I can't argue with that. You'd have a lot of explaining to do. And with our corrupt criminal justice system, they'd flip that on you in the worst way possible—unless you went to the police first."

"That's why I just need some time to think and clear my head."

"Well, your brother, he's just worried about you. You're his baby sister, and he loves you very much. He doesn't want anything else to happen to you, especially after what happened to Crystal."

"Well, if that's the case, he needs to stay as far away from me as possible. Those dudes only kidnapped me to get to him. They used me as a pawn, like my life meant nothing. Did he tell you that he actually considered not paying the ransom and just letting them kill me? He told me to be strong, because even if he paid them, they would still kill me. I've never felt so alone in my life."

"Well, I'm sure whatever he said to them fools, was only to throw them off their game long enough to rescue you. Your brother loves you a lot more than you think. He would've died trying to rescue you, girl. Believe that."

"Then he needs to end his damn obsession with Sincere. Because it almost cost me my life."

"Maybe now, after all of this, he will. But trust me, I've tried to talk him off that ledge before. He's even pulled both of my brothers and my cousin into their war. Honestly, I think he feels like he has too much invested to stop now. When it comes to men like him, their pride tends to be stronger than their will to live. Trust me, I grew up in a house full of men like Dante. I'm sure right now, as we speak, he is out there hunting down any and everyone thought to be involved in your abduction. I'm talking about all the way down to the cashier who sold them the duct tape."

"You don't get it. I don't want any of that. That's not me. I just want my life to return to normal, which I know it never will. I went to college to avoid situations like this, yet here I am. All because of Dante and his stupid ass vendetta. Crystal is dead! No matter what he does or who he kills, she still isn't coming back. Everything he does from now on only affects those of us still living. Why doesn't he get that? Crystal knew exactly what she was getting herself into by running the streets and selling her body. It's not fair that her poor life choices are still ruining our lives. He needs to just let her rest in peace so we can go on with our lives."

"I feel you 100% on that, sis. But right now, what can I do to help you cope? So you can start to move past this whole ordeal. C'mon now, give me something—since you made it clear you won't accept any professional help."

"Honestly, I just want to be alone with my thoughts. I appreciate the breakfast, though—it was thoughtful of you."

"Okay, well, I'll let you be alone with your thoughts. I have to go check on them badass kids anyway. You know if you need anything at all, all you have to do is holla, sis."

"A'ight, thanks, Nique."

Domonique walked over, gave Angela a consoling hug and a kiss, then left the room, closing the door behind her.

CHAPTER FOUR

• • •

Face had already decided that it was Sincere's fault his mother had been shot as he walked toward the entrance of the hospital. That was why he blew up Sincere's phone the entire way there, trying to give him a piece of his mind. As soon as Face hit the main lobby, Banks flagged him down aggressively like he was prepared to let him have it. Therefore, Face immediately looked to the twins and Lil' Chris for help, but they were nowhere in sight.

Face asked, "Where are the twins and Lil' Chris? They a'ight?"

Banks replied, "Yeah, you just missed them. They let them go in to visit Tonya. Lil' Chris is in the bathroom."

"Now, what happened to Mama?" Face asked inquisitively.

"Nigga, you tell me!" Banks stated angrily.

After his sudden outburst, Banks looked around in embarrassment, realizing he was making a scene. Then, he quickly checked his tone and pulled Face away from the other visitors for more privacy.

Banks said in a less aggressive tone, "I told you not to let your beef follow you back to Mama's house."

"My beef? How do you know that had anything to do with me and my business?" Face replied.

Banks quickly closed the distance between them and said, "Why else would somebody go to Mama's house to shoot her and CJ? They ain't involved in no street shit. Only through the grace of God, my girls weren't there. But Lil' Chris was. And guess what? He had to cry over his father's dead body before calling nine-one-one. You better pray this don't get me violated and taken away from my girls again. Now who's responsible for this shit? And don't play wit me, blood."

Face placed his hand on Banks' shoulder and said, "Look, I need you to sit down and relax, bruh."

Banks gave Face a cold stare as he sat down next to him, clearly expecting to hear some bullshit. He didn't even notice that Lil' Chris had come out of the bathroom and had sat at the far end of the visiting room next to the window.

Face said, "Listen, bruh, to be honest, I don't know who's responsible for shooting up Mama's house. Sincere got us into all kinds of extracurricular activities. It's more goin' on than just some beef with Sav."

"Like what, blood?" Banks asked, interested.

"This might sound crazy, but he accidentally killed the brother of our connect. A cat out of LA named Taz. Now he's out here wit a hit team ready to kill everybody involved in his brutha's murder. He even got a million-dollar bounty out."

"How the fuck did he accidentally kill the brutha of y'all's connect?"

"He claims he didn't do it on purpose. He didn't know he was related to him. It was on some spur-of-the-moment type shit when he caught the nigga trying to throw some bitch in his trunk while coming out of his studio. He thought he was a weirdo doing some weirdo shit."

"Since when did he give a fuck about a bitch?"

"Oh, it gets deeper. The girl he saved is a chick named Sorya, and she's the sister of El's bottom bitch Honesty. They're both hiding out at his house."

"Whose house? El's house?"

"Nah, Sincere's. Shit, I don't even think El knows about that part. It's been so much goin' on I haven't even had the chance to sit down and holla at him about it yet. But on top of that, he got blackmailed by a dirty ass detective for five million dollars. He had to borrow some dough from me to pay him off. It was the same detective who interviewed me downtown about the pistol. We had to pay him off for the evidence he had linking Sincere to the murder. The only thing is, I fear now that they're in our pockets, our relationship is far from over."

"You think?"

"But here goes the worst part. After dropping off the money, me and Sincere were supposed to meet up at the trap house on 102nd, but he never showed up. Remember that fool Donnie?"

"Yeah, why?"

"Well, he's running that spot now. So anyway, he had a couple of hoodrats trappin' fo' him when I got there. I had noticed one of them giving me a weird look, but I didn't pay them hoes no mind. Well, those hoes ended up stealing the trap and escaping through a bedroom window. A few minutes later, a hit team aired the house out with us inside. Me and Donnie were the only ones who survived. Now mind you, I haven't heard shit from Sincere since the drop off to the pigs. He completely disappeared off the face of the earth. I'm guessing he's either in custody or the same team that came after me ran a play on him. Only he wasn't as lucky."

"Speaking of, what happened with that play y'all ran on Sav's sister? How did that turn out?"

"To be real, your guess is as good as mine."

"How the hell is that? Dumbass, you orchestrated it."

"While I was locked up, I received a call confirming the package had been picked up, but when I got released and contacted the handler for delivery, nobody answered."

"So they could've run off and did some rogue shit for all you know then, right?"

"Man, at this point, I believe anything is possible."

"At least tell me you used some reputable soldiers to get the job done."

"Yeah, I hand-picked 'em myself."

"And that'd be who exactly?" Banks asked skeptically.

"Our potnas Cell-Bo, Tyson, and Reiko."

"Reiko? You talkin' 'bout lil' square ass Reiko? Pretty boy nigga?"

"Yuuup, he jumped off the porch late, but he's wit the function now."

"Yeah, I bet. Wait, you put emphasis on 'was' with the function. What do you mean by that?"

"Shit, it was on the news. They found a dead body inside his house late last night. Somebody burned his house down following a shootout. I'm assuming it was to destroy any evidence they may have left behind."

"What the fuck!"

"Yeah, I know. I was gonna smash past his spot to see if the car they used to pick up the package was there. But I looked at the clip on the KTVU website, and there it was, sitting right there in the background. Now, I don't know what the fuck to think. If Reiko left anything inside the car, sooner or later, the police are gonna find it unless he gets to it first."

"Who is he?"

"Justin. I hit him up and told him to steal the car as soon as the coast was clear so he could check it for evidence before torching it."

"Smart, but I'm assuming whoever killed bruh either got the girl, or they know where she's at. You told them to take her to his house?"

"Hell nah. That's what got me puzzled. I think they panicked and did something reckless after I stopped answering their calls."

"The Cell-Bo I know crazy, but he is far from game goofy. I have a bad feeling about this. That whole scenario just ain't adding up."

"I know, bruh. That's why I really need your help figuring this shit out. You've always been the smart one. So what do you say?"

Banks thought about it for a second, then chose his words wisely before speaking.

He replied, "Look, bruh, I called CJ's sister Sonya to come get the kids. She's on her way here from Bushrod. They're gonna stay with her until we figure this shit out."

Face said with a smile, "So you're gonna help me?"

"Man, I ain't doin' this for you. I'm only doin' this because I know Mama's stubborn ass is still gonna wanna live in that house. So our only option now is to eliminate the threat by any means necessary. Ain't no rules when it comes to protecting your family. But if I do this, you'll have to do everything I say from here on out. Fuck what Sincere talkin' about. He's letting one muthafucka dismantle his entire empire. And I'll be damned if you think I'm gon' let him destroy my family."

"Yeah, you're right. Speaking of, what's Mama's condition like?"

"I'm not sure. She just got out of another surgery. I'm waiting for the doctor to give me an update. Oh! Here he comes right now."

They both walked over to meet the doctor halfway. He was a forty-four-year-old, well-built, brown-skinned brother who resembled a younger Denzel Washington. His name was Dr. Reed. They could tell by the look on his face that the news they were about to receive would not be pleasant. Dr. Reed shook both of their hands before executing his duty as the bearer of bad news. He had only introduced himself to Face since he had already been acquainted with Banks.

Banks said, "Just give it to us raw, doc."

Dr. Reed said, "Okay, well we've removed all of the bullets except one, because it is lodged in her upper vertebra. I'm sorry to have to inform you of this, but she will be permanently paralyzed from the waist down. Attempting to remove the last remaining bullet could potentially paralyze her from the neck down. So you can understand why we've elected to leave the bullet intact."

"Yes, I understand, doc," Banks replied.

"Can we go in and see her?" Face asked.

Dr. Reed replied, "I'm sorry, sir, but that won't be possible due to the unfortunate circumstances. That can't happen until she is conscious and able to add you to her visitors list."

Face barked, "What? Muthafucka."

"But it shouldn't be too long a wait. She was recently transferred to the intensive care unit for observation. I'm worried her diabetes might cause some complications. I promise to notify you as soon as you are approved to visit her. I normally don't do this. But if you have a number I can reach you at, you can leave it with me so you can go home and get some rest."

Dr. Reed dealt with enough post-traumatic situations to deduce angry family members hanging around the hospital never helped the patient's recovery. Contrarily, it often meant a recipe for disaster.

Banks said, "Yeah, I appreciate that, doc."

Dr. Reed then pulled out an ink pen along with a business card and handed it to Banks. Banks subsequently wrote down his cell number and returned the stationery to Dr. Reed, who immediately took it.

Banks said, "Thanks, doc. I'm sure you did all you could to help my mother."

Dr. Reed replied, "It was all her. Your mother is a strong woman, you know. I only did what I took an oath to do. The rest is up to God. So, all we can do now is pray for her. Believe me, it works."

"Yeah, a'ight," Face mumbled disrespectfully.

Dr. Reed understood Face's misdirected anger was a characteristic commonly attributed to the victim's family. Therefore, he disregarded his comment and alternatively smiled, nodded, then walked away undisturbed.

Banks said, "I don't know whatchu gettin' mad at him for. He ain't the cause of this. That's the last person you should be coppin' an attitude with."

Face just looked at Banks with a stupid expression because, deep down inside, he knew he was only trying to transfer his guilt to Dr. Reed.

Banks said, "What the hell?" sounding surprised.

Looking over Face's shoulder, he spotted El walking through the corridor, looking stressed out.

Seeing Banks' expression caused Face to snap his head back toward El.

"El!" Face shouted.

When El heard his name called, he whipped his head toward Face and immediately spotted them. He gave them a head nod to acknowledge he'd seen them, then headed in their direction. Once he reached them, he gave them both dap and pretended to be joyful.

"Wassup? What are y'all doin' here?" El asked curiously.

Banks replied, "Man, fuckin' with this fool, my mama's house got shot up this morning. CJ is dead, and I just found out my mama will never walk again."

"What? Who the fuck would shoot up Auntie's house?"

"Ain't no tellin'. Him and Sincere got a whole lot of bullshit goin' on right now. But we're definitely going to need your help narrowing it down, though."

"Anything y'all need. You know she's like the mother I never had. I'll do anything for her. Just say the word, and it's done. But tell me that at least one of y'all has an inkling of who did that shit."

Banks looked at Face as if to say, 'Go ahead and talk.' Face quickly caught on to their vibes as they both stared at him, anxiously awaiting his explanation.

Face said, "The hit was orchestrated by that fool Sav or a cat named Taz out of LA. You already know the situation wit Sav."

El replied, "But you and Sincere spoke highly of Taz. Why the fuck would he be ordering a hit on Auntie's house? What y'all robbed the connect or something?"

"Nah, worse. Sincere accidentally killed his brutha on some Good Samaritan-type shit. You know your hoe Honesty got a fine ass sister named Sorya, right?"

"Yeah, I've have been trying to turn her out for the longest. Why?"

"Well, apparently, Taz's brutha hunted them hoes down 'cause they stole two hunnit thousand dollars from him. Sincere caught him outside his studio, trying to force Sorya into the trunk of his car, and smoked him. Now Taz is out here wit a hit team offering up a million-dollar bounty on whoever did it. On top of all that, a dirty ass detective named Jones just blackmailed us for five million dollars. We had to pay it because he had evidence linking Sincere to the murder."

El rubbed his chin as he fell into deep thought.

"What is it?" asked Banks.

El said, "Shit! That's gotta be who shot her then. I went by their house last night to pick up Honesty, and I found her lying on the floor with a gunshot wound to her head. That crazy bitch was still alive. That's why I'm up here. They said they got her in a medically induced coma until the swelling of her brain goes down. Taz must've caught up to her. I hope they don't think I had shit to do with it."

Face said, "If that's true, that would explain why Sincere's been MIA all day. I think that bitch gave my boy up. 'Cause when I went by his house yesterday to get the rundown, her and her sister were there laying low. But why would she go back home, though, knowing Taz was looking for her?"

"I don't know. She told me her sister was goin' through some shit. I came up here hoping to run into her so I could get some answers. But I wasn't expecting this revelation. How I see it, ain't none of us safe now."

"Shit, who you tellin'? I just barely escaped a shootout with my life. Some hoodrats tried to set me up. I had to shoot my way out of one of our trap houses. We got one of them suckas though. The only thing is, I didn't recognize him."

"Well if he's rockin' like that, he might be comin' after all of us. Our safest bet is goin' on the offense, especially if he believes we had something to do with it. 'Cause I'll be an easy target coming back and forth out of my club throughout the day. I don't like lookin' over my shoulder, pimp. He might try some Player's Club-type shit. I can't go out like that."

Banks interjected, "You forgot to tell him about the Reiko situation."

Face said, "Oh yeah. Fed up wit Sav's bullshit, Sincere decided to have his sister kidnapped to draw him out. He had me send a team to snatch her up from Chico State. Well, I got confirmation that they snatched her up. But late last night, the police responded to a shootout at the driver's house. By the time they arrived there, the house was already engulfed in flames. After putting out the fire, they found a dead body. The fire chief said it was arson. And I ain't heard shit from the other two fools."

El asked, "So how do you know Sav didn't somehow rescue his sister?"

Banks said, "He doesn't know. At this point, he doesn't know shit."

Hearing the unnecessary drama Face was involved in caused Banks' blood to boil. It took everything inside him not to fire on his dumbass again.

El said, "You got a whole lot of shit goin' on, Face. But we're family, and family sticks together no matter what. Now, we have to prioritize each situation according to its threat level. The highest threat level is whoever's responsible for shooting up Auntie's house. I think the best way to do that is by using the process of elimination. We all know the shooter wasn't after Banks because, according to you, they also tried to stamp you at the trap house. We also know Honesty got hit. The only thing linking y'all together is Sincere and Taz. You said you had just seen her at Sincere's spot right before she got shot, right?"

"Yeah, that's right," Face replied.

"Well, it sounds to me like she got scared and gave y'all up. That would explain why Sincere isn't picking up his phone. He's probably dead. I think with a million-dollar bounty out, somebody tried to cash in and tried to kill two birds with one stone. So it had to be somebody you know. Because not only did they know where you were going to be, but they also showed up at yo mama's crib."

Banks nodded. "That checks out."

"But on the other hand, if they botched the kidnapping or did some snake shit, that would bring a whole other element into play."

"Whatchu mean?" Face asked, fully invested.

"Was Reiko supposed to take her back to his house, or was there another plan in place?"

"Nah, we got a warehouse for shit like that. The cat who ran it said it looked like someone had recently been there, though."

"So, for all we know, the other two could've smacked him and kept the ransom money for themselves. Or Sincere could've just been tying up some loose ends. Who knows, maybe they'll discover the other two fools dead somewhere."

"I doubt it. Sincere don't rock like that. He's the most loyal person I know. And Cell-Bo wouldn't backdoor us like that, either. It has to be something else. I can feel it."

"You sho got a lot of faith in 'em."

Banks said, "Well, whatever it is, we've gotta get to the bottom of it before Mama gets out of the hospital. I'd say it's time we took this investigation to the streets, where we can actually make some progress. Face, you need to track Sincere's ass down so you can find out everything there is to know about Taz. If he hasn't moved on Sincere yet, this gives us the advantage of knowing he eventually will. We got the streets. All he's got is a couple of goons looking to make a payday. If we use every resource we have in the streets, that muthafucka will be dead by this time tomorrow."

El said, "Yeah, there ain't too much we can do from here. The way I see it, our best chance at finding out who's behind this is those bitches at the trap house. If we can find out who had them sittin' on the spot waiting to make the call, that trail should lead us directly to the source. I'm sure Sincere is just as lost as we are if he ain't already dead."

Face said, "I was thinking the same thang. We already have an APB out on them hoes. They can't get too far."

Banks said, "Hopefully, they don't get scared and run straight to the cops first."

"They won't. They think they're hood. Plus, those hoes are the ones that set it all in motion."

"You think you got it all figured out, huh? That's exactly why they might go to the police. They're probably nothin' but scared little girls who realize they bit off more than they can chew. And now they're looking for the quickest escape route."

El said, "That's a possibility we gotta consider, but I doubt it. Just be prepared in case they do, though."

"So what? You think I should skip town?" Face asked nervously.

Banks said, "Hell nah, blood. This is your mess we gotta clean up. You're gonna stay yo ass right here and deal wit this shit. Look, I'll wait here for Sonya until she comes to pick up the kids. Then, I'll canvass the neighborhood. Hopefully, somebody saw or heard something, because

Lil' Chris wasn't any help. You need to go find Sincere. Then find them set up artist before they end up in the wind. Ay, El, if Taz put out a bounty, there's gotta be a way to contact him. I need you to find it. You have strong roots in The Town. I know somebody knows who cashed in."

El replied, "You know that's gonna be a tall task, so we can't just rely on that. But I will definitely do my research. Hopefully, Honesty wakes up out of her coma so that I can get some intel from her."

"Yeah, that's if that bitch's circuits ain't fried. That's probably a dead end, too."

El didn't like hearing those words coming out of Banks' mouth because even though Honesty was batshit crazy, he still loved her ass. Fortunately, Banks noticed that his words hit a soft spot because he immediately tried to walk back his words out of sympathy.

He said, "But she'll probably a be a'ight though. I've seen people come back from worse."

An awkward silence filled the room as they suddenly realized that Banks had only taken back his statement out of pity for El. His uncharacteristic emotional connection to Honesty totally caught them off guard.

El asked, "So, did y'all already visit with Auntie?"

Banks replied, "Hell nah, she ain't in stable enough condition to give her consent yet. She will be soon, though. She just got out of surgery."

"Consent? Man, that's yo mama."

"I know, but that's how they protect gunshot victims now after them idiots from the west ran up in here and killed Rashad. They admit them under aliases now, so the shooter can't come finish the job."

"Oh, I know the script. I just can't believe this shit happened to Auntie out of all people."

"Well, it did. Now we gotta find a way to come from under it, and fast."

Face said, "A'ight, I'm about to paint The Town to see if anybody's talkin'. What do y'all say we huddle up at my house at about eight?"

"Yeah, that's cool wit me," El replied.

Banks said, "Might as well. I'm gonna need you to text me your address though."

Face said, "A'ight," and texted his address to Banks' cell phone. "So we done here?"

"For now," Banks replied.

"Alright then, y'all. I'll see y'all tonight."

Face spent off like he was mad at the world, but he could only be angry at himself since he played a major role in everything that transpired. He constantly tried to convince Jamela to move out of Oakland because he feared the possibility of his street life one day catching up to him. He knew the streets were cold. So what, he operated under mob rules, like no women or children were to be harmed. The new generation didn't give a fuck about no rules, making Jamela a liability.

El watched Face walk away, shaking his head in disbelief at the burden he had brought down on their entire family. Then, once Face had finally cleared the corridor, he turned to address Banks.

He said, "Check it out, bruh. I know you just came home a bunch of bullshit. But right now, y'all need each other more than ever. I know you want to get off in his ass because lord knows I do. But please stick to the script. At least until we've weathered the storm. After that, I'll help you beat his muthafuckin' ass for this shit. A'ight?"

Banks said, "Oh, don't trip. I know I gotta play it cool."

"Wassup witcha though, dog? You've got that look in your eyes."

"What look?"

"The same look you had after your pops got killed. I ain't ever seen a look so cold."

"Well, we handled our business, didn't we?"

"Yeah. I still be having nightmares about that night. But whatever you're planning, I'm witcha one-hunnit percent. I'll see you tonight. Until then, be safe, lil' bruh. I love you."

El hugged Banks passionately, fixed his clothes, then headed down the corridor toward the exit. Following his departure, Banks sat down feeling relieved to finally be alone with his thoughts because now he could plot out his revenge on whoever shot his mother. After ten minutes of brainstorming, he got up and walked to the vending machine to grab a Pepsi. Next, he stood before the vending machine and downed the whole soda without even taking a breath. He subsequently crushed the can before throwing it into the recycle bin. When he turned around, two detectives were suddenly standing in front of him. He could tell they were detectives because only detectives wore their badges like he used to wear his gold chains. He didn't see his parole officer around, so he figured that was a win for the home team.

Detective Jones said, "Well, if it isn't the infamous Mr. Banks. You were only out for what, two weeks? And you already started running up the body count."

Banks replied, "I don't have the slightest idea of what you're talking about, officer—"

"Jones. And this is here, Detective Johnson."

"Well, Detective Jones, I know nothing about a body count. I'm just here to visit my mother, sir."

Johnson glanced down at his notepad to inform Banks they were investigating documented intel. It was his way of insinuating they were in complete control.

Johnson said, "That would be a Jamela Harris, correct?"

"Yes, that's her name. Why? You found out who shot her already?"

"No. Not yet, at least."

"Then may I ask why you're here questioning the last person on earth to have a motive to shoot either of them?"

Jones said, "You see, we're not here to accuse you of killing Christopher. But I do have a hunch that today's shooting and last night's explosion are related. I mean, you get out of the joint, and then all of a sudden, your estranged wife and her new lover both get blown up. It's no secret he was known for having criminal ties in East Oakland. So I'm guessing the nexus is, the next day, your mother's house gets shot up. It sounds to me like a retaliation murder. Or did I miss something? Feel free to fill me in."

Banks said, "First off, if you truly believed that, I would be in handcuffs right now."

"Don't tempt me."

"I would never do anything to harm the mother of my children. So I'm sorry to say, but y'all are barking up the wrong tree here."

"Is that so? Well, where exactly were you last night between seven and eleven p.m.?"

"I was with a lady friend of mine all night. I've got the scars on my back to prove it. If you know what I mean."

"Is that right? Well, does this so-called lady friend have a name and number? So she can corroborate your alibi. I'm sure you don't have a problem with that, right?"

Frustrated, Banks pulled out his cell phone and began scrolling through it.

He said, "Yeah, her name is Tiffany. Here's her number. I also notified my PO, just in case you're wondering."

Banks handed Johnson his phone cunningly, like he had nothing to hide. Consequently, Johnson jotted down her name and number in his notepad before returning it to him.

Johnson said, "Thank you for your cooperation. We will most definitely be checking into your alibi."

Banks wasn't too worried about his alibi checking out because Tiffany had already started to fall for him. She couldn't help it after the way that he put his dick game down. Shit, she was already sprung after just one night of pure hedonistic fucking. In their short time together, she had already revealed to him that one of her brothers used to work for Johnny, up until the day that Johnny had him killed for allegedly stealing from him, making her the perfect alibi.

Normally, Banks wouldn't involve a chick he just met, but he knew he'd need an alibi if the police came knocking. And who better to use than her? Since he strongly believed in turning the enemy of his enemy into one of his allies. Luckily it panned out this time, because his lust for revenge made him sloppy. It was the combination of Johnny setting him up and the way that he treated his daughters that clouded his otherwise keen judgment.

Jones said, "We ain't done yet. I still have some questions. So, what was your relationship with Johnny like? I know you couldn't have been too happy with him parading your kids around town like they were his."

Banks replied, "I didn't have any issues at all with the brutha. The way I see it, he took care of my kids when I was unable to do so myself. If anything, I owe him a thank you."

"A thank you, huh?"

"Yes, sir. I don't harbor any ill feelings toward the brutha, nor do I have any animosity toward the mother of my children. I went away to prison for ten long years, and she moved on with her life. I can't be mad at her for choosing to be happy."

"Let me get this straight. She left you sitting high and dry while playing house with your kids, and now you just get out as if everything is fine and dandy? I'm not stupid. I know you two were rival drug dealers.

"It is fine and dandy. Look, I see what you're trying to do. You're trying to spin this like I had a motive to kill him out of a jealous rage. Well, it isn't going to work because I wasn't jealous of their relationship. And we most definitely weren't rival drug dealers. That theory just makes you sound desperate."

"Well, that's not what Ms. Jenkins said. How do you think we knew you were down here? She claims a few days ago, you two had it out over the custody of your two children. She also claimed that you and your mother tried to stop her from seeing them, forcing her to threaten calling the sheriff's department to get them back."

Banks didn't like the direction this investigation was heading, so he knew he had to act fast to put out the fire.

He said, "It wasn't even like that. Tonya basically said she was tired of taking care of the kids, and she wanted some time to do her. I felt I needed to spend more quality time with them, so we agreed to let them stay with me at my mother's house. But the other day, she came over there all drunk and belligerent, talking about how she was going to take my girls. Now, what father in his right mind would allow his children to get in a car with someone, mother or not, knowing that person was heavily intoxicated?"

"So now you're saying the only reason you refused to let her take them was because she was intoxicated?"

"That's right," Banks said proudly.

"Well, I highly doubt that, because Tonya and her doctor both informed me she was fourteen weeks pregnant. And now you're claiming she was drunk? You know, the more you talk, the less convincing you become. Look, I want to give you a break here, but you need to give me something concrete to work with. Who could possibly have had a reason to shoot up your mother's house?"

"I really have no clue, detective. But I promise if I come up with somethin', you'll be the first to know."

"You know what I think?"

"No, sir. What's that?"

"I think you know exactly who did it, but you and your hoodlum brother want to take them out yourselves. As a matter of fact, where is your brother? I just had to interview him down at the station a few days ago. It seems to me like trouble tends to follow you two everywhere, doesn't it?"

Johnson said, "Hey Jones, lay off him a bit. His mother just got shot."

Jones replied, "Alright, well, where is your brother hiding? We need to ask him if he has any possible suspects in mind."

Banks said, "Y'all just missed him. If you leave me a card, I could have him call you as soon as possible."

Jones reached into his blazer pocket and pulled out a business card.

He handed it to Banks and said, "I'm personally holding you responsible for making sure he calls. You got that parolee?"

"Yeah, I got that. Oh! By the way, whose case are you working on? My mother's? Or Tonya's?"

"Both. Because, like I said, we think you and your brother are the connection. So expect to be hearing from us real soon."

"Okay, you have a good day now," Johnson added.

As Jones and Johnson headed down the corridor, Johnson asked, "Why didn't you tell him that we knew Johnny was the one who set him up?"

Jones replied, "I figured we could keep it as our ace in the hole in case we hit a dead end. Who knows, maybe we'll even be able to use that information to secure another big payday."

"From who? He doesn't have that kind of money. He just finished serving a ten-year bid, remember? He's been out of the game for a while."

"Then it looks like he'll have to borrow money from his brother, won't he?"

CHAPTER FIVE

— • • • —

Javier sat at his sister Sophia's house, waiting patiently for his recklessly dangerous nephew to walk through the door, as he was prepared to tear him a new asshole. He glanced at one of his men positioned at the window, who gave him a nod to signal that Betho had finally arrived. He downed one last shot of tequila before heading out the front door to intercept him. Because the house was filled with family and friends mourning Maria's death, Javier chose not to make a scene.

As Betho approached the house, he smirked as if he had just accomplished something spectacular and wanted the entire world to know. What he didn't know was that Javier was waiting to wipe that smug expression off his face. Once Betho got within arm's reach, Javier snatched him up by his shirt and pushed him through the garage door, which was held open by one of his men. He aggressively slammed Betho's back against the black Chevy Suburban parked inside the garage.

Betho exclaimed, "What the hell, man?"

"Tell me you didn't do it," Javier replied.

Javier's soldier closed the garage door and stood outside to ensure that no one interrupted his boss while he handled business.

"Do what?" Betho asked, confused.

"You know what I'm talking about. Not only did you take one of my men to do an unsanctioned hit, but you also failed. And you shot an old lady in the process. You're lucky you didn't kill a small child, or you would be lying next to Alejandro."

Javier then opened the back of the Suburban, revealing Alejandro lying there, beady-eyed, bound, and gagged.

Javier quickly closed the door and stated, "He told me everything. I'll deal with him later."

"Hey, I'm sorry, Javie, but I had to do something in honor of Maria's name. I promised my madre I would–"

"Shut the hell up. Your actions dishonor Maria's memory. Not only did chu' shoot innocent people, but chu' also alerted the real targets that we were coming. Now, who's to say they haven't skipped town? I told you to wait, and have someone sit on the house. You said you were just going to check it out. You stupid idiota—now we can't even do that!"

Javier knocked all the arrogance out of Betho by pinning him against the truck. As a result, he stood still, looking like a disobedient little boy sentenced to time out.

Betho begged, "Please, Javie, give me a chance to fix this."

"And how do you plan on doing that?" Javier asked, uninterested.

"By killing those fuckers."

"And why should I trust you again after what you pulled?"

"Because no one wants to make those muthafuckas pay more than I do. I'm willing to do anything to get revenge for Maria."

"You sound like a small child, eager to open his Christmas presents. I've seen many men lose their lives because their impatience caused them to act impulsively. So you will not, and I repeat, you will not go anywhere near that house again. You leave that to the professionals. Do you understand?"

Because Betho didn't respond quickly enough, Javier grabbed him by the face, squeezing his jawline as tightly as he could.

"I said, do you understand me?" asked Javier.

"Yes, I understand," Betho replied. All the while thinking, *I'll show him.*

CHAPTER SIX

• • •

Banks had been knocking on doors all afternoon, trying to gather any information he could regarding his mother's shooter. Unfortunately, he eventually ended up at Co-Co's house. He had been purposely saving her for last since he tried his hardest to stay away from her scandalous ass. You see, Co-Co was a cougar who had grown up with his mother, meaning they had been neighbors since they were kids. She had been trying to give Banks some pussy ever since he was thirteen years old. She used to pay him to do little chores around the house, like cutting her grass every two weeks to get him home alone. Finally, after vetting him for a while to make sure he wouldn't snitch to Jamela, she decisively threw the pussy at him. At the time, he had been making puppy love to a fourteen-year-old girl named Gina, who lived on Eighty-Ninth and Dowling while her mother was at work. It was fucked up because it was the first time he had ever slapped skins bareback, and Co-Co just happened to give him gonorrhea. Since he was inexperienced in sexually transmitted diseases, he confronted Co-Co about the burning sensation he felt whenever he urinated after sleeping with her. Ironically, she had the nerve to blame him. She said he was the one who had burned her and told him to stop sticking his dick inside those little fast-ass girls. Although he knew he had gotten it from her since she was the only one with whom he had ever exchanged bodily fluids. He'd learned that much from sex education. Of course, she was concerned about getting caught, so she took him to the Planned Parenthood in Richmond for treatment. However, once she dropped him off, she drove herself to Kaiser hospital in North Oakland to get a shot of her own. Since then, Banks had kept his distance from her trifling ass.

Co-Co answered the door wearing a dingy black robe with white lint balls all over it.

She said, "Hey, Banks, I'm sorry to hear what happened to your mother and CJ. He was hella cool. Do you wanna come inside?"

"Actually, I do. I have a few questions. But I promise not to take up too much of your time."

"Well, come on in."

After Banks entered the house, she closed the door behind him. Then, she escorted him to the dining room table, where a steaming cup of coffee was waiting.

Banks heard a raspy voice shout, "Yo! Co-Co! Who is that?"

She replied, "None of yo goddamn business! This is my house!"

She then turned to Banks and said, "Damn, you give a nigga some pussy, and he swears y'all are married. I'm sorry about that. What can I do for you, sugar?"

Banks replied, "I've been canvassing the entire neighborhood all afternoon, questioning people to see if anyone saw anything that could help me find out who did the shooting. I know you stay at the end of the block, but you may've seen a suspicious car lurking around or fleeing the scene."

"Nah, I'm sorry. I wish I could say I did boo-boo, but I would just be blowing smoke up ya ass. But I'm pretty sure somebody saw somethin' they aren't comfortable relating to the police. Or they're just waiting for a Crime Stoppers reward to get posted."

Banks was surprised to see the 5'9" sugar daddy who walked into the room eating a greasy piece of Church's chicken, wearing a 1970s-pimp suit.

The man said, "Who is dis negro, Co-Co?" while smacking irritatingly.

Co-Co replied, "This is my neighbor Banks. That was his mother's house that got shot up this morning. Banks, meet Darrell. And Darrell, stop smacking. Don't nobody wanna hear all that"

"Whatever, woman. Anyway, I'm sorry to hear about your mother, young blood. Did they catch whoever did it?"

Banks replied, "Nah. That's actually why I'm here. I've been questioning all our neighbors to see if someone saw anything helpful, like a car skirting off or something."

"Nah, young blood, we were laid up in the bed watching TV all morning. I didn't even hear the gunshots."

"Okay, that'll be all Darrell," Co-Co said, irritated.

She was visibly offended by the way Darrell was openly volunteering her business.

Darrell mumbled, "Shit, I don't know whatchu gettin' mad at me for?" as he turned to leave.

Suddenly, Co-Co gently caressed the back of Banks' hand.

"I'm sorry, baby. I really wish there was more I could do for you," she said sympathetically.

Banks immediately slid his hand from beneath hers, still feeling repulsed by how she tried to play him back in the day. He always thought he should've told his mama so she could've beat her ass for that shit. However, it would've still been considered snitchin', so he had to keep it a secret.

He stood up and said, "Don't even stress over it. But I do need you to keep an ear to the streets, though. I'll give you my cell number in case you see anything out of the ordinary. Like some unusual cars lurking around the block or somethin', a'ight?"

"Okay. It's the least I can do. You know your mother is like a sister to me."

Banks thought, *If that were the case, why did you seduce your nephew, then.*

"You got a cell phone?" he asked.

"Yep, one second," she happily replied.

She turned and disappeared down the hallway leading to her bedroom. Fortunately, she returned quickly with a phone in hand. She quickly handed it to him and watched admiringly while he stored his number.

Once he was finished, he handed it back to her and said, "There. I stored it under Banks."

"Alright, well, I'll let you know if I see or hear anything," she said, leading him toward the front door.

"A'ight, y'all take care now," he replied as he stepped out the front door.

Banks was frustrated because he couldn't go home to change clothes or grab his hygiene essentials. CSI was still at their house investigating, which meant he had no choice but to call Face for assistance. He had also decided to stay away from Tiffany in case Jones questioned her. It was a wise decision because her statement would not appear to be coerced.

After hearing Face's voicemail pick up, he climbed into his truck and slammed the door. Next, he started up the truck before redialing Face's number one last time for good measure. But still no answer. Now highly agitated, he threw his phone onto the passenger seat and banged his hands against the steering wheel. Ironically, his phone rang just as he had his outburst of frustration. When he picked up the phone, he was relieved to see that it was Face returning his call.

Banks answered, "Wassup, blood? Where you at?"

"I'm on Seven-One hollerin' at my folks, trying to find out who shot at me. Where you at?" Face said.

"I'm down the street from the house. CSI is still there, and I need to shower and change clothes. Plus, I have something important to fill you in on—but not over the phone, though."

"So whatchu sayin', blood?"

"We need to meet up at your house so that I can wash my ass and shit. I'm about to slide through Durant and grab something to wear real quick. I'll meet you there in about an hour, a'ight?"

"Durant? Bruh, you trippin'. You can have some of my clothes."

"Man, I ain't trippin' on no damn fashion. I've been wearing state blues for the past ten years."

"Look, blood, I got some brand new shit for you. Just meet me at my house in twenty. Ain't no brutha of mine about to be shopping at no damn indoor flea market. And I keep extra toothbrushes and shit for my smash parties."

"A'ight, man, I'm on my way there, then."

"A'ight, peace."

Banks sat outside Face's house for about fifteen minutes, waiting for him to arrive. He was expecting Face's nosey-ass neighbor to call the police, since she walked her German Shepherd past him three times. She was obviously curious about why he was sitting in Face's driveway. Finally, the sixty-seven-year-old Caucasian woman built up enough nerve to tap on his driver's side window. Banks slowly rolled down his window, bracing himself to be racially profiled for being unaccompanied in a predominantly white neighborhood.

"Yes, ma'am, how may I help you?" he said in a square-ass voice.

"Don't try to play me, fool. You got some of that good shit?" she replied, catching him totally off guard.

"Excuse me?"

"I said, do you got some of that good shit? 'Cause lately, I've been coppin' from the Cannabis Club, and they're taxin' a bitch like crazy."

Banks looked at her blankly, utterly shocked yet deeply amused by her candor.

She said, "Oh, I see. I bet when you saw an old white lady walking past, you thought I was one of them neighborhood watch motherfuckers. Well, I ain't. Shoot, those sons of bitches be narcin' on me, too. Every weekend me and the golden girls get together for a little enhanced bingo, if you know what I mean. It's my little side hustle. Plus, it helps with the glaucoma."

"Is that right?"

"Yep. By your strong resemblance to Face, I'm assuming you're the jailbird he's been blabbing on about. Banks right? He told me you were supposed to be getting out soon."

Banks turned in his seat, feeling blindsided by her bluntness.

She said, "Don't be alarmed. He's bangin' one of my granddaughters, so he comes over and smokes me out from time to time. And he's always speaking highly of you."

"Okay, that's fine, but I don't have any trees, ma'am. I'm sorry."

"Speaking of the devil, here he comes right now."

Face pulled up into his driveway and parked adjacent to Banks.

Banks said, "Hey, I never caught your name."

She replied, "Me, I'm Nancy," then patted her German Shepherd and said, "And this here is Clarence."

"As you already know, I'm Banks. Nice to meet you, ma'am."

Face got out of his whip with a blunt of kush tucked behind his left ear, cheesing for no apparent reason.

He said, "Hey Nancy, whatchu up to?"

"Nothing, just admiring this fine specimen of a man. Why, you got some trees?" she replied.

"Yeah, I gotcha."

He then pulled out a freshly rolled blunt from behind his ear and tried to hand it to her.

She frowned and said, "What the hell am I supposed to do with that? I need at least a pound, fool."

"Oh. Well, I don't have that much on me right now. You gotta wait 'til later on. Give me a couple hours, a'ight?"

She said, "Alright," and snatched the blunt from his hand. "This should do for now."

As she walked away, Clarence barked at the blunt because he enjoyed the smell just as much as she did. Shit, he'd been her smoking buddy for years.

Banks got out of the car and said, "She's crazier than a muthafucka, huh?"

"Yeah, I love her old ass though. Come on, let's get inside," Face replied.

"She reminds me of Mama."

"I ain't gon' lie, bruh, that rap shit you've been talkin' 'bout sounds real good right about now."

Face unlocked the door, walked inside, and immediately disabled his alarm system. Banks followed closely and shut the door behind him.

Face said, "So wassup, bruh? It sounded like you had something real important to tell me."

"I do. Look, right after you left the hospital, I got a visit from the same detectives who blackmailed you and Sincere. Now they're trying to link me to the murders of CJ and Johnny."

"What the fuck do you mean Johnny's murder? That nigga Johnny is dead?"

"Uh, yeah. That's how Tonya had her accident. They said somebody blew his car up, and she just happened to be with him. Their theory is I may have done the shit in a jealous rage. Then his folks shot Mama's house up in retaliation."

"Wow! On the phone, you said she had a car accident. Now you're telling me her car blew up? Why didn't you say that at the hospital in front of El? You're putting everything on me when you could've been the reason Mama got shot. You and I both know if Keno thought you killed Johnny, he wouldn't hesitate to slide. He probably knows Johnny was the one who set you up. That would give you the motive and the means to knock him down."

"That's why I didn't say shit about it earlier, 'cause I knew you would try to weasel your way out of accepting responsibility. That shit was your fault, and I'm gon' prove it."

"Well, tell me this—were you the one who blew up his car? And don't lie, bruh."

Banks stared at Face intently, contemplating whether he should tell the truth since he might need his help later.

He said, "Yeah, I did it. I was doin' what I had to do to protect my family, though."

"Bullshit, don't try to sugarcoat yo fuck ups while persecuting me for mine. You wanted revenge for him stealing your bitch and sending you off to prison as a parting gift."

"Regardless of any of that, it ain't the reason Mama's house got shot up."

"Yeah, let you tell it. By the way, how do you know they were the same detectives that blackmailed us?"

"Because I know how they think. One of them was a dark-skinned brutha, about six-one. His first initial is a T, and his last name is Jones. The other one's name was Johnson. He was obviously the sidekick."

"Yeah, that's them."

"Good. Now that we're on the same page, here's his number. He wants to ask you all that formal bullshit. Like if you know anyone who would do that to Mama."

"What? I'm good."

"Here, bruh, take the card. It's best you just call him and get it out the way because he could make shit worse for us."

Face angrily snatched the card from Banks' hand because he felt he was betraying the code of the street.

"A'ight, I'll call his ass later," he stated.

"Don't forget, blood. 'Cause I know how you are."

"Aye, bruh."

"Yeah?"

"You must've really been mad at Tonya to try to blow the bitch up. What'd you have, some C4 or some shit?"

"Nah, bruh. And I wasn't trying to blow her up. She wasn't even in the car wit him. She followed him to some bitch house that he was fucking on the side. Out of nowhere, she pulled up alongside him, arguing and shit right before his car blew up. And I definitely wasn't finna save the bitch."

"Daaaamn... Was that nigga running around on fire, screaming and shit like a lil' ol bitch?"

"Nah, man. It wasn't like in the movies. I'm sure the concussion from the blast killed him instantly."

"Damn... That's some sick shit, bruh. I love you for that, though. That's gangsta."

"Anyway, have you heard anything from Sincere ass yet?"

"Hell nah. None of the lieutenants from any of the traps have, either."

"On the real, I think we need to slide by the house he hiding that bitch at wit all that money on her head. And she better have some answers for us, before I collect the bounty my damn self. This shit's all her fault anyway, ain't it?"

"Yuuup, it sounds like a plan to me."

"Oh—before I get in the shower—what happened with that Cell-Bo situation?"

"Still no word from him or Tyson. When we get back, we'll dip through his spot to see if he's been there. The shit's weird 'cause nobody's seen him or Tyson around. But they left the getaway car parked in front of Reiko's crib."

"Yeah, that shit's crazy. I'll do some serious brainstorming while I'm in the shower—it used to work for me in the pen."

"A'ight, c'mon, I'll get you some clean clothes and shit."

Approximately thirty minutes after Banks had showered and brushed his teeth, he stepped out of the bathroom, looking and smelling fresh. He walked uncomfortably into Face's master bedroom, where he was busy packing a suitcase. The room appeared to showcase precisely the right amount of sex appeal a bachelor pad represented—an erotic atmosphere created by exotic furniture and cheap paintings, but nothing too corny.

Banks said, "Damn, blood, why you got me wearing these tight-ass skinny jeans, bruh? I'm gonna get a yeast infection on my nuts, blood."

"Ha! Them ain't skinny jeans. They're fitted jeans, man," Face replied jokingly.

"Shit, what's the difference?"

Face paused, considering his response.

"Shit, I don't know, but they're Gucci, though," he said sarcastically.

"I just got off the phone with Tiffany. She said the detectives called her to verify my alibi."

"That ain't no surprise. The million-dollar question is, did they buy it?"

"She said they did."

"They must be on some lazy shit if they didn't push to see her in person. Everybody knows they like to get a good read of a muthafucka to see if they're lying or not."

"Yeah, well, I'm just glad they didn't. Now we can focus on our objective without suspicion looming over me."

Banks suddenly noticed that Face was packing a suitcase.

"Ay, man, whatchu packing that bag for?" asked Banks.

"This just in case we gotta skip town in a hurry."

"Skip town? Nigga, we ain't goin' nowhere. What? You forgot I have two daughters to look after?"

"C'mon, bruh, you know I ain't forget about them. But you never know where the yellow brick road might lead to."

"I know for damn sho it ain't leading me away from my kids. Ya, feel me?"

"Yeah, I feel you. Are you ready to bounce? Because you know it's gonna be traffic on Eight-Eighty."

"Yup, let's get up out of here."

It took them thirty-five minutes to reach San Jose due to traffic. Luckily, the commute wasn't as congested as usual, or it would have taken at least fifteen minutes longer. As soon as they passed the San Jose city limits sign, Face's phone started ringing. He looked down and saw Justin's name in bold black letters. *Finally, I'm about to get some good news,* he thought.

Face answered, "Wassup, bruh? Gimme some good news."

Justin said, "Well, I got some good news, and some bad news, big dog. The good news is, since the car was parked on the street, I was able to get it. The bad news is it was wiped clean. Not even a hotel receipt was left behind."

"Fuck! Make sure you burn it, man."

"A'ight, dog, I'll take care of it. Lata."

"Peace."

Disgruntled, Face put his phone inside his cup holder and said, "That was Justin. He had no luck finding anything in Reiko's car."

Banks said, "You should be happy. That would've meant them fools was sloppy as hell. And more than likely, they would've left a trail leading them right back to yo ass."

"Yeah, you've got a point there. What now? Is the question."

"Shit, now we just gotta follow the breadcrumbs. They usually lead straight back to a rat."

"Whatchu mean by that?"

"Think about it. If your spots keep getting hit by the same person, somebody's gotta be in bed wit 'em, helping him to mastermind."

"Dontcha think we thought about that already? There are too many damn people in our machine to just narrow one snake down like that. All we can do is tighten up the security on all our spots. We can't watch everybody. Shit, the whole hood knows what goes on inside them trap houses."

"I'm thinking it's one of y'all lieutenants."

"Why did you say that?"

"Because the streets are just like the penitentiary. In there, every race is a card, and each race card is broken up into smaller cards—like Bloods, Crips, Skinheads, et cetera. But on the streets, we got subsections within the hood. Now, peep game. Every one of these cards has a head nigga in charge with keys to the yard. Every nigga with the keys has a lieutenant waiting in line to take his place should the opportunity arise. The thing is, every lieutenant has sergeants backing him with the mindset that they should be next in line. Just like every turf is broken up into little cliques that really don't give a fuck about each other. Everybody's just sitting around waiting for a come-up. Well, sooner or later sergeants get tired of waiting, so they create an opportunity to move up in the ranks by knocking off the boss. In this situation, I would call a meeting with your lieutenants and their right hands to see if they are campaigning for a promotion. Because y'all just might have a mutiny on your hands."

"Yeah, that sounds like a viable approach. I'll run that by Sincere and see what he says."

Ten minutes later they exited the freeway and headed toward the San Jose hills. Shortly afterward, they entered a high-end neighborhood primarily inhabited by tech giants and corporate sharks—a seemingly safe and quiet place to raise a family. One would not have expected the carnage that had recently taken place to have occurred in such a sublime neighborhood. They instantly noticed the local Bay Area news vans parked near the center of the cul-de-sac as they pulled onto Sincere's block. There were spectators gathered on both sides of the street, trying to figure out how such a horrendous crime could have happened in their coveted neighborhood—a neighborhood many of them held in such high regard.

Carol whispered to her neighbor Lucy, "I knew he had to be a drug dealer because my husband said he wasn't a major athlete. And he dressed like one of those gangster rappers."

"Now that's just plain racist, Carol," Lucy replied sternly.

"Hey—if the shoe fits."

Face pulled into an empty driveway, assuming the homeowners were at work and wouldn't notice. They exited the car and casually walked up the block to join the crowd of bystanders.

Afterward, Face snuck up behind Carol and asked, "What happened here?"

"I think it was a drug deal gone bad, from the looks of it," Carol replied.

"Why'd you say that?" asked Banks.

Carol whispered, "Because they were colored folks."

Carol was unaware of who she was talking to, so Lucy gave her a quick elbow nudge, followed by a head nod, alerting her to look over her shoulder. Taking the hint, she turned to her right and saw Banks, causing her to gasp. Then, when she turned to her left and saw Face standing there, it almost gave her a heart attack.

"Come on, Lucy, let's get out of here," Carol demanded as she pulled Lucy through the crowd.

Banks stepped up and tapped a heavyset white man on the shoulder—he was wearing tan Dockers and a plaid shirt.

"Excuse me, sir, but do you know what happened here?" asked Banks.

Considering the man's reaction to seeing Banks, it was apparent he hadn't recognized him from the neighborhood. Therefore, he immediately darted his eyes to Face to see if he recognized him.

The man said, "You two aren't from around here, are you?"

Banks replied, "No sir. We were just checking out the area looking for a home to purchase, and spotted the news vans. This doesn't look very welcoming, does it?"

"Oh, well normally this is a serene environment. But nowadays nowhere is safe, ya know."

"Yeah, I hear ya."

"The police are saying they believe it was a home invasion gone wrong. There were three bodies found inside the house, including the homeowner. They showed a couple of neighbors his ID to verify that he actually lived there. It's sad, ya know. You aren't even safe in your own home anymore. We've gotta do something comprehensive about these gun laws."

"Yeah, man, we live in a cold world. And it seems like it gets colder every day."

Face eventually noticed that Carol and Lucy had moved across the street and were now talking to their neighbors. Oddly, it seemed like they had somehow become the topic of their conversation. Suddenly, Face felt unwelcome, and the feeling quickly spread to Banks.

Banks said, "C'mon, bro, let's check out some more properties."

"Sounds like a good idea," Face replied.

Banks said, "Alright, sir, you have a blessed day now. I'll be sure to keep that family in our prayers."

"Okay, thanks. It was nice talking to ya. And I'm sorry if this tragic incident scared you guys off."

They then hurried to the car before the police noticed them and decided to question them. Banks knew he was playing with fire because any line of questioning could've easily resulted in him being arrested. Therefore, he acted cautiously since initiating police contact while on parole was a sure violation. Given the circumstances, that was the last thing they needed, especially with everything else transpiring.

They were both dead silent the entire ride to the freeway as they tried to process the devastating news they had just received.

Face shouted, "Fuck, blood! Sincere is really dead. Now what the fuck are we supposed to do?"

"Try staying calm, for starters. 'Cause gettin' all amped up ain't gon' help nobody," Banks stated.

"Stay calm? Bruh, not only did I just lose the head of my organization, but that muthafucka owed me two-million dollars. Whatchu forgot? And now I don't even know where that bitch at. She was our only lead."

"It looks to me like El's bottom bitch gave her sister up before she took a bullet to the head. The part that has me puzzled is, why would they kill Sincere and take the broad? Why not just kill her, too? If Taz got money like that, it couldn't have been about locating any money. Do you know if he had two other soldiers at his house?"

"Nah, but I know for a fact, if it was two dead bodies in his house, Sincere killed them. Because I was the only person he trusted enough to know where he lived."

"Shit, at least he went out like a gangsta. He took a couple of them suckas wit him. I think the bitch somehow got in the wind. I don't think she's dead, blood."

"Man, knowing Taz, he probably got her somewhere peeling off her flesh with a skin grafter."

"Either way, the bitch is useless to us now. Did Sincere keep any work at his house?"

"Yeah, but not at that house. He constantly rotated stash houses, keeping their locations secret. After every major transaction, he got on some James Bond, 007-type shit.. He always said no one could force me to reveal what I didn't know."

"Well, remember that lieutenant's meeting I was talkin' 'bout?"

"Yeah, why?"

"'Cause it looks like we're gonna have to expedite it."

"Why you say that, bruh?"

"Think about it. Sincere is dead now. If a mutiny is on the rise, what better time than now to campaign for the keys to The Town? Who is normally in charge of pickin' up the dough during daily operations?"

"I am, why?"

"Because we need to snatch all the money and dope from the trap houses before they find out that Sincere's dead."

"Why? You think they're gonna steal that shit?"

"You've gotta expect the worst at a time like this. Some of them cats are gon' panic, thinking their run is over and get on some grimy shit. Plus, I'm willing to bet that whoever believes they deserve to be running the show will show their true colors now. And that's when you assert your authority once and for all in front of all your lieutenants. That will ensure no one else questions your position. Ya, feel me?"

"Yeah I feel you, blood."

"And on top of that, we don't know if Sincere left any records linking him to any of the trap houses. Lord knows, if he happened to slip like that, the DEA could be kicking in doors within a week."

"I doubt it, but we could never be too careful."

"Do you have a discreet location where we could fit all your soldiers at once?"

"Yeah, Kaion has a warehouse off Mandela Parkway."

"Well, there it is there."

"We're going to need your truck to fit all that work in. Call El—tell him to meet us at my house ASAP so he can trail us. Then all we have to do is pick up one more shooter we can trust."

"Who?" Banks asked optimistically.

"Awol. He's been puttin' in work since you've been gone. He called me last night and said he just got back from Atlanta."

"Don't he still be having them grand mal seizures, though? He a fuck around and seize up, and shoot everybody."

"He said they weren't as frequent as they were when we were kids. But yeah, he still does."

"Ay, remember that time when we tried to rob the pizza man, and that nigga had a seizure?" Banks asked jokingly.

"Hell yeah, Awol ass seized up, and the pizza man started beating his ass. We had to run back and save that fool. We're the reason none of the pizza places deliver in The Town now to this day. We was some bad ass kids wasn't we?"

"Man, those were the good old days."

"Yeah, that's when Pops was still alive."

Banks' smile slowly faded, and a brief emotional stillness hinted at his discomfort.

Banks said, "A'ight, I'm about to call El so we can get this show on the road," before pulling out his cell phone and dialing El's number.

CHAPTER SEVEN

• • •

Awol had spent the whole day in Fonk Town shooting dice. He was trying to win back his money from a mark who wasn't even from his hood. Unfortunately, his luck had been bad all week. First, one of the three strippers he'd been trickin' with at a hotel in Atlanta stole his iced-out Rolex. Then, his layover flight was delayed, forcing him to stay overnight in Phoenix, Arizona. Now, he was down seventeen hundred dollars to this off-brand-ass nigga named Yukon, who was up about fifty-five hundred dollars in total.

Yukon finally crapped out, and Awol had him faded so he was next on the dice. Therefore, Yukon purposely took his time handing Awol his money so he wouldn't have to fade him, but Awol peeped it. Next, Awol shook the dice and rolled double treys. By then, he was in his feelings about losing to a buster like Yukon, so he took his side bets personally.

Since Lobo was the one that had him faded, Awol said, "Bet five hunnit on the six-eight, Yukon. You got it?"

Jarvis said, "Ooooh..." trying to instigate the bet since everybody knew Yukon was a pump-up case.

Yukon said, "Bet, nigga. I ain't never been scared to take a sucka's money. I need me some new Gucci loafers anyway."

Awol then rolled the dice again. He first rolled snake eyes, then a four, followed by a shaky nine. Afterward, he picked up the dice, and blew on them once for good luck, before rolling an acey-deucey.

He said, "C'mon, bitches! Dance for daddy," as he spun the dice.

Both dice spun around like the old school children's toy spinning top. The anticipation increased the longer they spun because they felt like they were both playing for their pride.

Awol yelled, "C'mon bitches!" as the first die landed on a four.

The second die tumbled around, flashing a four, then a one, then a six, before eventually landing on a heartbreaking three.

Awol yelled, "Fuuuuck!"

"That's what I'm talkin' 'bout," Yukon exclaimed.

They were playing hand fade, so Marcel quickly handed Lobo twenty dollars to get on dice next. Suddenly, a silver Audi pulled up, knockin' Philty Rich. The driver was a jazzy BBW, rockin' bright red hair with blonde highlights. She quickly double-tapped her horn, causing everyone to look up at her suspiciously.

Yukon said, "Alright then, y'all, I'm about to cut. I gotta go handle some shit."

Awol said, "What! You can't hit and run wit my money, family. Fuck that fat bitch. I'm still fading. You gotta give me action!"

Nigga, this my money now!" Yukon said, stuffing his pockets with cash. "I'll be through here tomorrow. That should give y'all enough time to break y'all kids' piggy banks open."

Yukon was feeling himself, so it didn't bother him that he was adding fuel to the already flaming fire. He walked off with a cocky limp, cheesing like he had just won the lotto. Then, he hopped into the passenger seat and started showing off his winnings.

He said, "You see this baby? This is how real bosses do it. We get it out the mud."

"Um hmm.. daddy, I see you. Are you ready to go eat?" she replied.

"Yeah, let's get the fuck up out of here. These fools is hatin'."

However, before she could even put the car in drive, she saw a hand holding a Glock 23 swing through the window, causing her to tense up instantly. All she heard was, "Bitch-ass nigga!" before deafening shots rang out, accompanied by fiery muzzle flashes. She was frozen stiff as the shooter snatched all of the money sitting on Yukon's lap, bloody and all. She just sat there traumatized, with her face covered in blood and brain matter. Her hands remained glued to the steering wheel, stuck at ten and two. Eventually, she looked over at Yukon to see if he was still alive, and if so, what was the severity of his injuries? After witnessing his disfigured face smoking, she threw up in her lap before scrambling out of the car. Hearing the gunshots caused everyone else to scatter like cockroaches trying to get somewhere safe.

Awol hurried to his car, hoodie stuffed with blood-covered money, wondering who could be calling at such an inopportune time. However, once he started up his car and peeled off, his caller ID prompted him to answer his phone.

"Wassup, cuzo?" he asked through bated breath.

"A lot. We gotta talk business. Meet me at my spot ASAP," Face replied.

CHAPTER EIGHT

· · ·

Sav pulled into the Cypress Village housing projects, driving his silver S63 Mercedes Benz with presidential tints. He parked next to a group of hoodrats kickin' it outside a Ford Focus. They were smoking weed and drinking Grey Goose vodka out of red plastic Dixie cups.

"Damn, sexy, can I come witchu?" one of them asked flirtatiously.

"Nah, not today, ma," he replied.

"Well, can I at least get your number?" she asked desperately.

"Look, I tell you what. If I come out of here with some good news, I'll take all four of y'all to the Ritz for a little private party. How does that sound?"

They all looked at each other hesitantly because they wanted to agree without sounding thirsty. Even though they knew, in all likelihood, he wanted an orgy.

"A'ight, we're down," said the outspoken one, speaking for them all.

He looked at the rest of their expressions to make sure they were really with it—so if push came to shove, he wouldn't end up wasting his time.

"I guess. Shit, we ain't got nothing else to do," said the one who was seemingly the ringleader.

"A'ight, well, I gotta go. I'll holla at y'all in a minute," he replied, laughing.

"Wait, we know who your fine ass is. But you ain't ask for our names."

"Because there's no need to. You're Keke, you're Lisa, you're Shonda, and you, you're Felicity. These are my projects, and I know everything that goes on in here. Now, if y'all will excuse me, I have some important business to tend to."

Then, he walked off like a boss, knowing he had just mind-fucked them with his god complex.

Keke's outspoken ass said, "Girl... I'm so gonna give him some pussy tonight."

"Shit...me too," Shonda added matter-of-factly.

Moments later, Sav reached the base of the steps leading to one of his many trap houses. There, he ran into one of his young soldiers named Wayne, who was supposed to be on point. He was sitting between the legs of a fine chocolate honey smoking a strawberry Swisher Sweet with only half his hair braided.

Wayne said, "Wassup, Sav? Wanna hit this blunt?" while holding it out in front of him.

However, Sav didn't respond until he got within arm's reach of him.

And when he did, he slapped the blunt out of Wayne's hand and said, "Nigga, ain't you supposed to be lookin' out?"

"Uh… yeah," Wayne replied, feeling completely embarrassed.

Sav immediately snatched his honey up by her wrist and asked, "So why the fuck do you got her sittin' here distracting you then?"

"My bad, boss. She's just tryin' to be down wit a nigga, that's all."

"That's all understandable. But y'all gotta do all that lovey-dovey shit on y'all own time. Right now, you on the clock, so lil' mama, you gotta bounce."

Sav didn't have to tell her twice; she already knew whose spot it was, and his reputation preceded him. Ironically, even after his chastisement, he couldn't help but watch her big booty cheeks jiggle in her black yoga pants as she walked away.

Wayne yelled, "I'll call you later!" regretting her departure.

Sav said, "I ain't gon' lie though, she's bad. Do she got a sista?"

"Yeah, and she be doin sliders. She ratchet, though."

"She might still be good for somethin'. Is she fine, too?"

"Yeah, she's like twenty-two."

"A'ight, yougin', get her number for me, I gotta go. And you better keep watch from now on, you know it's Fonk Season."

"A'ight, big dog, I gotcha."

Sav entered the apartment and saw four of King's curb servers sitting around watching television. He slowly scanned the room, quietly evaluating them, trying to gauge the professionalism King upheld while running his place of business. It was no secret that Sav prided himself on running a tight ship because it was how he lasted as long as he did in the game. He claimed he ran his trap houses like an authentic business establishment, except the customers weren't always right, and you didn't receive any medical benefits, either. So if you were ever to get sick, you would have to take your ass down to county just like everybody else. Hence, in all actuality, it wasn't run anything like a legitimate business, he just made it sound good.

After Sav finished his evaluation, he decided everything looked in order. However, that didn't surprise him because it usually was at that particular trap house.

Sav closed the door and said, "Wassup wit y'all, niggas?"

Suddenly, they all bounced up like they were kids who just got caught watching porn.

"Wassup?" they all replied before giving him dap.

"Shit, just came through to holla at King. Where is he at?"

"He's in the back room. He said he was expecting you earlier," one of them replied.

"Ay, what had y'all all mesmerized with the TV?"

"The Wire, this shit off the hook, blood."

"Oh yeah, I be off that too. That fool Omar reminds me of myself. A'ight, I'll holla at y'all in a minute. I gotta holla at King real quick."

"A'ight."

As Sav reached for the doorknob, he could hear J. Stalin's music blasting. Once he opened the door, he could hear King's younger brother, Egypt, wincing like a little bitch over the music. He had a nurse named Zakia on his payroll for delicate situations such as avoiding hospitals. Hence, there she was bent over stitching up Egypt's arm. He knew now that they were using the loud music to drown out Egypt's moans while she worked on him.

Sav said, "She's just now gettin' here? Get out for a minute, Zakia."

Afterward, he held the door open until she exited the room, then quickly closed it behind her.

Sav said, "Please explain to me how y'all go to do a hit, and you get shot?"

King replied, "Man, Sav, this spot wasn't like any of the other ones. We was on a narrow ass street, and they had gunners wit choppas posted on the porch. We knew we couldn't use the usual approach, so I parked in front so Egypt and Quan could bounce out. They got the drop on the first two niggas, but somebody started bustin' through the window of the house on some Kamikaze shit. Quan got hit first. I knew he was dead, so I told bruh to c'mon. He started running back to the car, and that's when he got hit."

"Where's Quan's body at?"

"He crawled up the sidewalk and collapsed. We had to leave him there. But don't worry, we didn't take anything that could link us. No cell phones, no IDs, nothin'."

"Man, you think I'm stupid, huh? You're gonna look me dead in my eyes and try to convince me that the hit was too hard? When y'all dummies really fucked it up on some greedy shit. All y'all were supposed to do was wait for Face to come out of the house and bark 'em down. But nah, y'all tried to run up in a secured trap house unprepared. Now, not only am I down a soldier, but now Face's guards will be up. Y'all just fucked up the perfect opportunity to down his bitch ass."

King just stood there shaking his head with a stupid look on his face. Meanwhile, Egypt didn't care what the hell was going on because he was too busy cringing in pain.

Sav said, "Where are the bitches that set the shit up?"

"They're in the other room chillin'. Why?" King asked nervously.

Sav then pulled out a 9mm pistol from his waistband and screwed a silencer onto the tip of the barrel.

He said, "Because thanks to y'all, now we've gotta kill 'em and get rid of their bodies."

"Why, man? They're solid," King replied, begging.

"Because y'all were just involved in a triple murder, as far as I know. And them bitches fingerprints are all over that house. Sooner or later, they're going to get questioned about that shit. If y'all would've just followed Face like I said, they would've been in the clear. So their blood is on y'all hands. Do you think they wouldn't spill the beans in a heartbeat if they got caught, leading the pigs straight to y'all? Because frankly, I don't trust that y'all wouldn't lead them straight to me. Then I'd have to kill all you muthafuckas. So to avoid having to kill you two niggas, we're gonna take care of that problem, right now."

"It's like that, bruh?"

"Yeah, stupid! Y'all fucked up. Now c'mon, so we can take care of these liabilities."

Sav turned to Egypt, smiled, and said contemptuously, "Stop crying, nigga. That's just a flesh wound."

When Sav opened the door, he saw Zakia standing idly in the hallway. By the look on her face, he could tell that she didn't want to be stuck in the living room with all of his goons. Which meant more than likely, they had been pressuring her for more than just some medical attention. Fully determined, Sav stepped into the hallway, hiding his gun behind his back, with King following closely behind.

Sav nodded at Zakia and said, "Go ahead and finish patching that fool up. They already paid you, right?"

"Yes, sir," Zakia replied bashfully.

"Well, we're all squared then?"

"Yes, sir."

"Good."

Next, Zakia walked back into the bedroom and closed the door behind herself. Meanwhile, Sav and King approached the door leading to the room Venus and Reina were kickin' it in.

"You go in first," Sav demanded.

King opened the door feeling sympathy for the girls because he knew his bad judgment was about to lead to their demise. Sadly, his mistake was beyond rectifying. At that point, nothing he could have done would have changed the inevitable. Therefore, he opened the door and casually walked into the room, followed by Sav, who rarely made a grand entrance. Sav then closed the door behind himself, hoping not to appear suspicious, while concealing his pistol behind his back. The room was blanketed in thick weed smoke after they closed the window and hotboxed a blunt of cat piss.

"Wassup wit y'all?" King asked deceitfully.

"Shit, blowing this blunt, trying to take the edge off," Venus replied.

King was praying they didn't slip and say anything about the money they had stolen from Sincere's trap house because that was some off-the-books shit.

"Wanna hit this blunt?" asked Reina.

"Yeah, let me hit that," King replied.

Venus could tell by Sav's cold, callous glare that something was awry. It caused her to watch King's body language, and she instantly noticed that he appeared tense. King accepted the blunt from Reina, then stepped to the side to assure he was out of range of any possible friendly fire. Reina was oblivious to the impending danger. She was only concerned with getting her next high. She was feeling herself but had picked the wrong time to zone out. She closed her eyes and started snapping her fingers to the beat of the music, joyously getting into her groove.

King reached his hand out and said, "Wanna hit dis Venus?"

"Nah, I'm good," she replied.

Reina said, "Here, I'll kill that shit," as she grabbed the blunt from King's fingertips.

By then, Venus was fixated on Sav, totally distracted by what he was hiding behind his back. Finally, she leaned to the side and saw the butt of his pistol, causing her heart to palpitate at an alarming pace. Venus and Reina knew they had fucked up, so they stayed quiet to avoid making things worse However, considering the circumstances, Venus felt it might be the only thing capable of saving their lives.

She said, "I'm sorry, Sav. I know we fucked up the lick—but we could easily make up for it."

"Oh yeah? And how are you going to do that?" Sav replied.

"I don't know just yet. But we'll definitely figure something out. I know some other ballers we could set up from North Oakland."

Hearing Venus' tone helped Reina finally realize some shady shit was about to go down. Then, all of a sudden, she had to pee like a racehorse.

Reina said, "I'll be right back y'all, I gotta pee," and attempted to step past King.

However, King pushed her back and said, "Damn, bitch! Can't you see the man is talking?"

"My bad," she replied and stood extremely still."

Venus said, "I promise, Sav. You got nothing to worry about. If we get caught, we ain't gonna say shit—I swear."

Reina darted her eyes back and forth from King to Sav, waiting for King to speak up for them. She felt it was only right since he was the one who had put their heads on the chopping block.

"Say something, King," Reina demanded.

King didn't respond, though. He just looked at her like, bitch, you trippin'.

Venus could tell by King's reaction that something was about to go down. She had a gut feeling they were planning on tying up loose ends. Which meant they were about to be the knot. It was no secret that Venus had been fighting boys all her life, and she never backed down from anybody. But in her lifetime, she had never felt a fear like she felt at that moment. Thankfully, the desperation and the basic instinct to survive gave her the courage to try and escape.

She stated, "Fuck this," then hopped off the bed, beelining straight for the doorknob.

Unfortunately, once she grabbed it, Sav put his pistol to her heart to confirm a kill shot.

"Please," she sobbed as she turned the knob and opened the door.

Sadly, her plea for mercy carried no weight against his instinct for self-preservation. Sav fired two shots into her chest, knocking her backward until she collapsed onto the bed. She died instantly, eyes wide open, tears still running down her cheeks. Reina stood frozen in fear because she had never witnessed a deadly act of violence. She merely orchestrated them, as most setup artists did. Therefore, she just stared down the barrel of his silencer, trembling in shock, unable to muster up the will to fight for her life. She was too paralyzed to even scream for help. Or maybe deep down, she knew her pleas for help would be futile because, in Cypress Village, no one called the police anyway. Nevertheless, she cut her eyes at King one last time for help, as Sav approached her for a better shot.

"Please," she begged as she reached out for King's arm.

"Pfft!" A quiet, metallic snap pierced the air, barely audible, yet unmistakable.

Suddenly, a bullet struck her chest, knocking her backward.

"Why?" she whispered as she slid down the wall into the abyss.

King just stood there, bug-eyed, hoping he wasn't next—especially after letting the one who had Angela raped and kidnapped get away. Sav pulled out a handkerchief, wiped his fingerprints off the gun, then handed it to King.

"Now clean this shit up. I got a date with some freaks," Sav said before walking out.

CHAPTER NINE

Special agents Robert Miller and Cynthia Hernandez entered Sacramento's Federal Detention Center determined to make a break in their case. Miller was a fifty-year-old Caucasian man with twenty-eight years of experience in the DEA. Given his reputation, everyone in the agency knew he kept a hard-on when solving big-time cases. Special Agent Hernandez was a twelve-year veteran who dedicated most of her time to infiltrating cartels. She was a thirty-seven-year-old Mexican woman with striking features that some mistook for Filipina ancestry. After checking in admittance, a US Marshal escorted them through a labyrinth of corridors to the facility's infirmary, where Cocaine was detained with one wrist shackled to a hospital bed.

Cocaine had been up all night mentally preparing for the inevitable cat-and-mouse game he was about to play. He had just finished his last bite of Jell-O when he heard his door unlock. He set his cup of Jell-O down and stared at Hernandez and Miller as they entered his giant cell.

Cocaine was momentarily captivated by Hernandez's beauty because she could've easily been a model.

Cocaine said, "Y'all came just in time, detectives. Now, y'all can fetch me some more Jell-O. And make sure y'all bring me the watermelon flavor this time. That cherry flavor nasty."

"Oh, I see we have ourselves a natural-born comedian," Miller replied.

Hernandez said, "Only we're not detectives. We're special agents, jackass."

"And you're in some deep shit," Miller stated as he inched closer to Cocaine's gurney.

Cocaine said, "Well, it sounds to me like I need to speak to a lawyer then. Y'all know what that means, right?"

"No, please inform us."

"It means y'all can suck my dick. That's what."

Miller stood at the head of Cocaine's gurney and said, "No lawyer is going to get your black ass out of this one. You know that gun you discharged recklessly in a residential area? It was linked to the death of a federal agent."

"Man, fuck you! I ain't kill no damn fed. And you can't prove I did. That gun was fresh out the box."

"Well, you see, that's where you're wrong. That gun you used was stolen during a gun heist in which an undercover DEA agent was murdered. Now we've linked the serial numbers from that gun back to the heist, which connects you directly to the murder of a federal agent. So it looks to me like you might be facing the death penalty, boy."

"I ain't your muthafuckin' boy, pig."

Miller had already read Cocaine's medical report, so he was completely familiar with the injuries he had sustained from the shooting. Therefore, frustrated by Cocaine's arrogance, he wasted no time exploiting his weakness. Miller casually pressed his thumb into Cocaine's left shoulder, exactly where he'd recently had surgery.

"Ahh!" Cocaine cried out in agony. "Ay, muthafucka, you can't do this to me. I'm the victim," Cocaine protested after Miller let him go.

Miller said, "Shut up! I know who you are. And I also know what it is you do. Now I know you didn't steal those guns or kill that agent—you're too damn stupid to pull off that heist."

"So why the fuck are you hassling me then?"

Hernandez interjected, "To get to the big fish. We know you're just a guppy, swimming along in a great big ocean. We want to talk to you about the deceased girl you were with. A Ms. Maria Lopez."

"Yeah? What about her?" Cocaine asked, frowning.

"We've done our research, so we know you're into the distribution business. With that being said, we know there is no way on God's green earth that you are simply dating Javier Guzman's niece for carnal pleasure. We know he is your supplier from video surveillance. We have you on video entering his restaurant with a backpack and then leaving with a duffle bag. We could've busted you then, but like I said, we want the big fish."

Miller said, "Think about it. With the video evidence we have linking you to The Faction, even if you were innocent of the agent's murder, the jury would convict you just to get you off the streets."

Cocaine said, "Well, if y'all are so smart, why do y'all need me? Man, fuck y'all! Y'all ain't got shit!"

Hernandez replied, "Because they are good at compartmentalizing. We know Javier wasn't present at your low-level drug transaction. They're not that sloppy. Now, if you want to avoid the lethal injection you only have one option. You have to set up a deal with Javier large enough to draw him out. I need something substantial enough to make him flip on a man who goes by the name of Grandpa. He is the head of The Faction's stronghold here in the U.S."

"Look, J-Lo, I wish I could help you, but Javier threatened to kill me. He said if I didn't find Maria's killer he was going to kill me in his place. So how the fuck do you expect me to call him up and set up a major deal?"

Miller said, "You seem pretty resourceful. You'll figure it out."

"Man, fuck you! Cracker."

"You see how easily we got you transferred to this federal facility? Shit can get a lot worse from here on out. Don't forget you're being detained on suspicion of killing a federal agent. Accidents do happen, you know."

Hernandez said, "But don't worry, we'll keep you safe as long as you play ball. You got forty-eight hours to think about it before we book you on murder charges. Until then—you should get yourself some rest. We need you all healed up because you have an important job ahead of you."

Miller then removed a card from his suit jacket and slapped it on Cocaine's chest.

"Take care," he said and pressed it against his body, causing him to wince in pain.

CHAPTER TEN

Banks and Face had spent the entire night securing the money and drugs from each trap house. According to the plan, Face tucked every last dollar into a wall safe at h. It was a secret stash house, unknown even to his mother. Face understood the critical importance of that re-up money since he had no idea where Sincere hid his supply, and all ties to Taz were officially severed. He had to admit Sincere was clever and elusive when it came to avoiding fed time. He methodically stashed large quantities of dope inside varying rental properties he owned using shell corporations until it was time for distribution. That made it nearly impossible to track his movements since each shipment arrived at varying times and locations. Also, Face was the only one allowed to pick up the drugs and deliver them to the lieutenant's stash houses. Once the lieutenant secured the drugs at their stash houses, they became responsible for controlling the flow of drugs through their assigned networks. Face thought about his recent conversation with Sincere and how he proudly claimed they were equals. It sounded reasonable at the time, but now that Sincere was dead, he felt like he was in a sinking boat without a life jacket. He realized it was some philosophical bullshit, to say the least. How could they have been equals? Because now, without Sincere supplying him with the product, he was no different than any of the lieutenants, and he knew it. Controlling the inventory long enough to find a new supplier was his only hope of averting a civil war. Since every lieutenant would now be searching for a cheap connection, leaving millions of dollars in the streets was not an option. Indeed, that would be the result if a network was left without product in such a demanding market. Luckily, Banks said he had a connection to at least sustain the network temporarily. All he had to do for now was solidify his position so he could keep their machine running.

It was 12:15 in the morning. All thirty-five of Sincere's lieutenants stood around Kaion's warehouse, awaiting an explanation for why all of the drugs and money were being extracted so quickly. Most of them felt insulted, assuming the precaution was taken because Donnie's spot had been shot up. Half of them eyed Donnie suspiciously, thinking he had complained to Sincere about his inability to hold his own. The other half knew it had to be something much bigger, like a federal indictment. Neither side realized the magnitude of the shake-up they were about to experience. Face had strategically placed all of the drugs on display for the lieutenants to see. It made it appear as though he had a stockpile of product to spread throughout their network.

Now holding all the cards, Face entered the warehouse, exuding total control. It was the first time he had felt that way since he found out Sincere was dead. He had left Banks, El, Awol, and Kaion at the warehouse to protect the drugs while he secretly hid the cash. Thankfully, he arrived just in time because the lieutenants had become restless and started questioning Banks about their recent incursion.

Banks, El, Awol, and Kaion stood united in front of the table where the drugs were displayed. Kaion and Awol clutched AK-47s in case anybody felt froggish and decided to leap. Banks and El had guns, too, but theirs were tucked in their waistband to avoid making the lieutenants feel any more threatened than they already did. Luckily for

Face, Kaion was as equally loyal to him as he was to Sincere. Primarily because after dealing directly with Face over the last eight years, a sense of loyalty developed organically. It was important it did because Kaion's trucking company was a crucial component of their operation, especially after Face decided that once he had acquired a sustainable network, he would expand as far east as possible. He already had it made up in his mind that he would be bigger than Sincere. So big that out-of-town niggas like Taz wouldn't have a chance in hell at knocking him down.

Kaion agreed to ride the wave because his wife had become accustomed to the extravagant lifestyle transporting the extra cargo provided. Hence, he knew that getting out so suddenly would've caused marital problems due to the decrease in her luxurious allowance.

As Face approached the table, the lieutenants gathered around him gradually, mentally preparing themselves for a game-changing revelation. Most of them looked around skeptically, wondering where the hell Sincere was. Face stood between Banks and El for visual effect. He made sure he took a position of authority before he even began to speak. Then he pulled out his .40-caliber handgun and sat it on top of the table to let everyone know he came to talk serious business. Seeing his demeanor made some of them nervous because every last one of them skimmed money periodically to maintain their lifestyles.

Face said, "I know y'all wondering why I dragged y'all down here for an emergency meeting. And why I extracted all of the dope and money from y'all trap houses."

The lieutenants suddenly began mumbling among themselves.

Face continued, "Well, I brought y'all down here to discuss Sincere's current status."

"What do you mean by his current status? Is he in jail? asked Deion."

"Nah, bruh, Sincere's dead."

"What! You lyin'."

They all gasped and then began to mumble amongst each other.

Face said, "Listen up! I wish I was lying, but they found Sincere dead at his house earlier today. They also found two other bodies. I'm assuming it was a hit team, but he managed to take two of them bitch-ass niggas wit him."

Ant asked, "Well, who the hell sent them fools?"

Stroll replied sternly, "Sav, nigga. Who else?"

Suddenly, everyone looked to Face for confirmation of Stroll's account.

Face said, "He's right. It ain't no secret. Sav's been chipping away little by little at our organization ever since his sister got killed. We all knew the street war between them two wouldn't end until one of them was dead."

Deion abruptly interrupted Face, "So what now?"

Face shot Deion a sharp look, making it clear he didn't appreciate the interruption. However, he knew then wasn't the time to draw a line in the sand because he needed every last one of his lieutenants to sustain their machine.

Face replied, "Like Sincere always said, this is a business. So keeping the operation running should be y'all's only concern."

Deion said, " So what are you sayin'? We ain't gon' ride for the homie?"

"Nah, nigga. Sav will get his, but right now, we have to stop the bleeding. Now that Sincere is dead, that nigga should relax, allowing us to patch up our wounds. We just got caught up in some personal beef between them two niggas. It didn't have shit to do with our organization. It was all over a funky-ass bitch. I'm sure that fool is feelin' himself right now. He's probably celebrating right now as we speak. Talkin' 'bout how he's finna consolidate Sincere's network and shit. But once they think they've won, that's when niggas get arrogant and let their guards down. He won't even see us coming."

"So you got everything under control then, huh? I heard he almost stamped you and Donnie earlier today. I also heard he smoked some of Donnie's shooters in the process. It sounds to me like you were the one caught with your guard down. Now let me guess, you expect us to follow you down a rabbit hole because you were Sincere's errand boy? That's funny because me and a couple of lieutenants were just talkin' about how our machine needed an upgrade."

Hearing Deion disrespect Face like that justified Banks' plan to move the drugs and money to his safe house. Face then looked over at Banks, who nodded, identifying Deion as the example that needed to be set.

Face said, "Is that right? So you and some of the lieutenants been making plans, huh? Maybe we should just have ourselves a little vote then?"

"Shit, I'm cool with that," Deion said, shrugging.

"A'ight then. If anybody else feels we should vote on who will be running the show from now on, raise their hand."

No one was stupid enough to raise their hand, since that would've been considered choosing a side when it was best to leave all options open. Despite most of the lieutenants feeling better suited to take over, now was not the time to make their move.

At first, Deion appeared to be alone, but when he shot Dre a piercing glare, Dre immediately raised his hand. Then, the dominoes began to fall. Next, Deion stared down Rome until he eventually raised his hand, making Face's job easy. He couldn't believe his co-conspirators revealed themselves so foolishly. Deion was suddenly feelin' himself and decided it was time to make his proclamation.

He said, "Y'all keep y'all hands up for a second. Everybody in this warehouse knows I've put in the most work. And I run the most lucrative spots in The Town. This nigga is just a middleman. Any one of y'all could replace him. I already got a connect in Houston. If y'all join me, I promise at least a twenty-five percent markup on what y'all have been bringing in. I'm talking purer shit for cheaper. So y'all can step on it, and the fiends still gonna love it."

Deion surveyed the warehouse, realizing his charming words had no effect on the rest of the lieutenants. Only his two disloyal flunkies were willing to risk a stable operation out of selfishness. Deion's treacherous smirk slowly dissolved as he realized his attempt to dethrone Face did nothing but expose his hand. It was apparent because the other lieutenants stared at him like he was dead meat ready to be served on a platter.

"You finished, nigga?" Face asked with a devilish smile.

By then, Deion's rebellious spirit was shattered into pieces. He knew his plan had been thwarted before it even grew any legs to walk.

"Yeah," he replied with a timid head nod.

Face said, "Good," then picked up his .40-caliber handgun and shot him in the left cheek, killing him instantly.

Dre and Rome went for their guns, but Stroll and Ant beat them to the punch. As soon as Face shot Deion, they quickly pressed their guns against the back of their heads.

"What do you want us to do with these sell-out ass niggas?" asked Stroll.

"Disarm 'em and bring 'em over here," Face replied.

Stroll and Ant subsequently retrieved the guns they had tucked away in their waistbands before pushing them in Face's direction.

Face said, "I got something special for these two bitches, since they like to raise their hands and shit. Bring 'em over here."

Face walked over to a carpenter's table, where a vise sat on top, and began loosening its jaws. Panic quickly overcame Rome, and he began to plead uncontrollably.

He said, "C'mon, Face. We ain't really mean nothin' by that shit, man. It ain't nothin' personal against you. I was just supporting them niggas, blood. Please don't kill me. You know I got six kids, man, please."

"Nigga, shut the fuck up! You don't give a damn about them nappy-headed kids," Face said, snatching Rome by the wrist. "This is the hand you raised, right?"

"Yeah, man, why?" Rome asked, trembling.

Face tightened the vise onto Rome's forearm and replied, "Because your actions have become cancerous." Next, he reached for a handsaw and said, "So now you have to cut the cancer out."

"What! You expect me to cut off my own hand, man? Please don't do this, dog."

Face calmly set the saw down on the table and replied, "You did this to yourself, playboy. Now you've got sixty seconds to get to hacking if you ever plan on seeing your kids again."

Face stepped back, pointed his gun at Rome, and began timing him. He was emphasizing the fact that he only had sixty seconds to cut off his hand. Rome picked up the saw, sobbing as he begged for mercy, but his cries fell on deaf ears. Face could not afford for their actions to go unpunished. Also, the punishment had to be so severe that it deterred anyone else from attempting an insurrection in the future.

"You got thirty seconds left, nigga," Face announced casually.

"A'ight, man, a'ight," Rome replied in a pitiful voice.

Rome picked up the saw and squeezed his eyes shut because it was the only way he could bring himself to do it. Then he slowly sawed into his flesh, causing him to scream out in agony. Naturally, seeing blood spurt from his wrist made him stop and beg, hoping Face would show even a sliver of mercy.

Nevertheless, Face just gave Rome a brief reminder, "Twenty seconds, nigga," he said coldly.

Therefore, Rome squeezed his eyelids shut before cutting through his soft tissue directly into the bone. It was so gruesome even Face scrunched up his nose as he watched Rome carve through his own flesh like a Thanksgiving turkey. The grinding sound alone was enough to induce anyone spectating to vomit, especially someone with a weak stomach. Face scanned the warehouse, taking in all the sickened faces. He was completely satisfied with the impact his brutality had on them. Then he looked back at Rome's hand as it dangled, barely hanging on by loose skin. He was in shock, barely clinging to consciousness from the sheer pain he was inflicting on himself. His legs suddenly began to buckle beneath him, so he leaned on the table for extra support while fighting to remain conscious.

"You're almost there, boy," Face stated supportively.

Suddenly, Rome mustered up the strength to cut off the only piece of flesh still connecting his hand and wrist, before passing out from shock. At that point, the vise was the only thing still holding him up. So Face walked over and loosened it, sending him crashing to the floor. Unfortunately, since he was incapable of bracing his fall, his head just bounced off the ground like a bowling ball.

"Somebody come get this bitch-ass nigga," Face demanded.

However, everyone just looked around at each other, waiting for a volunteer, but no one did. So, Face was forced to select one randomly.

Face said, "J-Slow, come get this nigga out the way, blood."

J-Slow then walked over to Rome, grabbed him by his legs, and dragged him out of the vicinity.

Next, Stroll pushed Dre in the back of the head with the barrel of his gun and said, "It's your turn now, nigga."

Dre could tell by the extensive amount of blood loss that without any serious medical attention, Rome would be dead within minutes. Seeing him suffer in such agonizing pain made Dre's decision easy. He wasn't goin' out like that. Not begging for his life only to be humiliated, self-mutilated, and then left for dead while he bled out. Hence, he turned toward Face and took a deep breath.

Suddenly, he yelled, "You expect me to go out like a bitch? Fuck you, nigga!" Then he charged Face.

Boom! Boom! Boom!

Face fired three shots, hitting him in the chest and neck. Surprisingly, Dre kept stumbling forward and collapsed merely inches away from Face's feet. He wisely used his last ounce of energy to wipe his blood onto Face's pants, hoping to leave some trace of evidence behind for the police to find.

Face kicked his hand away. "At least he ain't go out like a bitch. Stupid as hell, but I gotta admit, he had heart. Now that we got all this bullshit out the way, we can get back to business."

Face returned to Banks and El, positioning himself between them before announcing his new plans.

He said, "It appears we have three new traps open. It looks like somebody's about to get a promotion."

Face hoped giving Rome's and Dre's territories to Stroll and Ant would earn their loyalty. He also knew that if he gave Awol Deion's million-dollar spot instead of giving it to Donnie, it would make Donnie resent him. Therefore, he was possibly causing more problems for himself later on down the road. However, rewarding Donnie after letting those two hoodrat bitches set them up like that would be an insult to the rest of the lieutenants. So he went with the candidate that would most likely help preserve his longevity in the game. Hoping his announcement wouldn't come off as a slap in the face to everyone else.

He said, "Stroll, I'm giving you Rome's block. Can you manage the extra responsibilities that come with it? You know, the more money, the more problems."

"Yeah, I know. I could handle it. Me and my squad run a tight ship," Stroll replied confidently.

"That's good to hear. What about you, Ant? You ready to take over Dre's hood?"

"I was born ready for this shit," Ant stated confidently.

"Well, last but not least. Awol, I hope you're ready for a seat at the round table. 'Cause I'm giving you Deion's trap."

Suddenly, there was an awkward silence because the remaining lieutenants were hoping for the promotion. So it came as a surprise to hear that Awol, a freelance hitman, got promoted instead of one of them. But no one dared to challenge Awol because they all knew he would kill them right there where they stood without blinking an eye if they did.

Face said, "Awol put in more than enough work over the years to earn his seat. He's both respected and feared throughout The Bay. So, I think running the most lucrative hood in Oakland is only right. What do you say, bruh? You in?"

"Fa'sho, my nigga. You know I don't turn down no money," Awol replied proudly.

"A'ight, well, you know that means no more of that freelance shit. If it ain't a matter of self-defense or protecting our organization, all hits must be sanctioned by me. You got that, Killa?"

"Yeah, I gotcha, bruh."

"Good. Because we gotta tighten up our structure now."

Afterward, Face stared into Awol's eyes for a brief moment. He expressed the importance of acknowledging that he was at the top of the food chain. He wanted Awol to know that he was running a tight ship from that point on, which meant no more antics.

Face said, "Well, welcome to the family, my nigga. Now, for those who ain't had the pleasure of meeting my brother Banks—here he is, in the flesh. This is the most solid nigga I know. And he is a truc mastermind when it comes to this street shit. So from now on, he is my right-hand man. That means y'all better treat orders from him as if y'all heard it directly from the horse's mouth. Understood?"

Everyone quickly acknowledged that they understood in one way or another.

"Great. Any questions?" asked Face.

Black Rob said, "I got a question. If Sincere's dead, where the hell are we going to get our product from? 'Cause if you ain't got a line on the same quality of shit, that could put a dent in all of our pockets."

Face could tell from their body language the other lieutenants were wondering the same thing. Hell, it was the same question he had repeatedly asked himself.

He replied, "Don't y'all niggas worry about the supply. I got a line on some better-quality shit. Plus, we're about to expand our inventory. I think it's time we start pushin' crystal meth—these young muthafuckas already hooked anyway. It's the new party drug. Them suburban niggas makin' a killin' off it. Might as well corner that market too. What y'all say? Y'all with me?"

"Yeah!" they all yelled, pumped about the increased profits they would receive after adding meth to their inventory.

"Well, a'ight then. Let's redistribute these drugs, so we can get this muthafuckin' money," Face stated, excited.

CHAPTER ELEVEN

Captain Williams stood gazing out his office window, trying to decide what to eat for lunch, when Detective Jones abruptly knocked at his door.

Williams yelled, "Come in!" then turned to face him.

Jones opened the door and stepped into Williams' office, bracing himself for a reprimand.

Williams said, "Be sure to close the door behind you. I have my air purifier on."

Jones shut the door, replying, "Lucille mentioned you wanted to see me."

"That's because I did. Where the hell is Colding? And why haven't you brought me a suspect on the Carter case yet? If you two inbreds don't have something by tomorrow, I'm giving the case to Conners and Ruiz."

"I have no idea, sir. Your guess is as good as mine."

"Well, I need you to locate him ASAP. I just received a call from a homicide detective down in San Jose. They found his son, along with two others, all dead inside his son's home. They need him to go identify the body."

"It sounds to me like somebody just made the streets of Oakland a lot safer."

"Fuck me. That was Colding's only son, for Christ's sake. Have some damn respect."

"With all due respect, sir, everyone in this department knows his son made a living selling poison to the community. And if that wasn't enough to destroy an entire generation, he was also pimping out their mothers. He used his businesses as a front. He was by no means a pillar of the community. He doesn't deserve my respect. Nor yours, for that matter."

"Then why wasn't he ever brought in on any charges, Sherlock Holmes? Huh? Please clarify that for me."

Jones just stared at Williams with a blank expression.

Williams continued, "A good detective gathers solid evidence then takes it to the DA for a warrant. They don't sit around making unprovable accusations to fit a baseless theory. Now get your head out of your ass and bring me a conviction. And by the way, have you two found any leads on the car bombing case yet?"

"Honestly, sir, there wasn't much to go on, but we're working an angle. We think the murder over on Ninety-Fourth was a retaliation for the car bombing."

"Oh yeah? How so?" Williams asked, intrigued.

"Well, there's an indirect connection between the two incidents. The woman who was shot on Ninety-Fourth's son is also the baby daddy of the woman from the explosion. His street name is Banks. He is a parolee just released from prison after serving a ten-year bid on a narcotics charge. And we all know Johnny was a big fish in the game. That explosion was meant for him. His pregnant girlfriend just happened to follow him, trying to catch him cheating. We think Johnny's boys believe Banks set the car bomb, and retaliated by shooting up his mother's house."

"Well, did you question this Banks guy?"

"Yeah."

"And?"

"He has a solid alibi. He was with his girlfriend the entire night."

"And you confirmed that with his girlfriend?"

"Yes, sir."

"Did Johnny's girlfriend give you any reason to think Banks is a legit suspect? Did he threaten them?"

"No, sir. Just regular baby mama drama."

"Alright, then talk to some of Johnny's associates to pick their brains. Then, I want you to see what your CIs can come up with. Because we can't afford for another street war to break out. I'm sure the streets are talking. I need you to find out exactly what they are saying. You got me?"

"Yes, sir, I understand. We're still waiting for the other shooting victim to wake up. The hospital said they'd notify us as soon as she's coherent."

"Good. Let me know once you've gotten something concrete. And if you happen to see Colding, tell him to report to my office immediately—it's important."

CHAPTER TWELVE

— • • • —

El stood next to Honesty's hospital bed, holding her hand, praying she would come out of her coma. He hated to admit it, but he loved her crazy ass. He especially missed her smart-ass mouth because it kept him amused. He was only allowed to visit her because she had him listed as her emergency contact along with Sorya, and Sorya was nowhere to be found. He was deep in thought when he heard a female voice call out his name.

"El?" she said.

He spun his head around and saw a beautiful, blue-eyed blonde with rosy cheeks smiling back at him.

"Aubrey?" he replied.

"Yes, it's me. How have you been, stranger?" she asked as she stepped inside the room and closed the door."

"I could be better," he replied sadly.

El hadn't seen Aubrey in years, but the impression she had left on him made it seem as if it were only yesterday. He could immediately tell she had her nose and breasts augmented, and he liked the new and improved Aubrey. She had worked for him for a little over a year to help pay for medical school. At first, she started dancing at Club Passion regularly until she began to accumulate complaints from the customers. They used to complain that her pussy gave off a foul odor during lap dances, which was a major turnoff. So, being the businessman he was, he offered her a job as a part-time escort. Considering she really needed the money, she accepted the demotion as an opportunity to continue pursuing her dream.

El said, "I see you've finished medical school. I must say, you're the first woman who worked for me and actually used her money for schooling."

Aubrey replied, "Yeah, I'm just glad that part of my life is finally over. However, the plus side is I don't have any student debt, and my credit is A1. So, I guess it was all worth it."

Aubrey's smile slowly faded into a concerned expression.

She said, "I wanted to ask you if this visit is business? Personal? Or is she a relative?"

El sensed something was seriously wrong and subtly closed the distance between them.

"Business. Why?" he replied skeptically.

Aubrey looked around like she was about to do something questionable.

She said, "I'm not supposed to be telling you this because it could cost me my medical license. So you can't implicate me, alright? But I owe you and think you deserve to know, especially in your line of work."

"You can trust me."

She quickly lifted the medical chart she was holding and flipped to the second page.

She whispered, "How about I just let you see for yourself?"

El stared into her eyes as he slowly took Honesty's medical chart from her. Then, he thoroughly scanned the lab results, looking for whatever Aubrey deemed so noteworthy. His eyes nearly popped out of their sockets once his gaze fell upon the results of her HIV test, and he discovered that it came back positive. He instantly went numb, causing him to drop the chart, sending it crashing to the floor, startling Aubrey. Feeling guilty for causing such distress, Aubrey quickly bent down and picked up the chart. She hoped it wouldn't cause anyone to rush in, fearing El might create a dramatic scene and expose her.

El's concerned countenance made Aubrey believe that he possibly had a sexual relationship with Honesty. Whether it was protected or not remained to be seen.

She said, "I don't know if you two were sexually active or not, but if you were, I suggest you get tested immediately. The disease isn't curable, but there are medicines now that help keep it in check."

El wasn't trying to hear that shit. He knew that in the Black community, HIV was equated with AIDS, and AIDS meant death. His whole life had flashed before his eyes. As far as he knew, HIV was only for homosexuals and drug addicts. How could a bitch that bad have the alphabets? But like most men, he didn't realize the prettier the woman was, the more men there were willing to have unprotected sex with her. This vastly increased her chances of contracting HIV, especially if she chose to be promiscuous. It really fucked him up because Honesty was the only woman he was having unprotected sex with. Also, he believed her when she said she was one hundred percent clean. Sadly, being irresponsible and taking your life for granted once is all it takes to create a lifetime of suffering. Aubrey could tell from El's abrupt withdrawal that he and Honesty had, in fact, been in an unprotected sexual relationship. Feeling sorry for him, she placed her hand on his right shoulder as a sign of comfort.

She whispered, "I'll let you two be alone for a while. I'll be back after I finish my rounds."

El didn't even respond to her. He just stood there staring down at Honesty, watching her cling on for dear life as a machine breathed for her.

After finishing her rounds of routine checkups, Aubrey headed back down the hallway to check on El. She was concerned about how he had responded to the devastating news. Then suddenly, she heard an alarm being emitted from someone's life support machine, indicating that the patient had flatlined. When she rounded the corner, she saw El walking past a nurse who was rushing toward Honesty's room, pushing a crash cart. After locking eyes with him for a brief moment, she knew right away that he had somehow killed Honesty. Therefore, she felt responsible and knew she had no choice but to keep quiet if she wanted to keep her medical license.

CHAPTER THIRTEEN

· · ·

Banks walked into Face's kitchen, where Face sat eating a bowl of Frosted Flakes. He set his phone on the countertop, then sighed as he took a seat on the bar stool. Face took another spoonful of cereal, then pushed his bowl aside.

"So, how'd the conversation go?" Face asked while still smacking.

"Nigga, close yo mouth when you're eating. You know I hate when you smack," Banks replied.

"Aw, my bad. Anyway, what happened, blood? What did he say?"

"He said it's good to slide through to holla in person. He set up the meeting for two o'clock."

"Where at?"

"In Frisco. He already texted me the address. We'll have to wait to see Mama until after we handle this first."

"Man, are you sure that nigga's straight?"

"I mean, I've never done business with him. But like I said, before I went down, I was coppin' from his uncle Hector. Hector was straight, though. We doin' business wit his nephew, a nigga named Mafi. I remember seeing him during a couple of our transactions. He said that after Hector got smoked, he took over the family business. The nigga got some kind of rank, though. He had the keys to the yard, and he only had a three-year bid. He was trying to fuck wit me on the yard. But after I got set up, I told him I was good. I couldn't trust nobody."

When Banks said, 'I couldn't trust nobody,' his emphasis on the word 'nobody' made it clear to Face that he too was deemed untrustworthy. Consequently, Face's guilty conscience forced him to avert his gaze. He couldn't stand to look Banks in the eyes after admitting that he had fucked Tonya while he was locked up. He felt terrible because not only did he betray his brother by screwing his baby mama, but he also betrayed his nieces' trust. Knowing his selfish actions had helped create an irreconcilable rift between their parents tore him up inside. But was it guilt? Or was it just embarrassment because his tender dick ass got caught? Either way, Banks could care less.

Face said, "A'ight, well, what's the game plan? 'Cause I'm thinkin' if he got some good quality shit at the right price, I'ma cop as much product as possible until I find a better connect."

"We both know the bigger the quantity, the cheaper the market price. But this is gonna be our first time doin' business with these cats. So I think we should only spend about two hundred and fifty thousand on the first transaction. Just to be on the safe side."

"Two hundred and fifty thousand? Nigga, that ain't shit unless we got a direct line to the cartel. We were gettin' our keys at nineteen thousand a piece unless we bought them in bulk. That means two hundred and fifty thousand will only get us thirteen bricks. And what the fuck am I supposed to do with thirteen bricks?"

"Survive, nigga. Look, we could do a test run to see if their numbers sound right. After that, you could test the water. But from my experience, you never go big on the first deal, lil' bruh."

"Okay, well, I guess we're gonna see what them niggas is hollerin' then.

"Before we do any of that, did you holla at them detectives yet?"

"Nah. I was about to call them after I got dressed. I'll use my house phone—I only use it for bill collectors anyway. I damn sho' ain't calling them from my cell phone so they can tap my shit. Callin' them from a burner won't do anything but make them suspicious of me. On another note, have you spoken to the twins?"

"Yeah, I talked to Alisha. She called and woke me up early this morning. She said she was up all night suffering from nightmares. She said she had a dream that somebody shot me. It ain't no reason my kids should be having damn dreams of me getting shot, bruh. The shit ain't right, my nigga."

"I know, that's fucked up, blood. You wanna mob over there so you can see 'em?"

"Nah. They're gonna be a'ight for now. I told Alisha I was out looking for the men who hurt Mama and Tonya. She understood. They look at me like I'm some superhero or some shit. If I was, I would've been able to figure out what the fuck happened to Cell-Bo and Tyson. You need to get in contact with that DA bitch to make sure them niggas ain't somewhere yapping."

"So what? You think them niggas got caught and turned state's evidence?"

"You never know. That's why I don't put my trust in nobody. You never know what a man is capable of doing until his back is against the wall."

"True dat. I'll get at her and see if she can turn over a couple of rocks. Hopefully, that ain't the case 'cause I got enough shit on my plate right now. I had to put a kill order on any out-of-town niggas inquiring about me. Just in case that nigga Taz thinks I had something to do with his brother's death. 'Cause I'll be damned if I go out like that nigga Sincere did."

"Shit, you almost did, nigga. Whoever had the drop on you just fumbled. That's why you gotta hurry up and find them hoes—'cause there's no telling if they have any other spots staked out."

"I also don't know if it was a hit on me or just a robbery gone bad."

"That's why the smartest thing to do is err on the side of caution. You can never be too careful when it comes to the streets. It's better to be caught with it than caught without it. You know that. If he is the one responsible for killing Sincere, there is a high probability he's gonna try to get to you before you have a chance to get him. That's what I would do."

"That's why I got my niggas on high alert. I ain't taking any more unnecessary chances until all threats have been dealt with. Donnie out combing the town with a fine-tooth comb, lookin' for them punk rock bitches right now. He said he's been calling their phones every thirty minutes. But their voicemails keep picking up on the first ring—like they got they phones off."

"I'm sure they did. If they were smart, they would've ditched those muthafuckas after orchestrating a triple murder."

"Right, so we definitely gotta find them bitches before the police do—'cause I know fa'sho they'll implicate me the first chance they get. I'm the big fish now that Sincere's dead. The pigs would give those hoes immunity just to close a case against me if they knew I was the one supplying the dope houses."

"Well, it sounds like we'd better get to work then. We can start by locking in this new connect."

"Now we're talkin'," Face replied excitedly.

Face stood up and smiled, realizing he had finally drawn the version of Banks he admired to the round table, except this time he knew Banks was unequivocally all in.

CHAPTER FOURTEEN

Mayor Tisdale's beautiful red-headed assistant opened the door to her office and peeked inside, her gorgeous green eyes and matching freckles on display. Mayor Tisdale was the epitome of a cougar. She was of German and British descent, but her evenly tanned skin made her appear French. She stood 5'11" with brunette hair and hazel eyes. Her curvy hips and 38D bust were capable of swaying any wavering vote in her favor.

"Sorry to disturb you, ma'am, but Councilman Chambers is here to see you," she said apologetically.

Mayor Tisdale replied, "It's okay, Jennifer. I was expecting him. Go ahead and send him in."

"Yes, ma'am."

Jennifer closed the door. Moments later, Councilman Chambers entered her office, looking like he had a chip on his shoulder. Chambers was a short and pudgy brown-skinned brother with a George Jefferson hairline. He always wore cheap suits and tended to sweat profusely through them.

Tisdale asked warmly, "How can I help you, Councilman? Over the phone, you sounded distressed. Is everything alright?"

"No, everything's not alright. You had one of your detectives murdered, for Christ's sake. And on top of that, you made all of us complicit."

"Exactly. So if I go down, we all go down. So don't you go gettin' all squeamish on me. I told you my boys would take care of it, and they did. So you don't have to get your little panties in a bunch. Everything has been swept under the rug."

"Swept under the rug? If a highly decorated homicide detective goes missing, the best of the best will come looking for answers—hell, there might even be an IAB investigation."

"And they won't find anything leading back to us or our little off-the-books meeting. Now keep your damn voice down."

"But how could you be so sure?"

"If you must know, I had my boys steal some drugs and a gun from an evidence locker and plant them inside Colding's home. It's an excellent insurance policy since there are already whispers of his son being a drug kingpin. It'll look like he's been on his son's payroll the entire time, ending any investigation. No one will want to shine a light on a dirty cop or bring any embarrassment to the department. And since you have a bleeding heart, you don't have to worry about his pension because he had no dependents.

"Councilman Chambers was at a loss for words, staring at Mayor Tisdale with his mouth open. He could not believe the level of crime he had become involved in.

Tisdale continued, "Oh, look at the bright side. If Colding were building a case against us or even decided to confide in someone else in the department, this would discredit him."

Councilman Chambers walked over to the couch and plopped down, stunned after hearing her diabolical plot to ensure their safety.

He said, "I must say, mayor, you've really outdone yourself. What you did was extremely excessive, even for you. You've broken so many state and federal laws, they would be fighting over who got the privilege to inject us."

"Oh, cry me a river, why dontcha. I didn't plan any of this. I simply improvised. And your manicured nails aren't clean, either. So you can spare me the choirboy routine. We both know if you're guilty of one element of the conspiracy, you're culpable for its entirety. So get your shit together. What you need to be doing is focusing on your children and the legacy you plan on leaving them behind. And keep in mind, as long as we continue investing in real estate, this will all have been worth it. Soon enough, it'll all be just a distant memory supplanted by your future. A future that will be very prosperous once we've removed all of the bottom feeders from our city. Because only then, can we reach our full potential. Just think about it, once we've pushed all of the low-income out, we could become billionaires through all the property we'll have acquired by then. All we have to do now is continue to buy up the properties and sit on them until their value appreciates."

"That's what I came to inform you about. Our shell corporation successfully acquired the land the Acorn projects currently sits on."

"See! Now, just imagine the luxurious skyscraper we can build there once we've torn down that crime-ridden roach motel. We already own eighty percent of the homes on Ninth and Willow. I figured a few proliferated home invasions would convince the rest to sell."

"Are you suggesting that we target innocent homeowners to force them into selling their property?" Chambers asked stupidly.

"Have you been listening to anything I said for the last five minutes? We're going to do what we must to secure as much land as we can before the tech conglomerates decide they want to bully the pot. Because, like it or not, within the next twenty to twenty-five years, Oakland will be filled with high-end skyscrapers. West Oakland's real estate will be much more valuable than any properties in the north or east because of its proximity to San Francisco. So, we must capitalize on our opportunity to have first dibs at all costs. Why do you think I went through so much trouble to steal Belford's portfolio? They already did most of the research for us."

"Yes, I'm aware of the intricacy regarding our investment portfolio. But like I said before, I'm not comfortable harming civilians for our personal gain."

"Well, to be frank, councilman, at this stage of our plan, you don't have much of a choice."

She gave Councilman Chambers a cold stare, letting him know she was done pacifying him.

She said, "Now, don't get me wrong—I'm not accustomed to violence either. But I must say, it's about time you grew some balls. Now, are you going to be a problem going forward?"

Councilman Chambers immediately considered how easily she'd had her dirty detectives kill Sorya back at the port. A part of him knew that graphic display of brutality was really a warning to the rest of her conspirators, reminding them that they, too, would become expendable if they ever decided to back out of their deal.

He replied, "No, Mayor. I will not be a problem going forward."

"Splendid. Because sometimes, sacrifices have to be made. If our forefathers hadn't taken the land from the Indians, we wouldn't have the great nation we call home today. Wouldn't you agree?"

"Yes, Mayor. And I, too, am currently satisfied with the economic status of our great country."

She leaned against her desk, folded her arms, and replied, "Phenomenal. Then give me all of the details regarding the Acorn projects."

CHAPTER FIFTEEN

Banks and Face coasted across the Bay Bridge, enjoying the beautiful weather on their way to meet their new connect. Face had just hung up the phone. Banks could tell from the tone of his voice that the conversation had been unpleasant.

"Wassup, blood?" Banks asked.

Face said, "Shit. That was that nigga Fred. He's a security guard at the Greyhound Station in West Oakland. He was on Sincere's payroll. He used to call Sincere when he spotted renegade hoes, runaways, or other potential prostitutes. Sincere would pay him five thousand dollars for every bitch that chose up. I had him keeping an eye out for Reina and Venus. He said he had no luck spottin' them, and they haven't purchased any tickets under their names."

"Them hoes gotta pop up sooner or later. That money is gonna run out. It ain't like they got you for millions or nothin'."

"I hope so, 'cause I don't like the feeling of knowing somebody came that close to killing me, and I don't have a clue of who orchestrated it. If I wasn't such a real nigga, they would've had me."

"Nah, it wasn't 'cause you're a real nigga. You just had God on your side, fool. All the realness in the world can't save you once your number is called. He just gave you a little extra time to get closer to him, that's all."

"Aw, nigga, don't tell me you went to prison and got all religious on me."

"Nah, bruh, religion ain't got shit to do with it. I mean, I read the Bible and the Qur'an, but that ain't my point. My point is, ain't nobody too hard to be humbled. You better read that part about the Pharaoh in the Bible. Real niggas get killed every day, and the one thing they all have in common is that they never saw it coming. The pen is full of niggas that thought they had it all figured out. And the Rolling Hills cemetery is filled wit hard-ass niggas that thought they were invincible. Feel me?"

"Yeah, I feel you, shit, Sincere is one of 'em. I still can't believe that nigga's dead, blood. After you got locked up, he became like a brother to me. That's why when I find out who killed him, I'ma gut they ass."

"Well, you know it costs money to go to war, so let's hurry up and lock in this deal. Then we can worry about gettin' some revenge for Sincere, Mama, and CJ, a'ight."

"Hell yeah, nigga! Let's get this muthafuckin' money then."

Face finally finished weaving his way through the congested streets of San Francisco and entered the Fillmore District, one of San Francisco's many drug and gang-infested neighborhoods. It was an area that truly contradicted San Francisco's stigma of only being full of homosexuals and hippies.

Banks examined the scenery because it felt like forever since the last time he had set foot inside the mean streets of San Francisco. It brought back a lot of fond memories, even though a lot had changed. When he looked to his left, he saw about thirty curb servers posted in front of a liquor store, many of them wearing either San Francisco Giants hats or 49ers jerseys to represent their city. As they eventually entered the neighborhood run by the Hispanics, he noticed the culture hadn't changed too much because they were also wearing SF hats and 49ers gear.

Banks said, "Bust a right up here at these apartments where them migos are standing."

"A'ight," Face replied.

The way the two men standing in front of the apartments stared at Banks made it evident they were the lookouts. Therefore, they were undoubtedly expecting them.

"Looks like we made it," Face said dryly.

Banks turned to Face and said, "Remember, just let me do all the talking since he doesn't know you. I know it's your operation, but let me make the introduction."

"It's all good. If you can get him down to a cheaper price, why wouldn't I let you do all the talking?"

"I'm just making sure we're on the same page."

"Oh, we're most definitely on the same page."

After Face put his car in park, he noticed the two lookouts quickly approaching in his rearview mirror. Then, they suddenly split up and moved to either side of the car. Both men subsequently opened their doors and motioned for them to get out.

"Damn, they got valet?" Face asked sarcastically.

Once they got out of the car, Face locked eyes with a cute Hispanic baby wearing nothing but a diaper. He was holding his bottle by the nipple and appeared to be taking a shit. *Damn, where is his mama?* Face thought as the two men frisked them.

"Whoa! Hol' up. I'm keeping my gun, folks," Banks stated as the man reached for the butt of his gun.

The man let it go and said, "I know. We're not searching for weapons. We're looking for recording devices. So be sure to leave your cell phones inside the car."

Banks gave Face a nod and said, "No problemo."

Afterward, they both pulled out their cell phones to discard them.

Face said, "Here, I'll put them in the glove compartment. I don't want nobody breaking into my shit."

After putting away their cell phones and locking up the car, they were escorted inside the apartment complex, where they were set to meet Mafioso. First, they turned left down a pathway, and then they turned right through a courtyard before eventually reaching the base of a pissy flight of steps. Seeing the projects filled with poor women and children reminded them of how the village looked before it got renovated and everyone accepted vouchers to leave Oakland. Banks looked across the courtyard and saw a twenty-something-year-old mother nodding off from heroin while still breastfeeding her infant.

Banks shook his head and mumbled, "Some shit just never changes."

After reaching their destination, one of the two men opened the door to the apartment, stepped inside, then motioned for them to follow. The other man remained outside, standing guard. Once they all entered the apartment, their escort closed the door and stood in front of it. He was clearly prepared to prevent them from leaving if need be. Both Banks and Face picked up on the vibe from the man as he leaned back on the door and crossed his arms. As Banks scanned the room, he noticed a total change in decor. With one look at the men sitting around a table full of coke and guns, snorting lines, he immediately realized that Mafi had surrounded himself with gangbangers rather than professional businessmen, as his uncle once had. Banks knew from past experiences doing business with the type of men he was staring at could prove troublesome. So, he decided he would take the more assertive approach. Then, out of the corner of his eye, he saw Mafi step out of the kitchen, drying his hands on a colorful sink towel.

He said, "Y'all fools hungry? I made enchiladas," with a cheap grin.

"Nah, we're straight. Thank you, though," Banks replied.

"You sho'? I have come a long way from making spreads."

"Yeah, I'm cool, dog. We just came here to talk business."

"Talk business, huh? My uncle always said you were a no-nonsense type of individual. I guess he was right. Well, come on and step into my office then."

It was ironic because all Mafi did was sling his dry towel over his left shoulder before walking back into the kitchen.

Face looked at Banks and whispered, "Is this muthafucka serious?"

Banks gave Face a forced smile, then followed Mafi into the kitchen so he could end their fiasco as soon as possible. Banks stared at Mafi in disbelief as he checked on his food instead of prioritizing their transaction. After witnessing Mafi's conduct, they knew they could not establish a long-term business relationship with him.

Mafi grabbed his Corona off the countertop, took a sip, and then asked, "So, who's your boyfriend?"

Banks replied, "This my brutha. We're in business together now. Shit didn't work out with our last connect. So now we're looking for a new supplier with old-school prices. You know me and your uncle go way back."

"Yeah, I know. But the last time I checked, he was six feet underground, eatin' dirt. And as you can see, we're under new management now. So does your brutha have a name? Or is he one of them deaf and dumb muthafuckas?"

Face interjected, "Yeah, nigga, they call me Face."

"Well, I'm Mafi. Welcome to my humble abode. It's a pleasure to meet you and all that other good stuff."

Banks said, "Well, now that we're all acquainted, let's talk numbers 'cause the suspense is killing me."

"I'm sure you know the prices have skyrocketed since the last time you've done business with us. Now, on average, a key is going anywhere from twenty-five to thirty thousand."

When Mafi uttered the numbers, he studied them both to see if his prices shook them. Considering if it did, it meant they didn't have deep pockets.

Banks replied, "Them prices are for rich frat boys trying to party at UC Berkeley for the weekend. We're buying in bulk like I've always done. So I need you to come down to the seventeen to twenty range."

"Seventeen? Aha, I don't know where the fuck you've been for the last couple of years, but El Jefe is sitting in a supermax prison cell. And if you haven't noticed yet, his untimely departure from the game caused a serious drought. So unless we're talkin' 'bout a major shipment, you'll have to bring them numbers back down to earth."

Mafi was fully aware that his unorthodox style of conducting business was getting to Banks. However, he couldn't care less, because he wanted the world to believe he was the man in the high castle.

Banks said, "Look, man, we've got a quarter million dollars we're trying to spend with you. And you and I both know a quarter of a million dollars is more than generous for an initial installment. I mean, we haven't even tested your product yet."

"Oh, don't you worry, my friend, my product is the best in The Bay. Here, see for yourself."

Then he opened a cabinet door, reached inside, and pulled out a kilo of cocaine. Afterward, he picked up a knife off the countertop and attempted to hand the kilo to Banks. However, before he could do so, Face reached around Banks and snatched the kilo out of his hand.

Face said, "Here, let me try that shit," as he gripped the kilo of cocaine.

Mafi let it go, stepped back, and leaned against the sink with an annoying expression because he knew he had some good dope. After Face snorted the cocaine, he knew right away it was some high-quality shit. He just couldn't let Mafi know how he truly felt for bargaining purposes.

After he rubbed some of the cocaine on his gums, Face said, "It's a'ight. It'll do, though."

"Bullshit! That shit's fire, and you know it," Mafi replied, animated.

Banks said, "So what if it is? We still haven't finished talking numbers. Remember, I'm fresh out, so I need a reasonable price."

"Reasonable, huh?"

"Yeah, man, we've got history."

"Alright, well, this is what I can do for you. If you can get me two hundred and fifty thousand by tomorrow, I'll give you eleven keys."

Banks' eyes wandered off into space as he tried to calculate the numbers in his head. Meanwhile, Face had already calculated the numbers and was busy devising a beneficial counteroffer.

Banks said, "That's almost twenty-three thousand a key. I know you can do better than that, my nigga."

"I'm sorry, Banks, but this ain't the Salvation Army, homie. Take it or leave it."

Face didn't appreciate being disrespected by that Antonio Banderas-looking muthafucka, so he decided to switch up their original plan.

Face said bluntly, "What about a million? Could you fill that order, big dog? Or is that too much for you?"

Face knew precisely what he was doing by initiating a pissing contest with Mafi. Since he read him as a prideful boaster, he figured he would be inclined to come down from the initial price if he couldn't fulfill the order. That way, he made himself feel like he was the one doing them a favor. Surprisingly, Mafi was stunned by the sudden increase in volume Face had requested. Mafi's reaction drew a proud smirk from Banks because he had never seen him at a loss for words before. Accordingly, he took it as a sign that their negotiation was about to take a turn for the better.

Mafi rubbed his chin and said, "Yeah, I can fill that order. I just have to make a few phone calls first."

Banks said, "Cool. I'm assuming the price per key is going to drop drastically."

Suddenly, Mafi started calculating random numbers in his head while staring off into space.

Then he stated firmly, "I can do fifty keys for that price. And that number is non-negotiable."

Banks instantly turned to Face for approval since Face was the money man.

Face said, "It sounds to me like we have ourselves a deal," and then reached out to shake Mafi's hand.

Mafi replied, "It looks like I should've been talking to you the whole time."

Noticing how Banks cut his eyes at him, Mafi quickly added, "Nah, I'm joking, dog. We're all friends here, right?"

"Yeah," Banks replied insincerely.

"So when and where is the meet?" Face asked, fed up with Mafi's bullshit.

Mafi replied, "Tomorrow. I'll text you the time and place. So be ready. I know how y'all bruthas are always late and shit."

Banks said, "A'ight, well, we're about to tear up out of here. We'll see you then."

"Of course. I'll have Victor and Armando escort you guys back to your vehicles. I don't want you fools getting jacked on the way out."

Once they returned to Face's car, Face didn't hesitate to express his feelings toward Mafi.

He said, "I barely even know the nigga, and I already can't stand that muthafucka. He talks too damn much. He is the most unprofessional muthafucka I ever came across in the game. With his attitude, he ain't going to last long."

Banks said, "Yeah, I know. But for now, he's just a stepping stone until we can get a more stable connect. Honestly, though, we got him close enough to a number you were looking for to continue doing business. At least for now. Dontcha think."

"Man, I'm gon' fuck around and kill that nigga if I continue to do business with 'em."

"Sometimes you gotta set your pride aside to see the bigger picture, blood. We may not be able to find a better connect this close to our stash houses. The shorter our commute to transport our dope, the less risk we take. The convenience of taking a short trip will make up for that fool's ignorance. And his dry-ass jokes."

"To keep it real, he's a lifesaver because I didn't have a connect that could plug me for those prices."

"You can save your praises until after we complete our transaction. Something about that nigga just rubs me the wrong way."

"You and me both. Now let's get the fuck up out of here."

CHAPTER SIXTEEN

Johnson and Jones sat inside their unmarked police cruiser, bouncing ideas off each other as they discussed how to approach Keno and his crew about Johnny's murder.

Johnson said, "Are you sure you want to bring these accusations to a hothead like Keno? I mean, this could easily blow up in our faces. If Keno starts a turf war based on the information we've given him, then the blood will be on our hands. And if it gets out, who do you think the captain will crucify?"

Jones replied, "Don't you worry. The only way anyone outside this vehicle will know what happens between us and Keno is if one of us talks—and I know for damn sure it isn't going to be Keno. All we're going to do is ask him a few questions to see what he knows. "Nine times out of ten, he'll play hardball anyway. At least this way, you can let your moral compass know you did a thorough investigation."

"Your sarcasm has never been one of your finer qualities," Johnson muttered.

"Well, let's go see if we can get a laugh out of this wannabe gangster."

"Alright, but if this shit blows up in our faces, you're the one taking the fall. Understood?"

"Yeah, yeah. Now come on, Bitter Betty, let's go stir up some trouble."

Johnson got out of the car, eager to witness the showdown that was about to take place between Keno and his impulsive-ass partner. From experience, Johnson knew that an old-school gangster like Keno wouldn't willingly give up any valuable information to the police. However, he was still eager to see what Jones planned to achieve.

Keno, Calico, and Blax Mobb were chilling on the porch, smoking a blunt, when Keno spotted the two detectives approaching.

Keno said, "Man, here comes T. Jones' muthafuckin' ass," as he went to put out his blunt.

Calico replied, "Whatchu put the blunt out for? This shit is legal."

"Because, nigga, everything else we're doin' ain't. Y'all don't say shit. Let me handle these fools."

Keno waited patiently for Jones and Johnson to reach the gate before acknowledging their presence. Once Jones locked eyes with him, he knew it was time to perform. When Jones grabbed the latch to the gate, Keno rushed down the porch steps in protest.

"Hey, hey now, hol' up. Y'all got a warrant?" Keno asked, pressing.

Jones replied, "No, sir, we don't. But our visit doesn't require one. We're not here regarding your illegal drug ring. We came hoping you could assist us in tracking down your boy Johnny's murderer. Now, if you have something in that house worth my partner and me seeking a warrant, I suggest you do your civic duty and cooperate. So we can take a brief statement and be on our way."

Keno took Jones' wordplay as a threat because he knew if the police ransacked his house, they would find enough heroin to put him away for life. So, he decided to at least pretend to play ball.

He said, "A'ight, y'all got five minutes. But y'all gotta stay behind the gate. I don't want y'all trying no funny shit. I know how Jones gets down."

Jones said, "Fair enough. We just have a few questions. Maybe you could help us clear up a few things."

"Like what? I already told the officers on the scene I didn't see shit because I was inside the house. Plus, I was drunk off my ass. So if somebody did tail us, I wouldn't've noticed them."

"Yeah, we read that part, but we wanted to question you about that. Are you aware of the shooting that took place on Ninety-Fourth, killing one man and wounding a woman? The news called it an attempted home invasion."

"Nah, I'm sorry I didn't get a chance to catch that. But what does that have to do with me?"

Jones then pulled up a photo of Banks on his cell phone and showed it to Keno.

"Do you know this man?" Jones asked.

Keno examined the photo thoroughly while keeping a poker face.

"Nah, I don't recognize him. Why should I?" he replied.

"Well, this, my friend, is the baby daddy of Johnny's girlfriend, Tonya. He was recently released from prison."

"Yeah, so? What does that have to do with me, though?"

"That's what I'm trying to figure out. Did Johnny ever mention to you or any of your boys that he was having any kind of beef with him?"

"No, sir. He never mentioned any such thing to me. Sorry, though. I wish I could've been more help to you, fine gentlemen."

"Are you sure? Because it sure seems like a hell of a coincidence. Not even twenty-four hours after your right-hand man gets blown up in a car that you were meant to be in. The house his girlfriend's baby daddy is paroled to gets shot up. It sounds to me like you went to get a little street justice. I'm sure your boy Johnny told you about how he was bangin' some cat's girl, and how they had some sort of altercation, right? And then what's the next thing you know, Boom! C'mon, man, fill in the blanks for me. I know the code of the streets. It's an eye for an eye, a tooth for a tooth. I just want to know if this is the guy who blew up Johnny's car. Help me solve your friend's murder. Now, did he threaten Johnny? Or say anything that could've been perceived as a threat? Give me something."

"Like I said, detective, I don't know what you're talking about. He never mentioned any baby daddy drama to me or any of my boys. But I tell you what, if I find out anything, you will be the first one I notify. Do you have a card, detective?" he asked condescendingly.

"You know what? You little piece of shit?"

Jones suddenly reached over the gate and snatched Keno up by his shirt. Immediately, Johnson stepped between them and pried Jones' hands away.

While pulling Jones away, Johnson said, "That'll be all, sir. Have a nice day."

Afterward, Keno threw a combination of shadow punches before mockingly fixing his shirt.

Then he turned to Calico and said, "Boy, he don't know how close he came to getting his ass knocked out."

Jones was pissed at the way Keno insulted his intelligence. He knew damn well he wasn't going to call him if he found out anything. What sent him over the edge was realizing Keno was, in fact, innocent of the retaliation murder. Fortunately, he interviewed enough suspects to infer when they were genuinely surprised by an unknown detail of an investigation. Jones stormed down the street like a pouting toddler about to throw a tantrum.

He said, "Don't you ever interrupt me like that again when I'm questioning a suspect. I didn't even get to ask him about his alibi."

Johnson replied, "You and I both know he had no idea what you were talking about. He's just not our guy, no matter how badly you want him to be. We need to focus on a lead that could actually produce results."

"Oh yeah? And what's that?"

"I think I may have something. Follow me, and I'm driving," Johnson stated authoritatively.

CHAPTER SEVENTEEN

Banks and Face arrived at Highland Hospital expecting to be allowed in to see their mother. That's why they were furious when, once again, they were told they would not be permitted to see her. Face paced back and forth in front of the hospital's administration desk, struggling to resist the urge to jump over the counter and beat the shit out of the receptionists. His toxic masculinity wouldn't let him accept the idea of two queers preventing him from seeing his mother. He didn't know what was worse—the rainbow colors in their hair or the way they obnoxiously chewed their bubble gum. He loathed how they unnecessarily made popping sounds while staring him up and down like fresh fish.

Banks, on the other hand, opted for a more diplomatic approach. He requested to speak with Dr. Reed, assuming he could help resolve the misunderstanding without adding fuel to the fire.

Face walked over to Banks and said, "Can you believe those two faggot muthafuckas? Talkin' 'bout how we still can't see Mama. Man, if you weren't on parole, I would've snatched one of those dookie chasers over that damn desk."

"And where would that have gotten you? Are you trying to catch a hate crime? It's the twenty-first century. You better leave them fools alone."

Surprisingly, Face didn't have a comeback. He just looked at Banks as if to say, 'You're supposed to be on my side,' then shook his head in disappointment.

Banks said, "Look, I'm pissed, too. But we just have to wait and see what Dr. Reed says once he gets here. Shit, think about it. How is beefing wit the people in a position to help Mama beneficial to her recovery?"

"You right, bruh. The shit just got me stressed the fuck out."

"C'mon now, we gotta keep our shit together for Mama's sake. I could only imagine what she's going through. And none of this has shit to do with her or CJ. They were just innocent bystanders caught in the middle of some bullshit. So, she only deserves our unwavering support from here on out. Feel me?"

Face said, "Whatever, here comes Dr. Reed," then pointed in his direction.

Dr. Reed had been hard at work for the last fifteen hours, so he was not mentally prepared to deal with any more of Face's bullshit. However, he still took the time to assist them anyway. As he approached them, he reached out to shake Banks' hand first since he was the only reasonable one.

He asked, "How are you, sir?" before reaching out to shake Face's hand.

"Pretty shitty given the circumstances," Banks replied.

Face rudely pointed to the receptionist and said, "Them two bitches said we're still not permitted to see our mother."

One of the receptionists then waved back at Face flirtatiously, knowing it would get under his skin—since nine out of ten super thugs from the hood were either homophobic or still in the closet, pretending to be straight.

Dr. Reed caught it and said, "Ignore them. I'll explain the situation from here."

"Be my guest," Banks replied, standing at attention.

"Okay. Well, as I explained before, you have to be cleared to see your mother. This is per policy because she's a victim of a violent crime, correct?"

"Correct."

"Well, I'm sorry to inform you, but once your mother awoke, I tried to have her add you two to her visitor's list."

"And?" Face barked.

"She said she didn't want to see either of you. She declined to add you to her visitors list."

"That's a lie. Why would she say she doesn't want to see her own damn family?"

"I never said she didn't want to see her family. Just not you two, for whatever reason. She did include some other names, but I'm not at liberty to disclose them. In my opinion, she just needs more time to mourn in peace. Try back tomorrow. Who knows? She may change her mind by then. If it were my mother, I'd stop by every day to let her know that I cared."

"Yeah? Well, thanks for nothing, doc. I'll be in the car, bruh."

On the way out, Face walked past the receptionists' desk and knocked over a stack of forms sitting on the counter.

He yelled, "Fuck you faggots" as all the forms flew through the air.

Suddenly, one of the receptionists stood up and grabbed the phone to call security, but Dr. Reed stopped him with a hand gesture.

The receptionist said, "Girl, he's lucky I just got my hair and nails done," as he sat back down and hung up the phone.

The other receptionist replied, "Or what? You were gonna get both of our asses kicked? 'Cause you know you can't fight, bitch."

CHAPTER EIGHTEEN

— • • • —

As Keno ascended the porch steps, Calico asked, "What were them pigs hollerin' about?"

Keno replied, "Them fools is investigating Johnny's murder. They think Johnny's main bitch, Tonya's baby daddy, had something to do with that shit. They called themselves tricking me into giving them a motive for why Banks wanted Johnny dead. They were trying to kill two birds with one stone."

"Whatchu mean by that?"

"Banks' mama's house got shot up less than twenty-four hours after Johnny was killed. If those detectives had left here convinced that I believed Banks killed Johnny and almost blew me up in the process, I would've become the number one suspect in his mama's house getting shot up. Right now, they're just fishing."

"So do you think Banks did that shit? 'Cause if he did, we need to smoke him before he comes back to finish the job."

"I don't know. From what I heard about him, he ain't the type to trip over no bitch. But on the other hand, it is a cold coincidence Johnny got killed right after he got out of the pen."

Blax Mobb said, "But we all know Johnny's loving personality made him a lot of enemies throughout the years. He chose to have people fear him rather than respect him. And a scared man is a dangerous man. It could've been anybody."

"That's true, too. That's why I can't say for certain what I think. But one thing I do know is whoever planted that bomb was planning on killing me, too, and I can't let that slide."

"So whatchu wanna do?" Calico asked, ready for whatever.

"Call up Hussein. We're gonna check out this fool Banks ourselves. If I get the feeling he did that shit, I'm going to kill his muthafuckin' ass myself."

CHAPTER NINETEEN

· · ·

Sav pulled into his driveway with a throbbing headache from all the partying he had done the night before. He had been up 'til daylight with the hoodrats from Cypress Village. Mixing molly, Viagra, cocaine, and alcohol felt amazing the previous night, but now he felt like shit. It was one of the worst hangovers he had ever experienced, and he had a lot of experience with party favors. He hoped Lil' D and his cousin Curtis were busy playing video games so they wouldn't bother him. The closer he got to the front door, the more his guilt swam toward the surface. He tried to drown it out with drugs and sex, but that only masked it temporarily until he sobered up. Now, he had to face the consequences of the choices he had made arbitrarily, disregarding Angela's well-being. Part of him felt embarrassed because he had always maintained an untouchable persona around everyone. The two women in his life he had sworn to protect probably doubted he was even capable of doing so anymore. How could he expect Angela to ever feel safe around him again, after everything she had been forced to endure simply because his enemies wanted to make him pay? He knew Angela's kidnapping would cause Domonique to question his ability to protect her and Lil' D. It made logical sense for his enemies to come after them next, knowing they provided more leverage than Angela did. Clearly, the only way he could regain their faith in him was to bring them Sincere's head. Considering he was the one who had ordered Angela's abduction in the first place, this was the only way he could redeem himself—by eliminating the threat through an act of vengeance. Well, that's how he saw it unfolding anyway. He had to kill Sincere to avenge Angela and heal the rift he had selfishly wedged between them.

Sav walked inside his home expecting to be welcomed by saddened faces and a gloomy atmosphere. So it surprised him to get a whiff of zesty aroma permeating from Domonique's signature dish, lasagna. It was by far his favorite meal, and Domonique was well aware of it. He knew off the bat that if she were cooking lasagna, it was an effort to cheer him up. It worked, too, because he was willing to accept whatever affection she gave, given the circumstances. The aroma got stronger as he approached the kitchen, where Domonique was busy cooking while being serenaded by Charlie Wilson.

Before he could make his grand entrance, Curtis spotted him and froze like a deer caught in the headlights. He was holding two Hawaiian Punch juice boxes and a bag of Doritos. He put his index finger in front of his mouth, signaling Curtis to stay quiet so he could surprise Domonique. Then Curtis smiled accordingly before taking off and running back toward Lil' D's room.

Domonique yelled, "I told y'all butts to stop running in this house!"

Sav snuck up behind her and said, "Hey sexy," in a seductive tone.

Domonique whipped her head around at the sound of her man's voice, instantly becoming elated.

"Oh my God! You scared me," she stated in a soft baby voice.

It was the same voice she used on him whenever she wanted to get her way because it seemed to always work. After all, there weren't many men alive who could've resisted Domonique's incomparable beauty and charm. She was 5'2", chocolate-skinned, and had ass for days. Her exotic features allowed her to rock the Halle Berry hairstyle with elegance. Oddly Sav wasn't a tittie man, so her 34B cup didn't faze him at all. However, he loved the stretch marks she acquired on her ass after having Lil' D, because it reminded him she'd been through some thangs.

She gently set her spatula down on the counter before grabbing him by the face and jamming her tongue down his throat.

"Damn! You smell like a strip club. You hungry?" she said, stepping back as she looked him up and down.

He replied, "Yeah, I could eat. How is Angela holding up?"

"I guess you could say she's doing fine, considering everything she's been through."

"Well, were you at least able to convince her to go to the hospital so she could get checked out?"

"Believe me, I tried, but she ain't having it."

"Oh, I know how stubborn she can get. Did she eat anything?"

"Barely. She hasn't come out of the room since you left. I've been taking her room service to keep her energy up, but she's barely eating anything off the plate. I wasn't going to say anything, but last night I heard her having a nightmare."

"And?" he asked, waiting for the punchline.

"She was calling out for your mother. Maybe you should give her a call."

"Call her for what? That bitch left us for dead. I was stuck raising my sisters while she chased the dragon."

"I know, baby, but blood is thicker than water. Sooner or later, you're going to have to forgive her."

"And cum is thicker than blood. That's why she chose her crackhead-ass boyfriend over her own damn kids. I don't even want Angela to know I found her. I only went looking for her so I could piss on her grave."

"Seriously, Dante? You need to cherish what little family you have left because tomorrow ain't promised to nobody."

"Man, that bitch done went and started a whole new family in Narf Richmond. That bitch ain't worried about us."

"Well, didn't you say she looked clean when you saw her? She may be a completely different person now. Don't sit up here and act like you haven't made any mistakes in your lifetime. How do you expect Angela to forgive you if you can't find it in your heart to forgive your mother?"

Sav just stared at Domonique, speechless because the harsh reality was he single-handedly fucked up Angela's life. And no amount of revenge could wipe away the pain and suffering she was forced to endure. She was lucky enough to have been saved before sustaining any irreversible harm.

"Daddy! When did you get here?" asked Lil' D.

"I just walked in the door, lil' man. You've been taking care of the house while I was gone?" Sav replied.

"Yeah. Auntie Angie is still sad, though."

Domonique stood idly staring at Sav, waiting to make eye contact, then mouthed, 'We'll finish this later.'

Domonique said, "Lil' D, you and Curtis go put y'all games away so y'all can get ready to eat. Because once I'm done cooking, I'm taking a power nap. Then y'all are on y'all own."

"Okay. Bye, Daddy," Lil' D said before sprinting out of the kitchen.

"I swear I'm going to kill them kids if they keep running through my damn house. Why don't you go see if you can convince Angela to come out of that room? She might listen to you. I think it's about time y'all talk anyway."

Surprisingly, before Sav had a chance to respond, they were interrupted by KO's signature ringtone.

He said, "Hold on, baby, this is KO," before stepping out of the kitchen.

"Tell him I said hi," she replied before returning to the stove.

Sav sat at the dining room table and pressed 'Talk' on his phone.

"Wassup, blood?" he asked.

"Wassup, cuzo? I got some news you ain't going to believe."

"Yeah? And what's that?"

"That bitch-ass he Sincere's dead, bruh."

Sav froze as he processed the bombshell KO had just dropped in his lap. It was by no means a phone call he was expecting to receive, but it was definitely a game-changer.

"Hello? You there?" KO asked.

"Yeah, I'm here. How do you know that he's really dead, though?"

"Shit, niggas been calling my phone all day talking about it. At first, I thought it was just a rumor until I checked it out online and saw it myself. Fa'sho, it's him."

"But I didn't see that shit on the news. When did it happen?"

"The other day. They said three black men were murdered inside his home in San Jose."

"That explains why I didn't see it on the news. I'm sure they put a gag order on that story. Three niggas getting killed in a rich white neighborhood can't be good for business. That's why they stopped showing all the violence in the Silicon Valley. They don't want to scare off any of them real estate investors. But anyway, did they give up the identity of any of them other fools?"

"Nope. The news said they were seeking the public's help to identify the other two suspects. It sounds like the police got Sincere down as the victim. I'm guessing it's because they invaded his house."

"More than likely."

"So what now, boss man?"

"We expand. With Sincere finally out of the way, the city is ours."

"What about that nigga Face? You don't think he gon' be a problem?"

"Nah, their organization is gonna crumble now. Soon, all his lieutenants will be asking me for a job. Until then, we're gonna keep our feet on their necks. And don't let any of them bitch-ass niggas breathe. Oh yeah! Domonique said wassup."

"Tell her I said what's good. What about Angela? How is she holdin' up?"

"I can't say. She said she wanted me to give her some space, so that's what I did. I can't blame her for hating me either. The shit was my fault."

"Yeah, but she knows you love her, though. You got her back, didn't you?"

"Yeah. Domonique said she hadn't been out of the room since she got here. I was on my way up there to see her when you called."

"A'ight, well, you go and take care of lil' sis. If you need me, you know I gotcha. Just hit my phone."

"A'ight. We have to hook up later on tonight to celebrate. I still gotta see that shit for myself, though."

"Fa'sho. You already know I'm ready to party whenever."

"A'ight bet."

"Peace."

Sav hung up the phone, then walked back into the kitchen, where Domonique was busy making a picture of lemonade.

"That was quick," she said as she turned to face him.

"I didn't go up there yet, smartass," he replied.

"I know. Don't tell me you got cold feet."

"Nah, I just came to tell you Sincere is dead. We finally got that mark."

"Really? Then why do I get the vibe you're not feeling too thrilled about it?"

"Because I don't think one of my niggas did it. If they did, they would've called me for the reward. But shit, I don't even know if any of them made it out of there alive."

"And how would you know if they were lying or not anyway? They could just be claiming the fame."

"Because I told them to bring me one of his fingers for verification. I ain't stupid."

"Wow, you really are sick, aren't you?"

"Shit, you asked. You know I'd do anything to protect this family."

"Well, if that's truly the case, why can't you just be happy that he is finally dead so that you can end your stupid war? And don't forget you're putting my family at risk, too. My brother and cousin look up to you, Dante. And they would do anything to earn your respect. Just be happy you won, and you're not the one dead or in jail. You have a loyal woman by your side and a beautiful son who adores you. I mean, what more could you ask for? I say it's time you became content with everything you have and move on before you lose it all, seriously."

Sav clenched his jaw, but said nothing. He hated when she made too much sense. So he did what he always did—he deflected.

He said, "I'll go try to talk Angela into coming to dinner."

However, Domonique wasn't a fool. She knew exactly what he was doing.

Hence, she placed her hand on her hip and said, "Umm hmm, you go do that."

Sav then gently kissed her on the forehead to concede his defeat without verbally admitting it. After she turned away, he watched her big booty sway down the hallway to see what was keeping the boys. *Damn, she's fine,* he thought. Feeling reluctant to do so, he turned and headed up the stairs anyway. It seemed like the staircase extended with every step he took, causing him to exhibit tunnel vision. He had been trying to conjure up the right opening statement the entire ride home. Nonetheless, none of the words he came up with sounded sufficient now that it was time to ask for her forgiveness. Eventually, he reached the top of the staircase but still hadn't come up with the proper words to minimize Angela's heartache and pain. Therefore, he decided to attack the situation head-on and hoped she would find it in her heart to forgive him.

Knock! Knock! Knock!

He stood nervously in front of his guest room door, expecting to be shut out, although it was something that he knew had to be done. He owed it to her to accept any verbal or physical punishment she felt needed to be released to regain her self-dignity. It was an unavoidable debt that had to be paid.

Knock! Knock! Knock!

"Angie, you up?" he asked.

Unfortunately, she didn't respond, prompting him to knock even harder.

"Hey Angie, you woke? I need to talk to you. It's important," he explained.

Then he stood knocking at the door for almost two minutes without a hint of movement on the other side. He resented the idea of invading her privacy but was becoming apprehensive about her. He thought, *she shouldn't be going through this alone anyway. She deserved better*, as he twisted the doorknob. After entering the bedroom, he immediately noticed that she had barely touched her food. Instead of being consumed, it was wildly scattered across a plate sitting atop the dresser drawer. Assuredly, it looked like a bratty toddler had been playing in it. Accordingly, he scanned the rest of the room and still didn't see her. Then, it quickly became evident that she was hiding inside the guest bathroom.

"Hey, Angie, you in there?" he called out as he approached the bathroom door.

She refused to respond to his voice, increasing his concern for her well-being. Suddenly, a part of him grew irritated because he hated being ignored, especially inside his own home.

"Hey Angie, you alright in there?" he yelled.

Bang! Bang! Bang!

He pounded on the door increasingly harder after it became apparent she was purposely choosing to ignore him. By then, his frustration was beginning to show. After calling her name and banging on the door for three minutes, he finally said "fuck it!" and decided to force his way inside. Luckily, he didn't need to because he realized the door was unlocked once he began twisting the knob. Then he slowly cracked open the door and peeked his head inside, hoping she was decent.

He stated, "We need to talk, Angie," as he gradually widened the door.

Sadly, what he saw next caused his knees to buckle, causing him to collapse onto the floor.

He said, "No! No! No! No! No!" as he crawled over to the bathtub, where Angela's body lay completely submerged under the water.

Afterward, he rose to his knees and pulled her out of the water, dragging her body onto his lap.

He yelled, "Domonique!" as he flipped her over onto her back.

Instinctively, he still gave her chest compressions even though he didn't have a clue what he was doing. By that time, Angela's lungs were so filled with water that every time he pressed on her chest, water just gurgled from her mouth. Trying not to panic, he pulled out his cell phone and dialed nine-one-one while continuously pressing down on her chest with his right hand.

He screamed, "Domonique!" before putting his phone on speaker and setting it down next to Angela's lifeless body.

Then he blew into her mouth three times while the phone rang, remembering how Pamela Anderson did it on Baywatch.

Suddenly, Domonique appeared in the doorway.

"Shit! What happened?" she asked hysterically.

"I don't know, but she's not breathing. When I found her, she was underwater—I don't know for how long," he replied.

Then, the nine-one-one operator's voice echoed through the phone.

"Hello! This is nine-one-one emergency," the operator said.

Sav handed Domonique the phone and said, "Here, talk to her."

Afterward, he continued to give Angela his version of CPR, hoping to succeed in resuscitating her. Next, the operator asked Domonique to be calm and briefly explain what happened. Truly uncertain, Domonique scanned the bathroom for any evidence of foul play, until she spotted two empty bottles of Oxycodone sitting next to an empty bottle of Vicodin. The first thought in her mind was, *fuck! She overdosed on my illegally prescribed medication.* She knew that if Angela had used her drugs to commit suicide, would almost certainly hold her accountable for her death.

"Hello? Ma'am, are you there?" asked the operator.

Domonique replied, "Yes, I'm here."

"Okay, now what is your emergency, ma'am?"

"It's my sister. She, she overdosed inside my bathtub. I think she also drowned. She's not breathing, but her brother's giving her CPR."

"Okay, ma'am, I need your address so I can dispatch an EMT."

Everything seemed unreal. Sav felt like he was in an episode of The Twilight Zone, utterly detached from all reality. Even from the grave, Sincere found a way to cause more turmoil in his life. He couldn't afford to lose his only remaining sister. Not over something he so selfishly refused to let go of. Something that could've easily been avoided had he just listened to Angela's supplications.

"Dante! Dante! Dante!" Domonique called out, trying to knock Sav out of his trance.

Finally, after snapping her fingers, he snapped out of it and gave Domonique a look of defeat. As if he had already accepted the fact that his baby sister was gone, and there was nothing he could do to bring her back. The big bad wolf was suddenly powerless because no matter how hard he blew, he couldn't breathe life back into Angela. He was humbled by the shock of her death because his God complex was shattered so abruptly.

"She's gone, baby," he said brokenly.

She replied, "The ambulance is on its way. Give me those bottles so I can tear off the labels because they can't find out they were my pills. They'll take Lil' D from us."

"Mama, what's wrong with Auntie Angie?" asked Lil' D from the bedroom doorway.

Trying to shield Lil' D and Curtis from seeing Angela's corpse, she rushed to the doorway and kneeled, blocking their view.

She said, "Baby, I need both of y'all to go into your room and close your door. I'll come get you in a little bit to explain what's going on, okay. You can play any video game you want, but whatever you do, don't come out of your room. Ya hear me?"

Curious, Lil' D tried to peek around Domonique's shoulder, but she gently grabbed his face, forcing him to look directly into her eyes. Aware of their curiosity, she protectively ushered them into the hallway and out of the bedroom.

She said, "Now promise me you will do exactly what I say and not come out until I tell you to."

"Okay, Mama, I promise. Come on, Curtis," he replied before sadly walking away with his head down.

When Domonique turned around, she saw that Sav had already begun carrying Angela's body toward the bed. Therefore, she hurried past him and snatched up the empty prescription bottles. Then, after peeling off the labels, she flushed them down the toilet, eliminating any evidence that could link her to the pills.

"What do we do now?" she asked as they stood over Angela's body.

"Ain't nothing we can do. Go outside and flag down the ambulance. I'm staying here with Angela."

"This is so fucked up," she stated on her way out.

Sirens blared up the street as the first responders quickly approached Sav's home. Meanwhile, Domonique jumped up and down, summoning the fire truck since it was the first to arrive. Once they parked, she ran to greet the firefighters before they could get out of the massive vehicle.

"My sister overdosed, and now she's not breathing! I think she's dead!" the fireman climbing out of the passenger side heard her yell.

He replied, "Okay, ma'am, can you take us to her?" while walking toward the house.

"Yes," she replied before jogging back into the house with the firemen in tow.

After reaching the guest bedroom, one of the firemen instructed Sav to step out of the room so they could try to resuscitate Angela. Meanwhile, another fireman was setting up a defibrillator on the bed next to her body.

"How long has she been unresponsive?" asked one of the firemen.

"At least ten minutes ago. He found her overdosed in the bathtub. I think she drowned, too. I'm not sure," Domonique replied.

"What kind of drugs did she take?"

"I don't know. But I found three empty pill bottles on the bathroom counter. They're still there."

He replied, "Okay, ma'am, we'll do everything we can to save her."

Then he shared the information with the firemen working to revive Angela.

Domonique stepped into the hallway and took Sav's hand, hoping to comfort him. Sadly, it was all that she could do during such a critical moment. They held on to hope that the firemen could revive her, although she was clearly dead before they even arrived.

From the top of the stairs, Lil' D asked, "Mama, what's wrong?"

"Boy, I thought I told you to stay in your room," she replied, walking toward the stairs.

When she reached Lil' D, she scooped him up with one arm and grabbed Curtis' hand with the other. Then she escorted them down the stairs to Lil' D's room. Finally, two paramedics entered the home, trying to locate the source of the emergency. A middle-aged, heavyset Caucasian man led the way, followed by a younger Portuguese woman with a curvy frame.

The man said, "It sounds like they're upstairs," before heading up the stairs.

One of the firemen standing in the hallway saw the paramedics and said, "She's in there," pointing inside the room.

The paramedics had to step over Sav because he was blocking the hallway as he cried into the palm of his hands. Immediately after stepping past him, the paramedics entered the room and placed their equipment on the floor beside the bed. Then, the fireman using the defibrillator on Angela suddenly froze, looked at them, and shook his head, signifying there was nothing more he could do. After examining Angela's body themselves, the paramedics conferred with the fireman before officially pronouncing Angela's time of death.

CHAPTER TWENTY

· · ·

Banks returned to Face's car, refusing to let their mother's rejection dictate his next move.

"You need to check your fuckin' attitude, bruh. You ain't doing anything but adding fuel to the fire with your antics. If them muthafuckas had called the police, it would've been my black ass getting violated—not you. And for what?"

Face replied, "My bad, bruh. That shit just had me hot. How the fuck is Mama gonna just disown us like that, blood?"

"Disown us? What are you, twelve? She's obviously going through somethin' right now. I'm sure she blames at least one of us for CJ's murder. She probably just needs some time to clear her head—especially now that she's paralyzed. Right now, all we can do is make sure that she has a safe home to be discharged to and kill whoever is responsible for the hit in the first place. That means we can't afford to be anything less than one hundred percent certain about who did it. No ifs, ands, or buts about it."

"So what now? You got any ideas inside that big-ass head of yours?"

"Nah, but you can take me to Mama's house so I can clean up and think. I have to analyze our options before making any wise decisions. Plus, I need to get at my PO before one of those crooked ass pigs tries to twist me up on some bullshit. You know they would love to fuck me over just because they can."

"Yeah, I feel you. Well, while you're doing that, I'll pick up Awol, so he can introduce me to his folks in Narf Richmond. He claims some cat named Brezz has the best crystal in The Bay, and he's looking to open a new pipeline."

"You sho you don't need me to roll witcha?"

"Yeah, I'll be straight. Go ahead and get your mind right. 'Cause I need you to be focused until we get over this hump. The way shit's been goin', ain't no tellin' what else is in store for us. So we have to be prepared for whatever may come next."

"A'ight, well, let's roll then."

Twenty minutes later, they pulled up in front of Jamela's house, feeling the unwelcoming stares of scared neighbors watching them like zoo animals.

"You see how they're looking at us, blood?" Face asked, concerned.

"Yeah, I peeped it. They're probably blaming me since nothing like this ever happened on this block. The optics definitely ain't in my favor. So I can't blame them, 'cause I would be thinking the same thing. Don't nobody want no hoodlums bringing stray bullets around their kids."

They looked on in disappointment as an old Cambodian lady hurried to usher her grandchildren back inside the house. She clearly held no reservations while peeking over her shoulder at them like they were potential kidnappers.

"Well, that's my cue to get the fuck up outta here," Face said firmly.

"A'ight, bruh, hit me when y'all get back from Richmond."

"Fa'sho. Be safe up in that house, blood. Who knows? They might double back to finish the job."

"A'ight, blood, I'm gone."

They gave each other dap before Banks got out of the car and slammed the door.

Suddenly he heard an unfamiliar voice say, "Wassup, Banks?"—causing him to whip his head around.

Face's reaction time was impeccable. He immediately snatched his gun from underneath his seat and shoved it out the window, aiming it directly at Keno's forehead.

Keno raised both hands and said, "Whoa, whoa, whoa, playa! I come in peace. I just wanted to holla at my boy Banks for a minute."

When Banks turned around, he immediately recognized Keno, who was in the back seat of a black Ford Explorer surrounded by three other men. Then he briefly swept the street for the police before clutching the .40-caliber pistol he had tucked in the small of his back.

"Do I know you?" Banks asked as he walked toward the SUV.

Keno replied, "Nah, but it appears you're becoming real famous in the eyes of the law. Wassup, Face? I heard about ya moms, too. That was some fucked up shit, homeboy. I send mines."

Face said, "So you mean to tell me you drove all the way over here to give me your condolences? Get the fuck outta here!"

Banks said, "Yeah, what the fuck does my popularity with the pigs got to do with you?"

Keno replied, "Well, if you could put your gun down for a second and give me a chance to explain my unsolicited visit, I'm sure we can reach common ground." He then looked around and said, "Besides, you're probably scaring your neighbors."

Keno then opened the door and stepped onto the street, reaching out his hand to greet Banks, who was now standing idly by the hood of Face's car, watching him skeptically.

"I'm Keno. I run Seventy-Third."

Reluctant to let his guard down, Banks elected not to shake Keno's hand.

Instead, he said, "Oh, I've heard of you. Wassup?"

"Well, I figured since we have a mutual enemy, we could converse like civilized adults. As the saying goes, an enemy of my enemy is my friend, right?"

"That's funny, 'cause the last time I checked, I ain't have no enemies."

"Not according to homicide detectives Jones and Johnson. They seem to believe you blew up Johnny's car in a jealous rage after he stole your woman. They even tried to threaten me into corroborating their theory so they could hurry up and close the case. Now, I took Johnny's murder personally because I was supposed to be in the car wit him when it exploded. Instead, it was Tonya who ended up being the casualty of war. So, of course, I decided to run a background check on you, and everyone I questioned spoke highly of you. They all said you weren't the type of nigga to kill Johnny over a bitch. So I gotta ask you man to man, did you kill my nigga Johnny?"

Realizing his response could easily make his already tumultuous situation worse, Banks chose his words wisely.

He stepped in close, looked Keno directly in his eyes, and said, "No, I didn't kill Johnny. But whoever did also hurt the mother of my kids, and that's unforgivable."

"So, one could only assume you're left seeking retribution."

"Who wouldn't be?"

"Not many. That's why I came over here to holla at y'all in person. I prefer to do so before those crooked ass cops try to play us against each other."

"What do you mean?" Banks asked curiously.

"Well, after they finished trying to pressure me into giving them a motive, they put me in their crosshairs. They claimed that I suspected you of trying to blow me up, which caused me to retaliate. They tried to make it seem like I was involved in shooting up your mother's house for revenge. So essentially, they threatened me with becoming a murder suspect since I refused to dry snitch on you. One thing about me is I'm old school. I know all of their fucking tricks. Them dirty muthafuckas are trying to play us against each other. I'm sure they'll be visiting you soon, accusing me of shooting up your mother's crib. So I came here to look you in your eyes and tell y'all I ain't got no beef with either of you. And I don't suspect y'all of killing Johnny over Tonya, either. Look, Johnny was my family, but he made quite a few enemies throughout the years. It could've been any one of them that did that shit. So, like I said, an enemy of my enemy is my friend. I'm sure you want whoever made the hit dead for what they did to Tonya. Likewise, I want them dead for what they did to Johnny. I'm sure if we combine our resources, we'll be able to come up with something. Maybe I could even help you find out who shot up your mama's house."

"Is that right?"

"No doubt. All we need is a name or address, and we'll handle the rest. Y'all ain't even gotta get y'all hands dirty on this one."

Banks immediately cut his eyes at Face for confirmation, which was something he rarely did. Even as a kid, he loved to assert the authority being the older brother gave him, especially since he seemed to flourish in decisive situations. Hence, he exploited the privilege any and every chance he got. Meanwhile, Face stared at Keno skeptically as if he could decipher his true intentions.

Keno looked at Face, threw his hands up, and said, "You know we're cut from the same cloth, man. I'm solid. Sincere and I may have had a few words regarding the expansion of territory, but the content of my character has never come into question."

Face stepped halfway out of his car, gun in hand, and replied, "I don't see why we couldn't work together. In a situation like this, we need all hands on deck."

Banks darted his eyes back and forth from Keno to Calico, trying to see if he could spot a tell, while also wrestling with the notion of making a pact with some fools he knew nothing about.

Finally, he reached out his hand and said, "Well, there it is there."

After Keno shook Banks' hand, he looked over his shoulder at Jamela's house and said, "Only a coward muthafucka would shoot up a house full of women and children. Hopefully, through our newfound partnership, whoever did it will be laid up on a metal slab soon enough."

"That part," said Banks.

Keno then reached into his pocket, pulled out a card, and handed it to Banks.

"Here, here's my number. Call me so I can have a direct line in case I come up with something valuable," said Keno.

"A'ight," Banks replied.

Afterward, Banks stared at the card while dialing the numbers written on it. Seconds later, Keno's phone began to ring.

Keno ignored the call, then said, "Well, I guess that concludes our business for now. I'll be in touch. Oh—and don't forget what I said about Jones and Johnson. They are two of the most corrupt cops in Oakland, so you better watch your back. 'Cause from the sound of it, they've got their targets set on you, young blood."

"Duly noted."

Keno nodded confidently at Face before climbing back into the truck.

After they drove off, Face said, "We gotta hurry up and get Mama out of this house."

Banks didn't respond, though. He just stood, spaced out, watching Keno's truck cruise down the block.

Calico turned around in the passenger seat and said, "Am I trippin', or did you just make an alliance wit them? 'Cause I was under the impression you was planning on smoking that nigga Banks."

"I was, if I truly believed he was the one who did it. But it wasn't him. I could feel it. I've been running these streets my whole life. I got a sixth sense for shit like this. Besides, I got bigger plans for them marks. Now that Sincere's dead, I'm sure that fool Face is planning to take over the operation. Luckily, he doesn't command as much respect in the hood as Sincere did. If I seize this opportunity to slide under him now, it might open the doors for us to take over his operation later down the line."

Blax Mobb said, "I knew you were up to somethin'. This old head always got somethin' up his sleeve."

Calico said, "So you expect us to try to find out who shot up his mama's house?"

Keno replied, "I gave the man my word, didn't I? It's a favor for a favor. He'll help us find out who killed Johnny, and we'll help him find out who shot up his mama's house. In the process, we gain some powerful allies. That way, we can utilize them until we're ready to take over their operation. We could do it without firing a single shot or starting a turf war. It's our best option since that's a war we would lose now that Johnny's gone."

"Shit, I'm always down for an upgrade. You ain't said nothin' but a word," Blax Mobb stated emphatically.

"Good. Well, let's head back to the trap. I got some shit I gotta get lined up."

Face got out of the car and approached Banks, who appeared deep in thought. Of course, Face was also skeptical about why Keno so desperately wanted to ally with them.

Face asked, "What do you think that was all about?"

Banks replied, "I don't know, blood. But from the sound of it, we've got one thing in common."

"And what's that?"

"Them two crooked ass cops are on both of our lines. They couldn't get him to snitch on me, so now they're trying to play us against each other. They're using the same tactics the COs used on me in the pen to get me to take off on my celly. That's the kinda shit they pull when you get into it with him. They searched our cell and only fucked my shit up. I mean, them punk muthafuckas tore through all my food and hygiene, talkin' 'bout, they were looking for a knife. I was so hot the shit almost worked. That dude Keno runs the spot on Seventy-Third, doesn't he?"

"Yeah, he does."

"Then, I'm sure those detectives threatened to shut down his operation if he didn't cooperate. It looks like he chose a side to me. At least we know he's not a snitch. As to his ulterior motives, only time will tell. We just can't let our guards down no matter what, because he's the least of our worries."

"I think he was fishing, trying to see if you acted guilty when he brought up Johnny's murder. So we're still gonna have to watch them snakes. 'Cause they're gonna be gunnin' for us if you didn't pass their so-called test."

"Yeah, I thought about that, too. Looks like I have to holla at my Muslim connect to stock up some artillery."

"Whatchu mean, blood? I already got guns."

"Exactly, you got guns. I'm talkin' straight-up military-grade artillery. He said they got some black market shit coming straight from the private sector."

"Damn, nigga! If you got it like that, why are you just now bringin' it up?"

"Because, bruh, I told you I was leaving that street shit alone so I could raise my daughters."

"Well, better late than never, I guess. Line that shit up then, cause I want everything he's selling. And make sure you relay that message, too."

"Yeah, a'ight. Now, go on and handle your business so we can be ready for tomorrow. I need some alone time to clear my head."

"A'ight. And you better stay on point in case them fools try and double back."

"Fa'sho."

After giving Banks a gentleman's hug, Face got back into his car and zoomed off down the street.

CHAPTER TWENTY-ONE

Face parked on 98th and C Street, where he observed Awol tongue kiss a scantily clad BBW wearing black sheer lingerie. *I can't take any more of this shit. I'm gonna throw up,* he thought.

Face yelled, "C'mon, bruh! Y'all can do all that square shit when we get back."

Awol held up the middle finger, signaling Face to wait while he snuck one last kiss in. Once he got in the car and closed the door, Face busted out laughing.

"What's so funny, blood?" Awol asked, looking confused.

"That was some nasty shit. I didn't know what I was watching. I thought that fat bitch was finna eat you, blood. What is she, a solid two-thirty?"

"Aw, man, fuck you. I love big bitches. They know how to treat a real nigga. I see I have to give you some game. A big bitch knows that she's fat, right? Ain't no hiding her weight because it's a part of her physical appearance. So she makes up for it by keeping her man fly. That way, all the other bitches be stuck trying to figure out how she managed to pull such a fly nigga. Science."

Face looked at Awol sideways and said, "Yeah right, you got your own money. Admit it, you just got a fetish for obese women."

"First rule of finance—never spend your own money."

"You know what? I'm going to leave that one alone. But you know you're crazy, though, right?"

"Whatever, let's get up out of here. Brezz is waiting on us."

Face started the car and said, "I hate going to Narf Richmond. Them niggas grimy as hell. They'll kill you just for giving them the wrong time."

"Yeah, they are cutthroat in Narf Richmond, but I've known Brezz for a while now, so we're straight. He ain't gonna do no snake shit for no crumbs knowing you got that long bread. Plus, all that would do is start some Oakland versus Richmond fonk. And we both know they already have enough enemies in their own city. So don't trip, bruh, we good."

"We better be."

Thirty minutes later, Face was driving over a set of train tracks, quickly breaking the threshold and entering the confines of North Richmond. Surprisingly, it was merely a set of train tracks that separated the city's most notorious neighborhood from the rest of the town. That part of Richmond was so infamous, it earned a distinct alias: Narf Richmond.

As they drove past the liquor store on Market, they couldn't help but notice how all of the men on the corner stopped what they were doing and stared them down. Some even clutched their pistols prepared to unload their clips if need be. They immediately recognized that they weren't from Narf Richmond. This was because that part of the city was so small, everyone knew each other's cars. And if there's one thing everyone in the Bay Area knows, it's that Narf Richmond residents don't like outsiders to cross them train tracks.

That's why I don't like coming out here, Face thought. Luckily, the car ride didn't last too much longer because they arrived at Breez's trap house within minutes. It was a typical dope spot full of gangstas in the front yard drinking and smoking weed. Also, there was a mediocre-sized dice game transpiring along the sidewalk. But just like at the liquor store, they stood out like a sore thumb. Once they got within thirty feet of the house, Face peeped a young teenager already clutching his pistol as they pulled up.

"Man, here we go," Face mumbled.

"Just be cool, nigga," Awol replied.

Awol tried to stop Face from reacting too soon and whipping out his pistol since that would've only made the situation worse than it already was.

Therefore, he stuck his head out the window and said, "Brezz is expecting us."

Still, they didn't budge. Luckily, just in the nick of time, Brezz's right-hand man, Nut, stepped out of the house and spotted Awol.

Nut said, "C'mon inside. We got some BBQ in the backyard."

Once Face entered the house, he could instantly tell it wasn't just your typical trap house. It was obviously someone's home because all of the sentimental pictures gave it away. The home had a Southern vibe to it. It wasn't surprising either because many of Narf Richmond's natives were originally from Louisiana. Fortunately, seeing the pictures of someone's grandmother made Face feel less likely to be killed inside that house. But the rest of the environment was no different from any other trap house he had been inside. It was full of drugs, guns, hoodrats, and niggas who didn't give a fuck, because they felt like they had nothing to lose. He noticed how the hoodrats lusted after him because, in their eyes, he was fresh meat on the line. He was someone who didn't know their dirty little secrets like everyone else in the hood did.

They followed Nut through the house and out of the back door, where the strong aroma of hickory BBQ permeated. Once he entered the backyard, he couldn't help but notice the big black man sitting in between two fine chocolate sistas playing dominoes. As they approached the table, the big Black Mandingo suddenly stood up and took a deep pull from his blunt.

Brezz said, "Welcome to my humble abode," after exhaling a thick cloud of gray smoke.

Then he looked down at the two men he was playing dominoes with and said, "Ay, y'all raise up. Me and my guest need to talk business."

"No problem," one of them replied before grabbing his drink and vacating his seat.

Brezz reached over, shook both their hands, then invited them to have a seat.

After they were seated, Brezz asked, "Are y'all hungry?"

"No thank you, I'm good," Face replied.

"Shiiit, I am," said Awol.

Brezz then looked down at the two beautiful ladies and said, "Y'all bitches go fix my guests some plates with everythang on 'em. And bring 'em both a cold beer to wash that shit down."

Brezz looked at Face, shrugged his shoulders, and said, "A to-go plate then? Trust me, that shit's fire."

"A'ight," Face replied respectfully.

Satisfied, Brezz sat back down and took another pull from his blunt.

He exhaled and said, "So Awol here tells me you're interested in conducting some very profitable business."

"That's right."

"So I could only assume you're looking to buy in bulk. What are you interested in, heroin or crystal?"

"Crystal."

"Well, let me stop you right there before we go any further. I gotta let you know, I don't do no backward hustlin'. So if I decide to do business with you, it's only under one condition."

"And what's that?" Face asked as he sat up in his seat.

"You gotta agree to stay on your side of the Berkeley city limits. Because when it comes to crystal, everything from Berkeley to Vallejo belongs to me."

Face glanced at Awol and said, "That's not going to be a problem. I have the clientele. I just need the product."

Brezz studied Face, deciding whether he wanted to do business with him or not.

"So how much product are we talking about exactly? Brezz asked curiously.

"Well, that all depends on your wholesale margins," Face replied.

"My wholesale margins, huh? You heard I got that top-of-the-line shit, or you wouldn't be here. I don't have that experimental bullshit they got floating around The Bay."

"Look, I don't fuck with the shit, so I wouldn't know the difference. But Awol vouched for you, and his word is golden wit me."

"Good, 'cause I sell my pounds for eight thousand a piece. What you want about ten of 'em?"

"Nah, I was thinking more like fifty of 'em at five thousand apiece. That's two hundred and fifty grand on our initial deal. And that's just for starters."

Brezz sat back in his seat, stunned by the large order Face had just requested. Hearing an opening bid of such magnitude on their initial business transaction caught him off guard.

"That's one hell of a discount you're asking for. But I think I'll be able to accommodate you. When could you have the money by?"

"Shit, I could have the money by tonight. The question is, how long will it take you to put my order together?"

"Aw, that ain't gon' take no time. I could have that packaged and ready to go by eight o'clock tonight. Is that soon enough for you?"

"That's perfect."

"Then we have ourselves a deal."

Suddenly, both women who went to fetch the BBQ and beer returned with their hands full. They carefully set the food and drinks on the table in front of Awol and Face.

Awol said, "Thank you, ladies, 'cause I was starving like a muthafucka."

The ladies giggled playfully at Awol's blatancy as they sat back down.

Face said, "So, what neutral location do you have in mind to make the transaction?"

"Shit, right here, nigga. Ain't no safer place I can think of."

Face suddenly looked around at all the grimy-looking ass faces like he'd beg to differ. Brezz took Face's reaction as a sign of distrust and didn't appreciate being disrespected in his own home.

Brezz said, "I know you didn't just come into my house, eat up my food, then accuse me of being untrustworthy."

Face looked at Awol sideways, letting him know without saying it: *If shit goes all bad after you vouched for Brezz, it's your ass on the line.*

"You can trust him, Face. He's solid," Awol stated confidently.

The tension built as Brezz waited for Face's response—his tone alone had his boys in go mode.

Unbothered, Face said, "Well, I guess we have ourselves a deal then."

Brezz replied, "Let's get this money then, baby," while extending his hand to Face, easing the tension.

CHAPTER TWENTY-TWO

· · ·

Detectives Johnson and Jones crept alongside Lieutenant Colding's house, hoping not to be seen by anyone nosy enough to investigate. Jones quickly reached across the wooden gate that led to the backyard and lifted the latch. After opening the gate in a single motion, Jones entered the backyard, ensuring there were no guard dogs. Meanwhile, Johnson followed closely behind him, holding a black plastic Sally's Beauty Supply bag. After verifying the coast was clear, they headed around to the rear of the house and approached the back door.

Jones said, "We've gotta be in and out, so keep an eye out. We can't afford to be identified by anybody."

Johnson replied, "I gotcha, just get to work," while looking around suspiciously.

Jones pulled a black plastic case from his pocket and extracted a set of lock picks. After selecting the proper lock pick, he quickly returned the case to his pocket. Next, he knelt on one knee and began fidgeting with the lock to trigger the mechanism to unlock the door.

"Dammit, man! This shit ain't working," Jones complained.

"Here, let me do it," Johnson replied.

"Be my guest."

Johnson handed Jones the bag and accepted the lock picks in return. Using the same technique as Jones, Johnson kneeled and began fidgeting with the lock. Jones instinctively looked up at the neighbor's window and noticed a little boy watching them. Luckily, the child appeared to be no older than five.

"Hurry up, man. There's a fucking kid watching us through the window," Jones said nervously.

"What!"

"I said there's a–"

"I heard you the first time. I'm almost in."

Improvising, Jones pulled out his badge and showed it to the kid while shushing him. Then he calmly pressed his index finger against his lips, hoping to gain the kid's loyalty. To his amazement, it seemed to have worked. The kid suddenly ran away from the window without ringing the alarm.

"You almost done? The little bastard disappeared," said Jones.

"Yeah, man, gimme a sec," Johnson replied, clearly frustrated.

Sweat began to trickle down Johnson's forehead, caused by the sudden spike in his heart rate.. Jones stared through the neighbor's window, praying the stupid kid wouldn't tell his mother what he saw. He knew it was too good to be true when he saw the little bastard reappear at the window, holding a pair of plastic cuffs and a badge. *This little muthafucka's crazy,* Jones thought. Fortunately, Johnson managed to unlock the door, allowing them to enter before the situation escalated. Jones then waved goodbye to the kid before trailing Johnson inside the house, hoping no one credible noticed them.

"I told you we should've just waited 'til tonight. Now we run the risk of getting IDed by a fucking toddler," Johnson complained.

"Yeah, well, we're here now. Let's just hide this evidence somewhere it could be easily found and get the hell out of here."

They went through the house, snooping while pretending to look for a place to plant the evidence. Surprisingly, Detective Colding's house was freakishly spotless, with every item neatly placed and precisely angled.

Jones said, "This muthafucka must've had OCD or somethin'. No normal person pays this much attention to detail. I mean, look at the symmetry of this shit. This fool had to have been crazy. That's how he was able to solve all those damn cases."

"You ain't lyin'. This is some *Hannibal Lecter*-type shit right here. Let's hurry up and get the hell outta here," Johnson replied.

"Okay. Let's plant this inside his bedroom closet since it'll be the first place they search."

"Alright, well, I'm right behind you."

Next, Jones led the way down the hallway toward the master bedroom. He pulled out the gun they had stolen from the evidence locker before checking the first of three bedrooms in the hallway. It was imperative that he made sure the house was empty because even though he knew Colding lived alone, it was better to be safe than sorry. The first room was no longer a bedroom because it had been converted into a fully stacked library filled with crime novels and other miscellaneous genres. The second room was filled with memorabilia, sectioned off by accolades for Colding, his deceased wife Mya, and Sincere. Everything else appeared exactly as they expected, spotless and freakishly neat. Jones shook his head as he backpedaled out of Colding's trophy room and turned down the hallway. Once they entered the master bedroom, Johnson headed straight for the closet in a rush to plant the evidence. It was clear he was determined to wrap up their B&E mission expeditiously. However, he was shocked by what he discovered when he opened the door, causing him to step back.

"What?" Jones asked, wondering what made Johnson react the way he did.

"This fool got some Fifty Shades of Grey shit goin' on, man," Johnson replied in a warped voice.

Jones asked, "What are you talking about?" before stepping in to view the contents for himself. "What the hell?" he asked.

Jones' eyes nearly popped out of his head when he saw the closet full of S&M instruments hanging, just waiting to inflict pain.

"I don't think it can get any weirder than this man," said Johnson.

"I see. Just put it inside one of those shoeboxes so we can get the hell out of here."

Johnson quickly opened one of the six shoeboxes stacked neatly in three rows. He was so stunned by what he had discovered that he couldn't express his shock intelligibly. Therefore, he quickly handed the shoebox to Jones before immediately opening another. Jones immediately knew what he was looking at because he had spent sleepless nights working their cases. It was a photographed collection of all five victims murdered during the Acorn Stalker's killing spree. Sadly, over a three-year span, five women were kidnapped, raped, and savagely murdered—all of whom lived in or around the Acorn housing projects. All of whom lived in or around the Acorn housing projects. Many believed it was the work of a sadistic, middle-aged white man with a deep-rooted hatred for African American women. No one would've ever suspected OPD's own golden boy since he was the detective working the cases. The same cases that helped destroy Jones' marriage and almost cohesively destroyed his career.

"Look, there's more," Johnson stated as he handed Jones another shoebox. "This sick bastard was keeping souvenirs of all his victims."

Jones sighed and said, "No wonder I couldn't catch the crazy son of a bitch. He knew all of our tactics and procedures. He was right there in my face the whole damn time, eating fucking donuts and drinking coffee."

"Well, we got his ass now. It looks like you'll get that promotion you've been going on and on about. Now you've got your smoking gun."

Jones, now inspired, rummaged wildly through the remaining boxes.

"That reminds me, do you still think we should plant the evidence?" asked Johnson.

"I don't see why we shouldn't. It'll just serve as icing on the cake."

"Okay, well, how are we gonna explain the chain of custody? We only got this evidence because we broke into his house. The plan was—"

"I know what the damn plan was! You think any DA, judge, or victim's family member gives a shit about the chain of custody? We have a chance to bring closure to all of the victims' families. Think about the boost our careers are about to receive."

"Shh!"

"What? Don't shush me."

"Wait! Do you hear that?" Johnson asked, animated.

"Hear what?" Jones replied, irritated since he assumed Johnson was being paranoid.

Johnson said, "That pinging sound," before kneeling and putting his ear against the hardwood floor. "You mean to tell me you can't hear that banging? It sounds like something metal clanking against a pipe. I think someone's locked inside the basement!"

Hearing the urgency in Johnson's voice brought Jones to the realization. It was possible that Colding could have died with one of his victims held captive inside his basement. The notion was not far-fetched, especially after what they had just discovered. Therefore, he tossed the boxes onto the bed, and kneeled beside Johnson so he could listen for himself.

"Ting! Ting! Ting!"

He could now hear the faint sounds Johnson had heard the entire time. A sound that was all too familiar in their field of work. It was the sound of handcuffs clanking against a metal object, which he believed to be a drainage pipe.

Jones said, "You're right. Someone is down there. C'mon, there is no telling how many girls there may be down there."

Suddenly, they both hopped up and scrambled to find the entrance to the basement. However, after checking every room inside the house, it became evident that there was no basement door. Soon after, Johnson walked into the kitchen, where Jones was stuck wrecking his brain. He was trying to figure out how someone could be held captive inside a basement if there wasn't one.

Johnson asked, "So what do you wanna do? Do you wanna call it in?" while pulling out his cell phone.

Jones then looked down at the large rug centered on the kitchen floor, shaking his head in disbelief.

He said, "No! Not yet. This is my collar, god dammit. We're missing something."

Johnson suddenly looked down at the rug and said, "That rug. Who puts an area rug in the middle of their kitchen?"

Jones thought about it, then immediately bent over and snatched the rug back, revealing a hidden door with a brass latch.

"Well, I'll be damned," said Johnson.

"C'mon, help me get this sucker open."

Johnson hurriedly assisted Jones in lifting the reinforced hatchway before unholstering his service weapon.

Jones asked, "What are you doing?" hoping to avoid accidentally shooting one of Colding's victims.

"Who's to say he doesn't have a partner down there? We could be walking directly into an ambush."

Jones unholstered his pistol and said, "You ain't gotta tell me twice."

Next, he walked eagerly down the stairs with the taste of victory on the tip of his tongue. He was finally about to solve the case that had haunted him day and night for years. His inability to deliver justice for the victims made him realize justice was nothing more than a figment of the imagination. Strangely, his ideology was strongly supported by every member of Congress. After all, lawmakers were paid to create laws based on figments of their imagination. So why couldn't he take matters into his own hands and deliver a little street justice? What made their ideal perception of justice more adjudicative than his? He knew they were capable of being bought, just like he was.

They eventually reached the bottom of the staircase, entering a dimly lit basement. Only a single lightbulb flickered dimly, making it extremely difficult for them to see. However, one thing that stood out despite the darkness was the walls. He noticed that they had been soundproofed, and not by professionals. It looked like a cheap setup that was secretly installed to avoid suspicion.

Suddenly, they heard muffled cries for help coming from behind a thick wooden door secured with a Master padlock.

Jones removed his cell phone from his back pocket and used its flashlight to illuminate the basement as they moved toward the cries for help.

Jones announced, "This is it," before angling his gun at the padlock.

He yelled, "If you can hear me, get back! I'm going to shoot off the padlock, okay? But don't you worry, we're detectives with the OPD!"

After making his announcement, he waited a few seconds to give her enough time to back away from the door. Her sudden silence indicated she had heard him and decided to comply.

Johnson said, "Wait! Let me stand on the other side of you, in case the bullet ricochets," while moving out of the way.

"You ready?" Jones asked sarcastically.

"Yeah."

"Here goes."

"Boom!"

Jones fired a single shot that made direct contact, immediately separating the padlock from the door's latch with ease. Then, Johnson tactically opened the door, while Jones covered him from behind, holding up his cell phone for light. Suddenly, they were both horrified at the inhumane living conditions the young woman had been forced to live in. Not to mention that she looked to be no older than eighteen years old. She wasn't sure who was actually entering the dungeon she'd been trapped in for God knows how long. Therefore, she crawled into the corner and hid behind a rusty old toilet. The room was also soundproofed, but there were no hanging light bulbs, which meant she had been living in almost pure darkness. Only a minimal amount of light from the adjacent room managed to squeeze its way through the base of the door.

Johnson said, "Don't worry, you're safe now. We are the police," in a soft, non-threatening voice.

They could now hear the chains that bound her hands together, clinking wildly as she covered her eyes in retreat. It was apparent that she had developed a sensitivity to light after spending so much time in the darkness.

Johnson looked back at Jones and said, "Put your gun away and show her your badge. And get that damn light out of her face—you're probably blinding her."

Jones holstered his gun, then laid his phone flat on the ground so the light would still illuminate the room. Then he slowly revealed his badge, which was tucked beneath his shirt because he hated how it dangled.

Jones said, "It's okay, I won't hurt you. We're police officers, and we're here to take you home to your family. What's your name, sweetheart?"

Jones thought *How could Colding do such a thing? He probably used his badge to get her to lower her guard.*

The young teenage girl slowly stood up after convincing herself she was finally safe because the two men standing before her were indeed law enforcement officers. It was heartbreaking for them to witness the living conditions she was subjected to at the hands of one of their own. One whom they perceived to be an overachieving golden boy unlikely to commit such an atrocity.

When she stood up, Jones noticed the chains that bound her led back behind the toilet like a leash, connecting her to a thick metal pipe protruding from the wall. It was ironic because the same tool Colding used to bind her was the exact tool she used to summon her rescuers.

Just by looking at the girl's frail, malnourished body, it was obvious that she hadn't eaten in days. *She must've been surviving off of the sink water all this time,* Johnson thought.

Jones asked, "What's your name?" as he took off his blazer.

She replied, "A.... Annette," before crawling out from behind the toilet and slowly standing to her feet.

Jones slowly inched closer to Annette. Sadly, the closer he got to her, the more he smelled the stench of musty ammonia and copper. He figured the copper smell came from a lack of access to feminine care during her period. Her clothes also smelled mildewed, like they had been wet and never had the chance to fully dry. Jones knew that poor innocent girl was in really bad shape mentally and physically, and she was certainly terrified for her life. He realized comforting her no matter what would be the humane thing to do, so he ignored the burning sensation in his nostrils, and wrapped his blazer around her shoulders. Annette's time in captivity naturally made her repellent to Jones' affection, causing her to tense up immensely.

Jones reassured her softly, "It's okay, I won't hurt ya."

Annette's eyes darted between Jones and Johnson like a scared kitten before she finally relaxed in Jones' comfort.

"Now let's get you out of here," Jones said, attempting to sound chipper.

Do you want me to call it in?" Johnson asked, gripping his cell phone.

"No! This girl has been through enough already. We don't need her to be stuck in the middle of a circus. I want you to call a bus and ride with her down to the hospital so you can take her statement. She may have information regarding other missing girls. I'll stay here and secure the crime scene. Looks like I'm finally going to get my just deserts. After all these years, we've finally managed to catch the bastard."

"Copy that," Johnson said, turning before jogging toward the stairway to dial 9-1-1.

Jones whispered, "You're gonna be just fine," as he escorted Annette out of captivity.

CHAPTER TWENTY-THREE

Banks was exhausted and gravely depressed after cleaning up all the blood spilled by his loved ones. He hoped the triple shot of Folger's he had drank would give him the spark he needed to finish off the night. He felt compelled because Face insisted that he accompany them on the crystal meth transaction. After spacing out on the couch for about fifteen minutes, the caffeine finally kicked in, causing his hands to sweat profusely. Suddenly, he grew restless from the surge of energy coursing through his body and decided to watch TV. However, when he walked into the living room to turn on the television, he noticed two bullet holes with spider web cracks spreading across the screen. So, he retreated into the bedroom where he had been sleeping since his release from prison. Then he sat on the bed and grabbed the remote from the nightstand, nearly knocking over a half-full glass of water. Next, he hit the power button on the remote and waited patiently for the picture to emerge on the screen. He hoped that it would help him escape his harsh reality, even if it was only temporary. He saw the news was on and instantaneously became uninterested, prompting him to change the channel, but it didn't matter because the same breaking news flash had interrupted the following three stations. Luckily, Detective Jones' face flashed on the screen just before he hit the menu button, or he would've missed his groundbreaking statement. He couldn't believe the bombshell Jones was dropping on the world during a live press conference. A highly decorated homicide detective was living a double life. By day, he was protecting the city, but at night, he moonlighted as a sadistic serial killer. If this turn of events didn't prove our justice system was broken, he didn't know what would. Since law enforcement officers played an essential role in our justice system, he felt they should be held to a higher standard than the average citizen. He believed that they should be subjected to a lie detector test investigating their motives for wanting to wear the badge, especially with the disclosure of systemic racism assisting the rampant killings of unarmed black men. Banks always believed that there were a few racist officers just waiting for the opportunity to shoot a person of color simply because a fascist, hate-filled ideology inspired them. So, a stricter screening process would be a small price to pay, given the circumstances. However, he knew that would never happen because there would hardly be any officers left to choose from. They left a loophole just wide enough for the corrupt ones to slither through the cracks.

Banks was so deep in thought that he jumped at the sound of his phone ringing. Still captivated by the press conference, he stood up and removed his cell phone from his front right pocket. Seeing Face's name on the caller ID, he knew they had arrived and were waiting for him outside.

He answered the phone and said, "I'm on my way."

"A'ight," Face replied.

"Click!"

Banks hung up the phone, then turned off the television, stunned by the unbelievable announcement he just witnessed. After locking up the house, he got into Face's back seat with a bothered look on his face. His distraught demeanor made Face look at him with concern.

"Wassup, bruh? Something wrong?" he asked.

"Blood, you ain't never gonna believe what the fuck I just saw on the news," Banks replied.

Face immediately thought about all of the illegal activities he was involved in and hoped it didn't have anything to do with him.

"What? It had something to do wit one of us?" Face asked nervously.

"Nah, blood. Sincere's pops is the Acorn Stalker. They got an APB out on that fool."

Awol said, "The Acorn Stalker? You talkin' 'bout that serial killer who was killing off all them hoes?"

"Yeah, bruh," Banks replied.

"Ain't his pops a cop, though?"

"Yuuup."

"Damn, that's crazy. That sick fuck was hiding behind that badge all that time."

Face said, "Shit, if he was going to be doin' some crazy shit like that, he could've been working for us. All of them bitches Sincere had, he ain't even have to take no pussy."

Banks said, "You know Sincere really didn't fuck wit his pops. You think he knew something was up?"

"Nah. He blamed that fool for the death of his mother and grandmother, as far as I know. He wouldn't've fucked with him at all if he knew he was on some shit like that."

"Yeah, you're probably right. I do know one thing, though. When they catch him, they're going to hang his black ass. And that's for damn sho. But enough about that fool. Whatchu got lined up with them shady-ass Richmond niggas?"

Face replied, "Exactly what I told you. And everything better go smooth too," while looking back at Awol.

"Bruh, I'm tellin' you, Brezz is straight. You be on that bullshit. You ain't got nothin' to worry about," Awol replied.

"Good, 'cause if he double-cross us you're gonna be the one puttin' the work in."

Banks interjected, "Well, let's just hope that's not the case, because we've got bigger problems to worry about, especially since Keno knows where we lay our heads at night."

"Keno? What's he got to do with anything?" Awol asked, completely out of the loop.

"Oh, Face didn't tell you? That nigga pulled up on us outside my mama's house talkin' 'bout how he wanna work together to find out who blew up Johnny's car."

"Wait, what? What would make him think you were willing to help him?"

"One could only assume it was because whoever blew up the car also disfigured Tonya's face. I guess he thinks I still give a fuck about the bitch. But if I had to bet my bottom dollar on it, I'd assume, as close as he was to Johnny, he would've known that Johnny was the one who set me up. And if that is the case, he was probably testing me to see if I still gave a damn about Tonya. Because the average man is always going to care about what happens to the mother of his children, no matter what. Unless she pulled some scandalous-ass shit like having him set up to get robbed and then sent off to prison for ten years."

"So you think he was basically just trying to read you, then?"

"That's what I think, but you know how the saying goes: keep your friends close and your enemies even closer. I know how to play the game. I greased the nigga a lil' bit and agreed to help his cause."

Awol said with a chuckle, "You really did that shit, huh?"

"Hell nah, man. And if I did, I sho wouldn't tell anybody. You know that."

"A'ight, a'ight, just checking. You know it don't matter to me if you did or didn't. I'm gon' ride wit y'all squares on whoever, regardless."

Face said, "A'ight, soldier. Well, how about we stick to handling one mission at a time? Them Narf Richmond cats got priors for double-crossing their own. So what the fuck you think they'll do to us? Until this transaction is complete, they'll be considered viable threats to the establishment. Ya feel me?"

"As they should be. But like I told you before, Brezz is a businessman. So he damn sho ain't finna bring no war to his front door. My nigga, believe dat."

"That wouldn't be smart," Banks added.

Face said, "Yeah, but some playas in the game don't gain their respect in the hood by being smart. They use fear and force. Those fools are the most dangerous because they're too stupid to see the ramifications of their actions. They only see what's directly in front of 'em. That's why I like meeting on neutral grounds for my initial transaction."

"Well, shit, bruh—if Awol says he's straight, then he's probably straight. If he's not, we'll play it cool, leave with our lives, then rain down the wrath of God on them muthafuckas."

"And that's what I'm trying to avoid having to do, because another war ain't good for any of us."

Awol snapped, "I'm telling you, bruh, it ain't no setup. Now quit being paranoid, ol' scary-ass nigga."

"Shit, paranoia is just the highest state of awareness."

Banks said, "Nah, he ain't paranoid, bruh. He's just shell-shocked from that shootout he just had in the hunnits. Trust me, I know the feeling. He a be a'ight."

Face gave Banks a piercing look like he wanted to make a brazen rebuttal, but what could he say? Banks was one hundred percent correct.

However, Face still countered with, "Well, even if that was the case, that's just more reason not to trust 'em. You feel me, bruh?"

Banks had already concluded that Face was nervous due to his near-death experience. Yet he refused to sound like a scared little bitch, so he appealed to him for support. One positive attribute Banks acquired from his stint in prison was his ability to read people. His extensive bid made it easier to analyze the motives of a shady hustler. So, from his experience, he knew there was no doubt about his brother's actions. He was still shook, causing him to categorize everything as a potential threat.

"Yeah, I feel you, bruh. We're gonna be straight, though. Let's just get this shit done so we can focus on the deal with Mafi," Banks replied reassuringly.

"Yeah, blood, now speed up before he sells that shit to somebody else."

Thirty minutes later, Face crossed over the train tracks that led to one of the Bay Area's most notorious neighborhoods. It was a bright full moon that night. Hence, the moonlight illuminated off of the crackheads, making them resemble zombies from the Walking Dead television show. They looked like zombies mostly because they stared at the ground as they trotted along, hoping to spot either a bundle of crack on the ground, or anything else they could flip for a few bucks. They noticed how every street dealer they passed clutched their guns as their vehicle approached and continued to do so until after they proceeded. But in the hood, that wasn't a secret. Everyone knew that if you saw a gangsta wearing a hoodie at night, there was a good chance he was using it to conceal his pistol.

When Face turned onto Brezz's block, he made eye contact with a fat teenage boy standing on the corner, who gave him a subtle nod.

"That must be his lookout," said Banks.

"Or his scout," Face replied argumentatively.

"Well, whoever he is, we're here now," said Awol.

Now that it was nighttime, Face felt a whole different vibe. He was ten times more on edge now than earlier. Unfortunately, Banks could see it all over his face. Therefore, he knew he wouldn't feel comfortable until the deal was finally concluded. It was evident that they were fully prepared for their arrival because once they reached Brezz's house, a tall, slender man was waiting to greet them.

"Pull up in the driveway," the slender man demanded.

"A'ight," Face replied before pulling into the driveway.

Next, the man followed their car up the long, narrow driveway and then waited for them to get out.

Once they exited the car, he said, "Follow me," leading them to Brezz's front door.

After opening the front door, he said nonchalantly, "Go ahead, he's expecting y'all."

Awol figured it was best if he went in first since it was his they were meeting. Banks followed closely behind, eager to see who had his normally fearless brother acting like such a bitch. When they got inside the house, they first noticed the thirty-something-year-old man chillin' with a girl that couldn't be any older than sixteen. She was sitting on his lap, holding a pint of Hennessy while smoking a blunt. It's sad because even though it is considered statutory rape in the state of California, growing up in the hood, everybody knew at least one person guilty of sleeping with a minor. Since the girls are post-pubescent, the men who took advantage of them were called ephebophiles. Even though many people frowned on it, they never reported it—because in the hood, it was all too common to see fast girls pretending to be grown. Sadly, most of them were only using sex as a tool to prove their adulthood. Shockingly, some of the younger mothers even encouraged that behavior, hoping their daughter would trap a baller—so she could get hooked up with one of his baller friends.

"Brezz in the backroom," said the ephebophile.

The young teenage gave Banks a flirtatious smile like she was ready to choose up. Banks quickly averted his eyes to avoid an unnecessary conflict, especially over a girl willing to do anything just to ride shotgun in a luxury car. The more they walked through the house, the more Face's anxiety subsided because he knew only a fool would kill them with that many witnesses around.

Awol was surprised to see the same two beautiful women from earlier. Now they were baby-oiled up, wearing nothing but panties, grinding on each other erotically. Oddly, the ladies were not bothered by their intrusion. In fact, being watched seemed to turn them on even more. Face was the last to round the corner and enter the room, and what he saw had him at a loss for words. All the qualms he had been contending with throughout the day suddenly disappeared.

Brezz was leaned back, puffing on a blunt while a nude, caramel-skinned woman with fiery red hair bobbed her head on his dick. She paused, glanced back at them, then kept doing her thing like she had no shame in her game. The freak was going to town and didn't even break a sweat. It was like having an audience made her perform significantly better. Brezz could see his little public display of affection made Banks feel uncomfortable. So he decided to use the opportunity to express his dissatisfaction with him showing up uninvited.

Brezz said, "Wassup Awol? Who is this fool lookin' at me like he ain't never seen a nigga get no head before?"

Both of the exotic dancers giggled at Brezz's joke while still freakishly grinding on each other.

Awol replied, "That's my cousin Banks. He is also Face's brutha."

"Well, the next time you decide to add somebody to your little guest list, make sure you clear it with me first. For all I know, he could be a fed. You a fed, nigga?" Brezz asked aggressively.

"Hell nah, I ain't no muthafuckin' fed," Banks stated firmly.

Brezz then stared at Banks intensely, waiting for him to break eye contact, but Banks held his gaze without feeling intimidated.

Finally, Brezz said, "Cool, y'all got the money?"

Face replied, "Yeah, I got yo dough," as he stepped forward holding a Gucci duffel bag.

Brezz said, "Well, let's see it," while reaching out his hand.

Face reluctantly stepped over to Brezz with the duffel, careful not to make eye contact—'cause no straight man wants to lock eyes with another man with an erection. Unfortunately, Face's plan to make a swift exchange didn't work. Moments before he made the handoff, Brezz retracted his hand and placed it on the back of the head doctor's head.

Brezz said, "Hol' up!" before tilting his head back and closing his eyes.

Everyone in the room knew what that meant. Face couldn't believe that weirdo was really about to make him stand there and watch him bust a nut in that bitch's mouth. *I ain't fuckin' with this psycho no more*, Face thought.

Brezz moaned, "Make sure you get it all, too," while his eyes rolled to the back of his head.

Once she finished topping him off, she grabbed a towel from the table and wiped most of her saliva off his dick.

Satisfied with her performance, she tucked his dick away, then stood up and said, "I'm finna go wash up, Daddy."

Face wasn't about to risk their hands accidentally touching during the handoff, so he quickly tossed the duffel bag onto the couch next to Brezz.

"It's all there," Face stated irritably.

Brezz replied, "I wouldn't accept anything less," before briefly sifting through the bag.

After confirming the agreed-upon amount of money was in the duffel bag, Brezz walked behind his bar, bent down, and retrieved a duffel bag of his own. Then, with a grim smile, he tossed the duffel bag to Face, who caught it with both hands.

Brezz said, "That's some good quality shit right there. The ladies are gonna love it. Just ask them," before pointing to his live peep show.

Face glanced at the ladies momentarily, then replied, "Nah, I'll just take your word for it."

Afterward, Brezz squirted two pumps of hand sanitizer into his hands before rubbing them together.

Brezz replied, "Shit, that's even better—because that means everything in this game," as he returned from the bar with his hand out.

Face met him halfway and shook his hand, slightly relieved that Brezz had disinfected them.

"Do you wanna toast to our newfound partnership?" Brezz asked jovially.

"I'd love to, but we're in a rush. We've got some urgent business we need to take care of," Face replied.

Brezz darted his eyes back and forth from Banks to Awol to see their expressions because he felt Face was blowing smoke up his ass.

He said, "Well, a'ight then. I'll let y'all be on y'all way. I don't wanna hold y'all up any longer than need be."

Brezz took the initiative to walk over and shake Awol's hand. Then he gripped it tightly and said, "Be safe out there."

Next, he shook Banks' hand and said, "Nice to meet you, big dog."

"Likewise," Banks replied.

After they were done embracing, Face walked up, shook Brezz's hand, and said, "It was great doing business witcha. I'll be back for a re-up real soon. That a'ight?"

Brezz replied, "Hell yeah it is, you got them crisp bills. Oh yeah! Drive cautiously heading out of here because the sheriffs have been trippin' ever since that little girl got smoked."

"A'ight, good lookin'. We out."

Brezz threw up the deuces, turned, and cha-cha'd over to the two freaks, who seemed to be having all the fun.

CHAPTER TWENTY-FOUR

Face decided to drop Banks off at Tiffany's house first since it was in Deep East Oakland, even farther from his place than Awol's. For some reason, he felt more comfortable riding dirty with someone else in the passenger seat, even though it increased his chances of getting pulled over—especially since cops saw two men in a car as a two-for-one bust.

After dropping Awol off, Face was so focused on watching for the police that he didn't notice the car tailing him until he pulled into his neighborhood. Once he realized a car was following him, he pulled over abruptly to see how the driver would react. Surprisingly, the car kept cruising at the same speed and didn't make any erratic moves. Face tried to look inside the vehicle as it passed, but the darkness and tinted windows made it nearly impossible to see the driver. The car subsequently made a right at the end of the block, heading in the opposite direction of Face's stash house. However, to be safe—even though the car turned away—he still waited three minutes before continuing to his stash house. He pulled into his garage a few minutes later, feeling overly accomplished. He routinely parked inside his garage to keep anyone from seeing him transport anything to or from his stash house. He also couldn't afford for anyone from the hood to recognize one of his cars and break into his spot.

Since Sincere suddenly stopped keeping overstock in the trap houses because of Sav, he had Face take twenty kilos and lock them in his safe. He left the rest of the drugs in the trunk of his transport car to be distributed to the lieutenants the following morning. He knew the extra trips increased the risk, but they were losing too much damn money to play it safe. So, he had no choice but to switch up how he ran the trap houses. It was either that or continuing to risk being hit for a bulk of their product, and that was entirely out of the question.

Feeling exhausted from ripping and running the streets all day, he thought, *fuck taking a shower. I'll do that shit in the morning.* So, instead of washing his nasty ass, he fired up a blunt and took a few puffs before putting it out. He just wanted to smoke enough to ensure a good night's rest before the big day. After putting his phone on silent, he climbed into bed, grabbed a pillow, and dozed off.

CHAPTER TWENTY-FIVE

Jones waited beside Johnson in the mayor's office, feeling elated. He had finally solved the case that had haunted him for years. Not only had he become an overnight celebrity, but now the sky was the limit. He knew that solving the Acorn Stalker case would undoubtedly bolster his career. It was the big break he desperately needed, and he could already envision himself sitting at the mayor's desk with his feet up, smoking a Cuban cigar.

"Jones! Jones! Jones!" Johnson called out, waking him from his daydream.

"Yeah, man. Wassup?" Jones replied.

"You alright? You were looking a little spaced out there."

"Yeah, I'm fine. I was just thinking about my future in politics. Why, what's on your mind?"

"I was just wondering what this early morning meeting was all about because she didn't sound too happy over the phone."

"I don't know what it is, but whatever it is, it better be some form of admiration for the two men who helped the city sleep better at night."

"I highly doubt that. I'm willing to bet she's jealous of our overnight success. You know this is going to overshadow her campaign efforts."

"Well, that's not on us. She knew exactly what she was getting into when she decided to run for office."

They both fell silent and instantly became attentive after hearing the sound of high heels quickly approaching. Seconds later, the mayor entered the room and shook her head in disapproval as she closed the door. Then she walked over to her desk, took a seat, and crossed her legs with calculated poise.

"What'd we do now?" Jones asked innocently.

Mayor Tisdale replied, "Take a wild guess. I mean, it's a shit show out there. I've got every damn reporter in America trying to shove a microphone down my throat. Can you believe one of those assholes dared to ask me if I was aware that the Acorn Stalker was working for the department? I wasn't even the one who hired the bastard. He was already here when I got into office. Those jerks are trying to derail my entire campaign. If it's up to them, there's no way I'll be reelected. You guys really screwed me on this one."

Johnson replied, "We screwed you? How? You were the one who told us to plant the drugs at his place to discredit him."

"Yeah, I said we needed to discredit him, not the entire damn department. Do you know how bad this makes us look? A serial killer right under our noses, and none of our detectives noticed."

Jones said, "Well, that's what made him so damn hard to catch—he knew all our methods. He knew exactly what we'd be looking for, keeping him ten steps ahead of us."

"Well, I'm sorry to say, but the public won't see it that way. Now I'll have to propose a stricter screening process to ease fears of a copycat. Oh! And I almost forgot to mention. The DA said he's been getting calls all morning from defense attorneys notifying him that they would be filing new trial petitions on behalf of their clients. It hasn't even been a whole twenty-four hours yet, and the sharks are already circling. I'll be stuck cleaning up this mess for the rest of my tenure while you two idiots march around town like fucking heroes."

Johnson looked over at Jones as if to say, 'See? I told you so.'

Mayor Tisdale leaned back in her chair and interlocked her fingers behind her head, exposing her cleavage.

She said, "So tell me about the victim you found. Did she give you any information that could help us solve other cases? Because I need something tremendous to spin this debacle."

"No. She said he kept her locked up in solitary confinement the entire time," Jones replied.

"So you two are sure no hippies hiking their dogs will find Colding's body? Because that is the last thing we need right now."

"Oh, you don't have to worry about that. Colding will be considered a fugitive from justice as far as the law is concerned," said Johnson.

"That's good to know because I have a quandary. I may need you two to handle it quietly. Our little anomaly at the port seems to have peeled back a layer of Councilman Chambers' stomach—revealing his yellow belly. His capricious change of heart was enough to convince me that he is willing to jump ship with all of our life jackets."

Johnson and Jones both looked at each other like, not again.

Jones said, "So let me get this straight. You're saying you want us to add a dead council member to our list of woes? I mean, right on top of our missing detective—who's wanted for serial rape and murder, I might add."

Mayor Tisdale paused for a moment while reconsidering her options.

She said, "Maybe you're right. I guess all this extra stress is clouding my judgment because, to be honest, I can't afford another blemish on my résumé—not this close to election time."

Johnson said, "I've got a better idea. While Jones and I are on our way to dig up some damaging dirt on your competition, we could always swing by the councilman's house—even if it's only to remind him of whose team he's playing for."

Mayor Tisdale then tapped her index finger against her chin, contemplating her decision.

She replied, "Fine, we'll do things your way for now. But if you can't keep him in line, you know what you must do to protect our interests."

"Don't worry, we'll make sure he gets the picture. Meanwhile, we were wondering about the status of our investments."

Caught off guard, she walked around her desk and sat in a burgundy leather chair. It was her way of stalling time before responding.

She said, "Things are going as expected. From here on out, you'll have to exercise some patience. But in the meantime, you can get out there and protect our investments by helping keep the property value down."

Johnson and Jones exchanged glances, then quickly stood. They suddenly realized it was best to leave before she came up with any more bright ideas.

Jones said, "Hey, you know what just dawned on me, counselor?"

"What?" she asked unenthusiastically.

"Looking back on it, Colding murdered his first victim on the anniversary of his wife's death. Her death must've triggered some sort of psychotic break or something. But I don't understand why he started back after so many years."

"Who's to say he ever stopped? People go missing every. He probably just relocated his hunting ground for a while."

Johnson said, "That sounds more plausible than him taking a hiatus."

"Whatever the case may be, the bottom line is that the streets are much safer now with him out of the picture. Now, will that be all, gentlemen?"

They exchanged subtle glances in response to her rudeness.

Then Johnson said, "Yes, that'll be all."

"Well then, carry on," she replied condescendingly.

CHAPTER TWENTY-SIX

• • •

Sav walked up the stairs to one of his newly renovated Victorian-style homes on Ninth and Wood. It was a hood often referred to as The Lower Bottoms, named for its secluded location at the city's edge. Most nonresidents only traveled to the Lower Bottoms for two reasons, and two reasons only: either for an illicit drug transaction or to visit a family member who lived there.

Once Sav reached the front porch, he dropped the Newport cigarette he had been smoking and smashed it under his shoe. Then, he looked over his left shoulder at KO, who stood directly behind him, watching his back.

Sav said, "C'mon, let's get this clown."

He subsequently opened the screen gate and proceeded to enter the house, filled with impetuous killers who didn't give a fuck. The living room was packed with thugs boasting about what they would do to Face if they saw him first. Most of them were so caught up in their gloating they didn't even notice that Sav had walked inside the house. To be sure his presence was felt, KO slammed the screen door shut and cleared his throat. The loud bang caused everyone to turn their attention toward the front gate, where Sav and KO stood, visibly displeased. The room immediately became so quiet that you could hear a pin drop because Sav's presence demanded respect.

"Are y'all finished?" Sav asked rhetorically.

A couple of his soldiers nodded yes in compliance.

Sav surveyed the room to make sure everyone he had ordered to be there had arrived on time for the meeting.

Sav yelled, "Where the fuck is Cash?"—pissed that Cash wasn't present alongside everyone else.

Antwan replied, "He said he was on his way from Stockton, so he should be here any minute."

Sav looked back at KO and said, "Call him and find out why the fuck he ain't already here."

KO replied, "A'ight," before pulling out his cell phone and dialing Cash's number.

Next, Sav dramatically cleared his throat before making an announcement.

He said, "Listen up! By now, everybody in this room should've heard that Sincere's bitch ass is dead. But that shouldn't come as a surprise. He suffered the same fate as anybody that ever decides to cross me. I ain't gotta waste no time with the gory details regarding his demise because it's irrelevant, especially since none of y'all flunkies can claim the fame. But what y'all can do is bring me one of Face's fingers to verify y'all loyalty. I want y'all to hunt that fool down to the ends of the earth. I got half a million dollars for anybody who can deliver Face's body, dead or alive. I don't mean just put the word out and sit back waiting for results while y'all are collecting money. Wait! As a matter of fact, I want all of the trap houses shut down until we get that bitch-ass nigga."

Diamond barked, "What! Man, you trippin'."

Consequently, Sav beelined toward Diamond with a devious smirk.

"Oh, I'm trippin', huh?" Sav asked calmly.

Diamond replied, "Yeah, man. Do you know how much money we'd lose if we did that?"

Suddenly, Sav whipped out a .45-caliber pistol from his gun holster and pressed the barrel against Diamond's forehead.

Sav said, "Bitch, my sister just killed herself because of what they did to her. Now you're gonna stand there and complain to me about some fucking money.

Hearing Sav cock back the hammer instantly made Diamond bitch up.

"Man, I... I didn't know, bruh. I'm sorry, dog. I was hella outta pocket," Diamond whined.

Sav eyed him intently while contemplating if he would release his pent-up stress by making an example out of him.

KO gently placed his hand on Sav's shoulder and said, "C'mon, bruh, it ain't even worth it. He was just talkin' out the side of his neck. Plus, we need all hands on deck to get that bitch-ass nigga."

After realizing KO was right, Sav lowered his pistol from Diamond's head and released the hammer.

"Does anybody else have a grievance they wanna express?" Sav asked sarcastically.

Everyone else in the room either shook their heads or said no, knowing any other response could mean death.

Sav said, "Then I'm glad to see we're all in agreement. Because we're going to destroy Face's organization before he even gets it off the ground. To make a statement, I want y'all to kill any muthafucka who even thinks about doing business wit him. My baby sister just committed suicide because she couldn't live with the way them bitch-ass niggas violated her. So we're not gonna rest until every person who even sympathizes with Face is dead. I want everybody to know that his money is no good in The Town. I don't care what y'all gotta do to make it happen. Just get it done. Until then, if y'all muthafuckas need some money, y'all better use your baby mamas to put in work."

Marco asked, "What if Face heard about what happened to Sincere and decided to lay low? I mean, what if that fool just falls off the face of the earth? Then what?"

"You would have to jump yo ass off after him then, wouldn't you?"

Sav's response made it evident to everyone in the room he wasn't bullshittin' about shutting down his operation. He was determined to use all of his resources to hunt down Face. His mind was set on conducting a relentless pursuit to take out Face and his entire network. It was genius on his part—what better incentive to give someone essential to your operation than withholding their livelihood?

Sav looked at the kitchen doorway and spotted an unfamiliar face staring back at him.

Sav asked, "Who the fuck is this pervert?" while rudely pointing directly at him.

The man immediately darted his eyes left and fixed them on a skinny Snoop Dogg look-alike who stood there looking bubble-eyed.

"Oh him, that's my cousin, Mel," said the Snoop Dogg look-alike.

"And, nigga, who the fuck is you?" Sav asked aggressively.

Low stepped between Sav and the Snoop Dogg look-alike and said, "That's my lil' brutha, Vic, and my cousin, Mel."

"Okay, well, why are they just standing there, looking at me like some fucking perverts? And why are they at a meeting that's supposed to be for my lieutenants?"

"That's actually why they're here. Vic informed me of some good news you would love to hear."

Sav then turned his attention to Vic and said, "A'ight, so what's so important that you had to crash my private party?"

Vic said nervously, "Well, we're here because of my cousin, Mel. He just got out of the pen, and while there, he was cellmates with Face's brutha Banks."

Sav pointed at Mel and said, "You talkin' 'bout this cousin Mel standing right here?"

"Yeah."

"So why the fuck am I wasting my time talking to you then?"

Vic just looked at Sav dumbfounded before finally turning to Low for support.

Sav stepped toward Mel and said, "Okay, so you were in the pen wit the nigga. Now explain how that's going to help me kill the cocksucker."

Mel replied, "Well, I wasn't just in the pen wit 'em. We were cellmates for two and a half years. I was a jailhouse lawyer, and he needed me to help him fight his custody battle. His baby mama was on some bullshit. The point is, I remember his mother's address—it's the one he said he was paroling to."

Sav rubbed his chin deviously while processing the information. The room suddenly sighed with relief because Sav had received a reason to keep the machine running.

While shaking his index finger at Mel, Sav said, "Now, see, I knew I liked this nigga. He doesn't even work for me, and yet he put in more work than any of you lazy muthafuckas. Mel, since you were the one who brought me this jewel, I'm going to give you first dibs on the bounty. I want you, Vic, and Low to sit on that address and see if he shows up. If y'all happen to get lucky, don't hesitate. Snatch that fool up and bring him to the junkyard if possible. And make sure nobody follows y'all. As a matter of fact, leave y'all cell phones here. I don't want them muthafuckas pinging and shit off no cell towers."

Vic said, "Well, what if he's not alone? What if Banks' kids, or his mother, is with him?"

"Shit—kill 'em. Don't let anybody stand in your way. And just to be sure y'all succeed, I'm sending Diamond and Wheezy as a contingency plan."

Sav turned to Diamond and said, "The sooner y'all handle this, the sooner y'all can get back to making money. And make sure you're positioned on the end of the block, too, in case y'all get into a shootout. That way, you'll have him boxed in."

It was obvious from Diamond's expression that he wasn't pleased with his job assignment, especially since it wasn't his beef in the first place.

Sav said, "Is there a problem?" baiting Diamond since he was still sour about being undermined earlier.

Diamond replied, "Nah, dog, everything's straight."

"Good. Now, I want y'all to leave me a copy of that address. It should be a pen and pad inside of that cabinet right there."

While waiting for Mel to write down the address, C-note decided to use that time to ask a stupid-ass question.

He said, "So does this mean we're back open for business?"

Even though they were all wondering the same thing, he was the only one dumb enough to ask the question.

"Man, what the fuck do you think?" Sav barked.

"Nah," C-note replied, looking dumb as hell.

Sav said, "I want the rest of y'all to continue pursuing that nigga in case that address is a dead end, a'ight. Because they might've moved. Now that y'all got your orders, it's time to take care of business."

Unaware that Sav had finished his speech, everyone stood by attentively, trying not to rock the boat.

Sav said, "What the fuck y'all still standing around for? Go get that muthafucka."

The atmosphere was filled with displeasure as Sav's lieutenants approached the front door. Meanwhile, KO walked up behind Sav and whispered into his ear.

He said, "Why don't we take a page outta his book?"

"Whatchu mean by that?" Sav replied as he turned to face KO.

"I'm just saying, if them niggas got his mother's address, we should just kidnap her and force him to come to us. That's what them hoe-ass niggas did to Angie."

"And how did that turn out for them suckas?"

"Shit, it went all bad for them suckas."

"Exactly. A wise man learns from other fool's mistakes. If we kidnap one of his folks, he is liable to call the FBI or some shit. Plus, God looks out for old hoes and babies. I'm trying to get away with killing that muthafucka. Not end up withering away in a cell for the rest of my life—for what? All because my emotions allowed me to get sloppy. Nah, not I. I got somethin' better planned."

"A'ight. Well, you know I gotcha either way."

"I never doubted that, blood. Now let's get the fuck up out of here, 'cause we have some other business to handle."

Sav and KO froze upon hearing an unexpected voice say, "Don't tell me I missed the party."

They all turned toward the familiar voice, surprised to see Cocaine standing in the doorway, propped up by a pair of crutches.

CHAPTER TWENTY-SEVEN

• • •

Banks and Face spent the whole trip to Highland Hospital debating why their mother had disowned them. Since it indicated she blamed them for the incident, neither of them was willing to own up to it. The argument would've continued if Banks hadn't suggested waiting to see what she had to say about the situation.

Face had to park at the bottom of the hill on which the hospital resided because of overcrowding. Between the hospital's visitors and the residents, the cars were parked bumper to bumper, leaving no parking spaces available. It was a quiet and shameful trek up the hill because they both felt guilty about what had happened to their mother. Sadly, what bothered them most was not knowing exactly why she was shot or who was even remotely responsible. They couldn't even tell her who had ordered the hit, let alone identify the shooter. All they knew was their mother had been shot and paralyzed while CJ bled to death beside her—and one of them was to blame.

When they entered the hospital's lobby, Face cringed at the sight of the receptionists, who had nearly made him blow his top during their last visit.

Banks said, "Be cool, bruh. We're here for Mama. Remember that?"

As soon as the oh-so-fabulous pair spotted Face approaching them, they both stopped what they were doing and stared him down, anticipating a confrontation.

Chauncey, the outspoken one, reached into his purse and said, "I'm about to get my mace, 'cause I ain't goin' for his shit today."

"Girl, me neither," said Tati.

Face took one look at their colorful braids and the way Chauncey was popping his gum like he was cute, then let out a dry, mocking chuckle.

"Is something funny, boo?" Chauncey asked, irritated.

"Nah, blood, we're just here to see our mama. And don't call me your boo, nigga," Face said

"Fine, 'cause we don't need no drama up in here today. Now, let me see y'all's IDs to check if you're even approved to visit her. Shoot, you're already giving me a headache."

Face and Banks reached into their pockets and pulled out their IDs before setting them down on the counter. Chauncey picked up their IDs and examined them skeptically, like he couldn't tell if they matched the photos. After his unnecessary screening, he finally handed back their identification cards.

"So is everything good?" Banks asked politely.

Chauncey replied, "No. Y'all still gotta fill out these visiting forms."

Suddenly, Tati pulled out two clipboards with forms attached and said, "Here you go."

Face snatched the clipboard, then walked to a row of chairs positioned alongside the wall and sat down. Banks followed closely behind him, cheesing with amusement over Face's crush.

When they turned to walk away, Chauncey whispered, "The tall one is kinda sexy," talking about Face.

"I was thinkin' the same thing, but he got an attitude problem," Tati replied.

Once they sat down, Banks said, "When we get done filling out this paperwork, I gotta hit up Awol to see where he at."

Face replied, "Yeah, 'cause he should've been up here by now. We can't let him make us late to our meeting wit Mafi."

After filling out and double-checking the visitor forms, they returned them to Tati for processing. Then, they waited patiently at the desk while Tati scanned the forms, ensuring they were filled out completely and correctly.

Once Tati deemed the forms met all the processing requirements, he stood up to address them.

He said, "Okay, everything seems to be in order. Now, y'all can sit in the waiting area until you're called. Processing might take a while."

"Alright," Banks replied.

However, instead of sitting inside the waiting area, he walked outside to call Awol. The first two times he called, the phone rang six times before going to voicemail, almost giving Banks a heart attack. Luckily, Awol answered the phone on the third try, sounding overly excited.

Awol said, "Wassup, blood?"

"Shit, we're still up here at Highland. Where you at?" Banks replied.

"I'm on Seven-One at this lil' broad house that I had been trying to fuck for a minute. At first, she was playin' hard to get, but she finally gave me the pussy. Now I'm about to get a key made so I can lay claim to her spot."

"You ain't got time for all of that, bruh. We have an important appointment in Frisco. Or did you forget?"

"Nah, I ain't forget. Have you even seen Auntie yet?"

"Nah, we're still waiting."

"A'ight then, I'll be done handling my business and on my way there before you're even done wit the visit. I'm just gonna run to Ace Hardware real quick. I got this, blood. Don't trip."

"A'ight, well, text me when you're on your way here."

"A'ight, bet."

As soon as Banks hung up, Face said, "What was that crazy ass fool talkin' 'bout?"

"Nothin', he still on that old school shit. Fuck a bitch real good, then get a key made so he could have an extra tuck spot. He on Seven-One. He claims he will be here before we're done seeing moms."

I know one thing—if they don't let me see Mama today, somebody gon' feel my pain."

"Like I told you in the car, they're only doing what the law permits. They don't have anything personal against us. They're just trying to protect moms and her wishes."

"Man, fuck all that. I need to see my mama ASAP."

"And you will, just as long as you relax and play it cool. You ain't gon' be able to see nobody from behind bars. If your ass gets arrested, you really ain't gonna see her. So you better be cool, bruh. Ya hear me?"

"Yeah, I hear you, blood."

They sat in the waiting room for what felt like an eternity, waiting to find out if they were approved to see their mother. Face couldn't help but spot Chauncey from the corner of his eye, wondering what the hell he was staring at. What made it worse was that he recognized that look— it was the same way he looked at a woman he lusted after.

Aw man, this faggot-ass nigga on some weird shit, he thought.

After realizing they had made eye contact, Chauncey smiled at him before batting his eyes bashfully. Face immediately took Chauncey's flirtatious advances as blatant disrespect, causing him to contort his facial expression into a mean mug. Next, Face gave him an aggressive head nod and mouthed the words, 'What the fuck are you lookin' at?' as he sat up in his chair. It pissed him off even more to see Chauncey respond to his aggressive nature by appearing to be turned on by it. Thus, Chauncey knew precisely what he was doing. It wasn't the first time he had to use his charm to see if a wannabe thug was just pretending to be homophobic. It was their clever way of hiding the fact that they were secretly on the down low. However, after seeing the deadly intent emitting from Face's gaze, he knew he was by no means an undercover booty bandit. So now, the only thing left to do was back off his unwanted advance and pretend it never happened.

Chauncey then hung up the phone and announced, "Y'all visit is approved. Go straight through them double doors, Dr. Reed is waiting on y'all."

Feeling relieved, Banks led the way toward the double doors, and once they reached them, he turned and said, "You know I peeped that shit, right."

"Man, fuck you," Face replied sternly.

When they passed through the double doors, they were greeted by Dr. Reed, who appeared to be in a blissful mood.

"How are you gentlemen doing this afternoon?" asked Dr. Reed.

"We're doing fine," Banks replied.

"Great. Then follow me so we can get you guys situated."

"A'ight."

Banks casually walked alongside Dr. Reed until he suddenly stopped in front of a closed door.

Dr. Reed took a deep breath and said, "Well, this is your mother's room. She's expecting you."

Face stepped forward and replied, "Thank you, doc. We'll take it from here."

"Okay, but feel free to have one of the nurses page me if I can do anything to help."

"Gotcha, doc."

Leading up to that exact moment, Face had been antsy about seeing his mother, but now that it was time to face the damage he had done, he hesitated. He felt a million butterflies fluttering against the walls of his stomach as he leisurely turned the doorknob. Banks didn't feel the sudden urge to rush into their family reunion either. It was eating him up inside, knowing their criminal lifestyles had caused such irreparable harm. When they entered the room, they both felt the unwelcoming vibe Jamela was emanating. She stared blankly out the window as if she were oblivious to their presence. Banks closed the door behind himself, seeking the right words to comfort her through this tragic experience. He had to choose wisely because he knew their support was pivotal to her keeping her sanity.

Face decided it was his turn to take charge, so he took the initiative and broke the ice before Banks could gather his thoughts. He walked over to the head of the bed and attempted to hold her hand, but she snatched it away before he could even feel her warm embrace.

"We're here for you, Mama. Anything you need, just ask, and we gotcha," Face exclaimed.

Jamela felt so distant, it was almost as if her consciousness had vacated her body, leaving nothing but a deaf-mute in its place. Not only did she fail to respond to him, but it was as though she wasn't even aware he was in the room. She just folded her hands in her lap and kept gazing out the window, undisturbed. Banks approached the base of her bed, determined to try his luck since he knew deep down inside he was her favorite son.

He said, "How are these people treating you here? Better yet, how are you holding up?"

After Banks' weak attempt at small talk, it became clear she wasn't going for any of their bullshit. So Banks thought he would try a different approach to get her to open up. Hoping her soft spot for the twins would allow him inside the invisible force field surrounding her bed.

"The twins said they love and miss you with all their hearts. We all do," Banks stated sincerely.

"Yeah, Ma, so let us be here for you," Face added.

"We're here to help you get through this. But you've gotta let us in first."

They both gasped when Jamela finally turned to address them, unsure how the interaction would unfold—or how much they'd be forced to reveal in their explanations. It wasn't a secret. They were aware that she blamed at least one of them, if not them both, for destroying her life.

Jamela said in a groggy voice, "So is one of y'all going to explain to me while I'll never walk again? And why I'm stuck raising a son without a father, 'cause I sure as hell don't have a clue."

Jamela darted her eyes back and forth between Banks and Face, waiting for a response since neither seemed to be in a rush to volunteer one.

"Well? Y'all had a whole hell of a lot to say a minute ago. Dontcha all speak at once now," she stated sarcastically.

Face said remorsefully, "I'm sorry, Mama, but it's my fault that shit happened to you. It happened in retaliation to a call made by Sincere. A call that also cost him his life."

"Well, it sounds to me like he got off easy, then. But that still doesn't explain to me why they would shoot up my house. Not unless you played a bigger role in whatever got that boy killed than you're leading me to believe. Now tell me the truth, what the hell happened?"

Jamela tilted her head sideways and peered at him intently. She was waiting for him to admit that it was also his fault, not only Sincere's, whom he so quickly threw under the bus.

Face said, "Yeah, Ma, I did play a bigger role. Remember that cat Sav—the one Sincere was fonkin' wit—that kept robbing our spots?"

"Uh huh, I remember. And?"

"Well, we tried everything possible to get that dude out the way. But he's always two steps ahead of us, so we had to do something drastic. Sincere had me put together a team to kidnap his sister, but we were never going to harm her. It was only so we could draw him out. Yet somehow, the shit still blew up in our faces."

"You did what? You know women and children are off-limits. You didn't care to think what would happen if they decided to retaliate against the women and children in your family? What if the twins were home? I thank God Lil' Chris wasn't hurt. I can't believe you did something so damn stupid."

Banks gave Face a piercing look as if to say, 'See, I told your dumbass.'

Face said, "Honestly, I thought I had everything under control. None of this shit was my beef to begin with. I tried to tell Sincere the money that girl was making wasn't worth the drama her brutha brought. But that fool's pride wouldn't allow him to let her go. Even after her brutha made it clear he was ready to go to war behind her."

"Well, I thought that Sav character was a brutha. I didn't know he was Mexican. And who the hell is Maria?"

Face looked confused momentarily before turning to Banks for an answer. Yet Banks just gave him a blank expression.

Therefore, Face replied, "Sav is a brutha. And I don't know no Maria. Not off the top, at least. Why did you ask that, Mama?"

"Because, before that crazy son of a bitch started shooting, he said, 'This is for Maria.'"

"Wait, so you're tellin' me it was some Mexicans that shot up the house?"

"It sure was."

"And he yelled out this is for Maria?"

"Mmm-hmm."

Banks said, "That nigga must've paid some Mexicans to do the hit in case Sincere's pops found out about their beef. It makes perfect sense. If a group of unknown Mexicans did the shootings, the police would suspect it was somehow related to a drug deal. Plus, it would've thrown us off his trail."

Face asked, "So why yell out the Maria shit?"

"Now that part, I don't know. I could only assume it's for the results they're getting right now. They got us second-guessing ourselves."

Jamela said, "So you mean to tell me I'm lying here paralyzed, mourning over my dead husband, and you can't even tell me who did it and why? Because to me, your theories sound like a bunch of random bullshit."

Feeling completely embarrassed, Face dropped his head, attempting to hide his shame.

She said, "No, you look at me when I'm talking to you, boy. Now ain't the time to be moping around looking for sympathy, 'cause you damn sho ain't gettin' none here. So, what you need to do is get your ass up outta here and go find out who the hell did this to me."

"I will, but–"

Jamela snapped, "But nothin'. Boy, you better get yo' ass up outta here."

Face stared at her in shock because her words cut through him like a serrated blade. Unsatisfied with his slow departure, she reiterated her discontentment with his presence.

She said, "Go on now. And dontcha come back around until your business is taken care of. Ya hear me?"

After snapping out of his trance, he said, "Yeah, I hear you, Mama."

Face approached her bed in an attempt to kiss her, but she flat-out gave him the hand.

"Uh-uh boy, I can't do this witcha right now. Go on! Get the hell outta here!"

Feeling completely lost and abandoned, Face turned to Banks, looking for verbal support. He hoped he'd once again play the big brother role and back him up like he always did. Unfortunately, Banks sensed his desperation and chose to side with his mother. So he averted his gaze out the window to avoid making eye contact. However, Face knew he was purposely staring out the window to avoid having to acknowledge him. He knew Banks didn't want to interfere with his chastisement, especially when he believed it was well deserved.

Face mumbled, "Yeah, a'ight," as he cut his eyes at Banks on the way out.

Once Face cleared the room, Jamela folded her arms and stared at Banks like he had shit smeared across his forehead.

She asked, "So, what you got to say?" in a don't-bullshit-me tone of voice.

Banks slowly walked toward her and said, "First off, I just wanna say I'm sorry that this happened to you, Mama. I wish I could've been there to protect you."

"Why? So you could've ended up dead, too? Then who would've been there to take care of your girls? How are they? I heard what happened to Tonya by the way. I know she's got her problems, but I don't wish death on anybody."

"They're doin' fine, Ma. Sonya is going to take care of them for me until we get things all figured out. Tonya should be released any day now."

"Why couldn't your brother have been more like you, huh? I mean, I know you went to prison and all that, but at least you had your shit together. You just trusted the wrong girl. But him—on the other hand—trouble always seems to find. It's never the other way around. Ever since y'all were kids, it's been that way. He would get himself into trouble, and you would always be there to get him out of it.

Now tell me, son, what did he get himself into this time?"

"Look, Ma, I wish I was in a position to give you all the answers you're looking for. Because I could only imagine what you're going through right now. But I'm still piecing shit together myself. Now that Sincere's dead, it'll be much harder to figure out who ordered the hit. Sav wasn't the only person out for blood. Face forgot to mention the LA cat named Taz runnin' around The Town looking to avenge his brutha's death. Supposedly, Sincere killed him while saving some random chick's life, which caused Taz to put a million-dollar bounty out."

"A million dollars? Shiiit, I would've turned his ass in myself for that kind of money. So you think your brother was involved in that boy's murder?"

"Nah. He said he wasn't, and I believe him."

"So what? You think they just came after us to get even or somethin'?"

"To be honest, I don't know what to think. Right now, all we can do is watch our backs until we find out exactly who called the hit. Until then, ain't none of us safe. But it shouldn't take long because we've got people canvassing the town lookin' for 'em."

"Well, if it was some LA cats, they're probably long gone by now. I'm sure they're not stupid enough to stick around waiting to get caught."

"Better safe than sorry. Because if there happens to be a bounty out on Face, this is far from over."

"Well, whatever it is, y'all better figure it out. Because I don't want my house gettin' shot up again."

"Ma, I hope you don't think you're goin' back to live in that house again, 'cause that's out."

"Boy, you don't tell me what I'mma do. I brought you into this world, not the other way around."

"I know. But that shit ain't safe, Mama. We don't even know who shot you yet."

"Well, you better figure it out quick. 'Cause I ain't about to let nobody run me out of my house."

"It ain't safe, Mama. Me and Sonya already talked about it. You're going to stay with her while we look for you a new home."

"Bullshit. Boy, I told you already. I'm not about to let anybody run me up out of my house. It has way too much sentimental value to just give it up like that. My mother died in that house. And so will I one day. Now that's the end of that discussion."

"Ma, why must you be so stubborn when you know we're just trying to protect you?"

"Listen, son. If you want to protect me, I suggest you find whoever's responsible for putting me in this hospital bed and kill 'em. Because I ain't hiding from nobody. Back in my day, we didn't run from our problems. We stood tall and faced them head-on—no matter the outcome. Now you know my mother and father were Black Panthers. And shit, your grandfather marched alongside Martin Luther King in Selma. So you think I'm going to allow some two-bit wannabe street thugs to take the memory of them from me?

"Nah, Ma."

"You goddamn right. So miss me with that punk shit."

"A'ight, well, can you at least stay with Sonya until we can eliminate the threat? And in the meantime, I'll have the house renovated for you. Deal?"

Jamela briefly pondered Banks' proposal before cracking a modest smile.

She replied, "Fine, but I'm picking out the decor. And I don't want none of that cheap-ass shit from Ikea, either."

"Deal."

"Now, what's goin' on with Lil' Chris? How is he holding up?"

"He's strong, Mama, but he's a child. I was only with him for a few hours before he left with Sonya. On the day of the incident, I don't believe he registered the severity of what had happened. He was too busy trying to grasp what was going on. Plus, we were focused on trying to find the twins. At the hospital, he became reticent and distanced himself from everyone until he finally broke down crying. I think being with the twins is the best thing for him right now."

"You know, once he finds out that Face is the cause of all of this, he will hate him for taking his father away."

"The thought never crossed my mind. But now that you mention it, could you blame him?"

"No. That's why you'll have to step up and be his father figure. I can't have my baby growing up wild and following in y'all's footsteps. Nuh-un, not this one."

"Don't worry about him, Mama, I gotchu."

"Mm-hmm... What about Tonya?"

"What about her?" Banks asked resentfully.

"What happened to her, boy? People's cars don't just blow up out of nowhere."

"I don't know what happened to her. It was probably her bad karma coming back to bite her triflin' ass."

"You sure? Because the timing seems a little too close to her not-so-pleasant drunken confession. But I know even under those circumstances, you wouldn't do anything to hurt the mother of your children, right?"

When Jamela asked the question, it wasn't to receive a verbal confirmation. Instead, she used it as an opportunity to read his body language. After all, she was the one who had birthed and raised him his entire life. Therefore, she could tell when he was lying ever since he learned how to talk.

Banks said, "Ma, you know me better than that. I wouldn't ever do anything to hurt the mother of my children. That shit had everything to do with that scandalous-ass nigga she was layin' up wit. Ain't no tellin' who else he done snitched on. Runnin' around Tha Town like he's invincible, knowing the streets are talkin'. I'm sure he brought it on himself. She was just in the wrong place at the wrong time."

"Guess we got that in common then, don't we?"

"Nah, you were exactly where you were supposed to be. That's what made you such an easy target for whoever did that shit. But don't you worry, 'cause I swear to God I'm gon' find whoever did this to you and make 'em pay."

"Whatever you decide to do, just make sure you be smart about it. Because the twins can't afford to lose you again."

"I know, Mama. This time I'm not going anywhere but to the top."

"I'm glad to hear you're so enthusiastic about the situation, because from where I'm sitting, I can only see dark days ahead."

Banks knew she was talking about being paralyzed and probably never walking again. Unfortunately, with her independent persona, having to live with such a hindering disability would be torturous.

He said, "Don't you let this obstacle kill your spirit or take your joy, Mama. Because you are by far the strongest and most intelligent woman I know. This is nothing but a chance for you to show the world how resilient you are. Plus, the whole family has your back, so we'll help you see this through."

"Family? Shit, ain't nobody else been up here to see me," she replied, disappointed.

"That's because we didn't want to endanger anybody else. We don't know how far whoever did this is willing to go. For all we know, they're watching the hospital right now as we speak. Everybody is waiting for you to get released. Then we can all meet up at Sonya's house. We can't afford to have anyone following our family members home from this hospital."

"Son, I don't know what kind of mess that boy done got himself into, but I don't like it one bit. I don't know if I should fear for his life, or kill him my goddamn self. In a way, I think it's just God punishing me for condoning y'all's criminal lifestyles all this time. Because Lord knows, I sho been spending up that blood money. Shit, I'm just as guilty as y'all are. But CJ, he didn't do anything wrong. He was the only innocent one in all of this, and he's the only one dead. Where is the righteousness in that? See, this is the kind of shit that makes me question my faith in God."

Banks felt devastated because he was forced to look on helplessly as his mother endured an insurmountable amount of heartache and pain. All of it resulting from the repercussions of their lifestyles. So he listened to her vent attentively without interruptions, knowing it was the first step of her healing process. A process that he was sure would last her a lifetime.

She said, "Anyway, so what do you have up your sleeve? Because I can see it in your eyes, you've got something big planned."

Banks struggled with himself, debating whether or not he should tell her the truth. He was conflicted because he knew the truth would only add to her stress.

Nevertheless, she caught on to him and said, "And you better tell me the truth, too, because I've been through too much to let you just sit up here and lie to me."

Banks could tell by the look in her eyes that lying was not an option.

He said, "Well, we're about to head across the bridge to handle some business. You know now that Sincere's dead, Face is gonna be runnin' the organization. So we gotta secure a new connection before he ends up with a mutiny on his hands. I figured the best way to look out for him is to be there personally to ensure his safety. At least now that he is in charge, he'll be able to find out exactly who did this to you. And I'll be right next to him, making sure he gets the job done right."

"He better handle his damn business, 'cause I ain't about to live the rest of my life looking over my shoulders, all paranoid and shit. "This is his beef, but you make sure y'all watch each other's backs because I have a bad feeling about this."

"Don't you worry, Mama. I got this. I'll take care of that knucklehead boy."

Banks met Jamela's gaze, hoping to reassure her, before bending over and kissing her forehead.

He said, "I'm gonna let you get some rest, Mama. I'll be back to check in on you as soon as I get things situated, a'ight?"

"Okay, baby. You be safe out there."

"I will. Bye, Mama."

"Bye, baby."

CHAPTER TWENTY-EIGHT

Banks hated having to maneuver through the ordinarily congested streets of San Francisco. Surprisingly, this trip wasn't like most, as they were lucky to have beaten the rush hour traffic that normally clogged the Bay Bridge— allowing them to sit back and enjoy a rare, moderate afternoon commute. All they had to do was cruise the speed limit and watch out for the highway patrol.

Banks said, "Do you think Mama was just terrified and hearing shit? Or Do you believe somebody really yelled out, 'This is for Maria'? I mean, who the fuck is Maria?' I don't know, no Maria."

Face said, "I fucked a couple of chicks named Maria in the past. But we never separated on any terms that would warrant no shit like this. Although if she did hear him correctly through all of the gunshots, it was only to throw us off. I don't think that statement holds any weight, blood."

"Well, there has to be a connection between them and Sincere. Even if it was just that Taz paid them to do that shit."

"A connection? Fool, that's like trying to find a needle in a stack of needles."

"Wait, bruh! Didn't you say that Cell-Bo missed and killed the bitch Cocaine had in the car?"

"Yeah, why?"

"And now you can't find 'em. What was the broad's name—the one them fools killed?"

"Shit, I don't know. Hold on, let me check."

Banks waited patiently as Face browsed his phone, trying to locate the article covering the botched assassination attempt.

Suddenly Face said, embarrassed, "Maria Lopez."

Banks briefly side-eyed Face, as if to say, 'You dumbass,' then said, "Nigga, that's the connection right there. They yelled the name out because they didn't expect Mama to survive. We know Cocaine didn't die. He must've told her folks that we were the ones who had her killed, and now they're out for revenge."

"At least now we're not in the dark. I know fa'sho Cell-Bo and them are dead now. That's probably how they got Mama's address. They must have tortured them fools until they spilled everything."

"The way I see it, them fools got what they deserved. Shit, dumbass niggas got my mama shot up."

"Damn, Banks, like that?"

"Yeah, nigga! Now, let me think for a second. I gotta clear my head."

After about ten minutes had passed, Banks looked back at Awol through the rearview mirror, noticing that he was deep in thought. Awol's inquisitive demeanor made Banks curious to hear his input on the matter. Mainly because even though Awol was burnt out, he was covertly savvy when it came to street shit.

"Wassup witchu, Awol? You ain't never this quiet," Banks asked, concerned.

"Shit, I'm just thinkin' about this lil' broad I used to fuck wit. She lived down there on Treasure Island. That bitch wasn't shit, just like Tonya."

Aw, he done got this fool started, Face thought.

Awol continued, "You know how they say the love of money is the root of all evil?"

"Yeah," Banks replied.

"Well, I was thinkin', every root has to have a seed first. And that's when I realized that the woman is the seed. Just think about it. Even in the Bible, it was that bitch Eve that convinced Adam to eat from the tree in the first place. And then I asked myself, where does the money come from?"

Banks and Face exclaimed in unison, "It grows on trees, nigga!"

"Everybody knows that," said Face.

"Exactly, but remember, God cursed the ground. And then he told Adam to toil the soil planting seeds and shit for listening to the bitch, right?"

"Yeah," Face replied, fully invested in Awol's crazy-ass philosophy.

"So now every seed we plant is destined to grow into a cursed tree, and yet we're still toiling the earth, willing to do anything for a dollar that grew on a cursed tree. That's why I go hard on a bitch, man—it's like the circle of life on some *Lion King* shit."

Banks said, "You know what? That shit sounded crazy as fuck. But it kinda made sense in a sick, twisted kinda way."

"I'm tellin' you, man, them bitches still trying to deceive niggas wit all this setup shit. Lying on rich muthafuckas to get a payday. They don't wanna see a conviction—they just wanna settle out of court for a fat paycheck."

Face said, "Nah, cuzo, some of them muthafuckas is guilty as hell. That one dude had a trap door in his office or some shit. They said when a bad bitch walks into his office, he hits a secret button. Then a trap door opens up, dropping her into a sex dungeon full of whips and butt plugs."

"Nigga, hell nah!"

They all burst out laughing at Face's exaggerated version of events.

Banks said, "Now that we got all the humor out of the way, can we focus on making sure this deal goes down smoothly? And Awol, when we get there, you'll have to ignore this fool's entitled personality. I know how you are. But we're here for one reason, and one reason only. And that's to make this business transaction. So remember not to let anything get in the way of that. That goes for both of you, especially any of Mafi's bullshit antics. I want to be in and out of there as quickly as possible. Ya feel me?"

Awol said, "Yeah, I feel you, blood. He must be on some real fuck shit to make you have to give a speech like that. I just hope he ain't too outta pocket, though, 'cause I'll double back on his bitch-ass."

Face said, "Put it like this, as soon as I find a better connect, I'm cuttin' all ties to that sadistic muthafucka. So let's just hurry up and get this shit over and done with before he makes me kill his ass."

"Well, alrighty then," Awol replied in a comedic voice.

The rest of the ride was uncomfortably quiet because no matter how many times you've done a drug deal, you always fear the possibility of it being a setup. Whether it's a robbery or law enforcement trying to lock you away until you're too decrepit to produce children. Either way, it was a fucked up feeling that sometimes made you second-guess your career choices.

Face announced, "It's almost showtime," as they entered the Fillmore District.

Banks said, "So be on the lookout for anything funny."

Now that they were near the rendezvous point, their spider senses suddenly shot up to full alert. Every passing car became a potential undercover cop. Presumably because they were unfamiliar with both the locals and the terrain, it made the pedestrians nearly impossible to distinguish from an undercover cop. The streets were packed with pale-faced, blood-sucking vampires, but these weren't just any vampires; these were day walkers. It was easy to tell who the drug dealers were, though, because their attire made them stand out. They were freshly cut, and some wore designer clothes, disregarding the advantage of remaining inconspicuous. It appeared as though they were welcoming law enforcement to investigate them by drawing their undivided attention. Banks always preached that a flashy drug dealer was a stupid drug dealer because, unlike pimps, they were supposed to stay low-key. Pimps dressed flashy merely to attract the gold diggers looking to make an easy payday. Contrarily, when a drug dealer dressed flashy, it made it more believable to the feds once somebody in his inner circle decided to start snitchin'. Because if there's one thing the cops hate, it's seeing a drug dealer doing better than they are. Not to mention all of the stick-up kids being flashy attracted. Standing on a corner flaunting your wealth was basically asking to be indicted—or worse, robbed and murdered.

Once they reached the block where Mafi's apartment complex resided, Banks quickly noticed the enforcers standing at the entrance to the parking lot.

"It looks like Mafi called in some reinforcements. What if he doesn't trust us?" Face asked rhetorically.

"Ain't no tellin' what that weird-ass nigga got goin' on," Banks replied.

Banks wasn't going to allow the idea of Mafi calling in more backup to faze him because it just made Mafi look scary, if anything. However, Banks knew that Mafi was anything but scary, so it had to be something else. This could be how he always did business for all he knew. After all, it was their first time conducting any sort of business transaction. Therefore, he refused to allow himself to become paranoid based on a bunch of uncertainties.

Banks said, "Lock and load," as they waited for a homeless woman who was standing in the street, begging for change.

Consequently, Banks reached inside his front pocket and pulled out a twenty-dollar bill. When the woman finally approached the vehicle, she hesitated momentarily to ensure she wasn't being an overly aggressive panhandler.

Banks said, "It's cool, ma'am. Here," then stuck the twenty-dollar bill out the window.

The woman took the bill and said, "God bless you."

"Just make sho you go buy yourself some food wit that."

"I will. I promise," she replied thankfully.

As soon as the woman walked away, Awol said, "Now you know that bitch ain't finna do nothing but buy some dope with that money. I don't know why you gave it to her dope fiend ass. You could've given that shit to me."

"Man, we all deserve a chance to do something better with our lives," Banks replied.

"Not with my money," Face added.

Awol said, "Look at these fools," as they pulled into the project's driveway.

"What, they got checkpoints now?" Face asked, staring down at the three men approaching them, wearing ten-gallon hats with matching belt buckles.

"What the fuck? Are these cowboys?" Awol asked sarcastically.

"Just be cool, bruh," Banks said calmly.

Two of the mysterious men said something in Spanish before splitting up, while the third man clarified he was strapped. One of the men quickly approached the driver's side window while the other walked around to the passenger's side. Then, both men briefly scanned the inside of the car before giving Banks the nod to pull in.

Banks rolled up his window and said, "That must be his connect."

Awol replied, "Them dudes watched too many damn Pablo Escobar documentaries. They got me feeling like I'm in a Western wit all that damn snakeskin on. Those fools are gonna get a yeast infection with those tight-ass jeans on."

Banks drove slowly through the parking lot, surveying the cars parked in the stalls. He was searching for anything that remotely looked suspicious. Eventually, he parked next to a teenage couple who looked like they had just been caught having sex. Moments later, Banks exited the truck and scanned the parking lot.

I remember those days, he thought.

Face stepped out next, followed by Awol, who carried a black duffel bag slung over his left shoulder. The duffel bag contained the funds needed to purchase their large order of cocaine and not a dime more. Banks suddenly recognized two of Mafi's soldiers hurrying toward them. He figured they were probably there to act as escorts to Mafi's trap house.

Banks said, "C'mon y'all, let's get this shit done," before heading toward Mafi's soldiers.

The two men stopped dead in their tracks and waited for Banks and his crew to reach them. Banks, feeling like he was being watched, glanced over his left shoulder and locked eyes with one of the cowboys from earlier. He couldn't help but notice how they were trailing them with an eerie, slow drag. When they finally reached their escorts, one of them attempted to grab the duffel bag from Awol.

"We'll help you with that," said the escort.

Awol aggressively yanked the bag away and replied, "Nah, I got dis, playboy."

The man calmly threw his hands up and said, "No problemo, follow me."

As they walked through the apartment complex, the trio scanned every visible nook and cranny, searching for any signs of a setup before the deal went down. They all understood that once the money changed hands, they were criminally culpable. Every hustler in the hood knew their chances were slim when it came to beating a federal case. Historically, the feds were so confident that they would sometimes set your court dates months apart—just to give you enough time to realize you didn't have a chance in hell of beating them at their own game. Also, if you didn't take the first deal they offered, they would often increase it drastically—just for wasting the taxpayer's money.

Banks and Face couldn't help but notice the change in the vibe of the environment around them. The last time they were in the complex, it was noisy, and the tenants were everywhere like it was the place to be. This time, it was damn near deserted. The only thing missing was a rundown tavern surrounded by rolling tumbleweeds. Banks figured the kids weren't outside playing because it was still during school hours. He figured a few might've been at work, but where was everybody else? There weren't even any dope fiends clucking, looking for a fix.

Banks couldn't quite put his finger on it, but something was off. Shit just didn't feel right. So, just before turning the corner that led to Mafi's trap house, he looked back to see if the two men were still trailing them.

Banks said, "Yo, Flacco, them cowboys wit y'all, right?"

Flacco stopped, looked back, and said, "Yeah, just think of them as Corporate."

Banks and Face then looked at each other as if to say, 'What the hell are they up to?'

Awol noticed their facial expressions and gave Face a look that said, 'I'm down for whatever.' Banks also caught Awol's gesture but disregarded it because he knew Flacco from doing business with Mafi's uncle. Luckily, he always conducted himself professionally. Having Flacco present during their transaction made Banks feel more comfortable dealing with Mafi's antics. He assumed his rapport with Flacco was the only reason he didn't get rechecked for a wire. Flacco knew Banks would've taken it as a sign of disrespect, so he didn't press the issue.

Flacco reached the apartment first, then opened the front door and stood aside.

"Go ahead, he's waiting on y'all," Flacco said quietly.

Once they got inside, Banks stopped to see if Flacco and his partner would be present or if they were ordered to guard the door. Suddenly, Banks became suspicious after seeing how Flacco looked everywhere except into his eyes. It was as if he had something to hide, immediately raising a red flag. To Banks' surprise, Flacco kept his head down as he reached for the doorknob, leaving them alone in the living room with two more unknown cowboys. Banks could see it all over their faces—these two men meant business. They weren't just some amateur gangbangers on Mafi's payroll. He had to assume that they were cartel members investigating their new clientele. One of the men had a sixteen-gauge shotgun across his lap; the other had a Chinese AK resting on his. Ironically, their handlebar mustaches made them look like '70s porn stars. This time, there were no drugs or party favors on the table, which meant someone had made Mafi clean up his act. *It must've been these so-called corporate muthafuckas*, Banks thought.

While Banks and Face were busy analyzing the situation, Awol was locked in a staring contest with one of the cowboys. Luckily, Mafi intervened before things got out of hand.

"Wassup wit it, my boy?" Mafi asked with an upbeat attitude.

Banks replied, "Shit, just here to keep up my end of the bargain," as he gave him dap.

Mafi followed through by shaking Face's hand before also embracing Awol.

"Wassup wit y'all?" asked Mafi.

"Shit, we good," Face replied.

Awol was too caught up in the pissing contest he'd just engaged in to even respond to Mafi's greeting.

"I see you got new security," Banks said, raising an eyebrow.

Mafi replied, "Yeah, you know, every now and then corporate sends someone down to make sure shit's running smoothly. You get it, right?"

"Yeah, sometimes we gotta make sure our money is secure."

"Speaking of money, let's get this show on the road. Yo Betho! Bring out the product," he yelled.

Face glanced at Banks to gauge his reaction when Betho's name was called, wondering if it was a signal for the DEA to bust through the door. However, Betho was as far from a DEA agent as one could possibly be. Still, they wouldn't relax until he turned the corner with drugs in hand instead of a team of federal agents wearing DEA insignias on their vests. Banks took one look at Betho and assumed he was nothing more than a gangbanger. And not just any kind, but the kind that would become a problem if a higher power didn't keep him in check.

Next, Betho dramatically rolled his neck before handing the duffel bag to Mafi. Then, standing beside him, he ran his tongue over his gold teeth, producing an irritating sucking sound. He gave off that too-hard-for-the-radio vibe as he eyed Banks devilishly while gripping his Desert Eagle.

Mafi raised the duffel bag and said, "I'll show you mine if you show me yours," like the shit was funny to him.

Banks reached back toward Awol, dismissively signaling for him to grab his own duffel.

After Awol handed the bag to Banks, he passed it to Betho and said, "It's all there."

"It better be," Betho snapped.

Afterward, Betho opened the bag, sifted through the cash, then dropped it beside him.

"It looks like it's all here," he said.

Banks didn't like how Betho dropped the bag so quickly, like he needed both hands free. It made him think even more meticulously than before. Suddenly, he knew he had to pay attention to every little detail because their survival could depend on his awareness.

Mafi handed the duffel bag to Banks and said, "You ain't gon' find better quality shit than this north of the border. You're getting a steal at these prices."

Banks replied, "We a see," as he handed the dope to Awol so he could test it.

Mafi attempted small talk while they waited for Awol to confirm the dope's quality. Unfortunately, a crucial side effect of crystal meth is excessive talking. It causes an otherwise tight-lipped individual to run their mouth in ways they wouldn't have if they were sober.

Mafi said, "This is my supplier, Betho. He came down from Sac to meet his new distributor. I told him you guys were solid, but you know how corporate is—they had to see for themselves. I was telling him how y'all gon' be runnin' shit now that y'all boss done took a permanent vacation."

"My boss?" Banks replied, puzzled.

"Yeah, my boy, everybody knows what happened to that fool Sincere. It was all over the news. Why you lookin' all surprised that I know? What? You thought it was a secret?"

"Nah, you got it all wrong, homeboy. I don't work for Sincere, and never did. You know that."

Betho interjected, "Nah? I know pretty boy over here did, though. He was his top lieutenant, I hear. Yeah, I did my research, homie."

"Then my reputation should've given me an A1 credit score," Face stated matter-of-factly.

Even though most dealers considered it mandatory to do a background check on anyone they planned to deal with, Banks knew something was off, although he couldn't yet pinpoint it. The circumstances of their meeting felt too much like an ambush to be a coincidence. Plus, there was still a huge question mark when it came to the mystery regarding who shot their mother. The only clue they had was that they were Mexican. That made Banks even more wary about their surprise introduction at such an inopportune time. Suddenly, Banks remembered the name that his mother had mentioned the shooter proclaimed revenge for. So, if there was a connection, it had to be her because she was the common denominator. It was like divine intervention the way Mafi ran his mouth so recklessly. He informed them that Betho was from Sacramento when that should've been on a need-to-know basis, especially since Sacramento was the same city that Maria was killed in. Now the only question was—what were the odds she was from there too? Whatever the case may have been, Banks knew that the only way to survive the ensuing war was to find out the true identities of his enemies. It was the only chance he had at gaining the upper hand, which meant that it was time for a moment of truth. He couldn't afford to overlook the possibility of there being a connection. Therefore, Banks wisely used their code phrase to signal Awol and Face to be ready to bust their guns.

He said, "Hey Betho, you remind me of my boy Jose. He's from Sacramento, too. He's from The Heights. You know him?"

"I don't know. I know a lot of muthafuckas, homie. Why?" Betho replied arrogantly.

"Because he had hooked me up with this badass Mexican bitch named Maria I used to fuck on. She sure loved anal."

Banks strategically made the derogatory comment about Maria to gauge Betho's reaction. He hoped Betho would slip and reveal his hand, knowing damn well he had never actually fucked a girl named Maria in his life. Remarkably, it worked because Betho turned as red as a tomato.

He leaned forward and said, "What the fuck you say?"

But before he could even finish his sentence, Banks had his .45-caliber pistol aimed at his face.

"Don't you move muthafucka," Banks barked.

Awol quickly followed suit, aiming his .45-caliber pistol at the cowboy who had been eyeing him. Likewise, Face didn't hesitate to press the barrel of his .40-caliber pistol against Mafi's forehead.

Face, filled with adrenaline, asked, "What are we doin' here, bruh?"

"We're gettin' the fuck outta here alive," Banks replied.

"No, you ain't, bitch. My boys got these apartments surrounded," Betho replied.

"Whack!"

Banks yelled, "Shut the fuck up!" as he cracked Betho across the forehead with his pistol. "Lock the door, Face."

Awol said, "That's what I'm talkin' 'bout," before jerking his gun toward his newfound friend.

Surprisingly, the man didn't flinch. Therefore, Awol shouted, "Say somethin'," trying to provoke him.

Banks pointed his gun at Mafi and said, "Bitch-nigga, you tried to set me up?"

Mafi replied, "I didn't have a choice. You stupid muthafuckas killed Javier's niece. Y'all are already dead, my boy."

Betho snapped, "Yeah, bitch, we're gonna kill you black muthafuckas."

Banks aimed his gun at Betho and said, "Yeah? And who the fuck are you supposed to be?"

"The Grim Reaper, puto. And I'm here to collect."

Betho's reckless mouth and emotional outburst confirmed Banks' suspicion—he was the one who yelled, 'This is for Maria,' before shooting his mother. Therefore, filled with hatred, he aimed his gun at Betho's knee.

Boom! The gunshot rang out, echoing in the small room.

"Ah... You bitch!" Betho screamed out in pain.

"I said, who the fuck are you?" Banks asked with an acute sense of authority.

"I'm Javier's nephew. You fuckers killed my sister Maria when y'all took a shot at Cocaine. Now, The Faction has a green light on you. And they're not going to stop coming until you're all dead."

"Is that right? Awol, take those fool's guns before they try something."

Awol yelled, "Keep y'all fucking hands up!" as he eased toward the one with the AK-47 sitting on his lap.

Once Awol secured the AK-47, he opted for heavier firepower. So, he tucked his .45 into his waistband and checked if the AK-47 was loaded.

Afterward, Face took the shotgun from the other soldier and said, "Lie face down. Hands behind your back. You know the drill."

Meanwhile, Awol ran and locked the front door, hopefully giving them enough time to devise an escape plan.

After the sicario complied, Face pulled the shoelaces from a pair of shoes lined up along the wall and used them to tie up both men. Suddenly, they heard the doorknob rattle as someone tried to turn it.

"Now what?" Face asked nervously.

"We get the fuck out of here," Banks replied.

Flacco called out, "Jefe," as he desperately jiggled the doorknob. Meanwhile, Betho tried to use the opportunity to scream for help. Unfortunately, Banks despised his foolish attempt at calling in the cavalry.

"WHAM!"

Banks cracked Betho across the head with the butt of his gun. The blow instantly opened a gash in the top left corner of his forehead.

"Now that was stupid," said Banks.

"C'mon, man, I'm bleeding out here," Betho pleaded.

"Shut the fuck up, punk!"

Flacco and whoever else was outside began kicking the door, trying desperately to knock it off its hinges.

Face grabbed Mafi by the back of his neck and said, "Order your men to stop kicking the fucking door! Or you're gonna be the first to die."

Mafi yelled, "Stand down, Flacco! Back away from the damn door—they've got us at gunpoint."

Immediately, the banging ceased as Flacco ran off to get reinforcements.

Awol said, "We gotta hurry up and get the hell outta here. I'm sure they went to get backup. The longer we wait, the harder it's gon' be to get the fuck outta here."

"He's right, bruh. We gotta haul ass," said Face.

Banks said, "I know. We're gonna have to take hostage to get out of here alive. Look out that window and see what kind of movement they've got goin' on."

Awol walked over to the window, pulled back the blinds, and peeked outside. "Aw fuck!" was not the response Banks or Face was hoping to hear.

"What is it?" asked Face.

"Blood, it's about fifty heavily armed shooters headed in this direction. We need to call for backup."

Banks said, "Nah, that would take too long. Besides, there is no guarantee they would make it before SWAT arrived. Just think, all of those gunshots are going to draw the entire police force, including the ghetto bird. There's only one way outta here. If they block the lot, we're fucked.

"We'll have to walk these sons of bitches out and hope there aren't any sharpshooters on the rooftops."

Banks grabbed Betho's shirt, pressed the barrel of his gun against his forehead, and asked, "Who the fuck is The Faction?"

Awol interjected, "I've heard of them. They're trying to take over the drug trade in the U.S. Word is after El Rey went down, there was a major drug war within the cartels over territory in Mexico. So, some of them decided to expand north to inherit all of El Rey's clientele. They're supposed to be some ruthless muthafuckas, too. They're cuttin' off heads and hanging dead bodies from bridges just to make a statement. When I was in Atlanta, they were allegedly the ones who left a trail of bodies throughout the west side. Apparently, the natives weren't too fond of them infringing on their territory. Which of course resulted in a turf war."

"Fuck! Man, I can't afford to be in another turf war," Face exclaimed.

After pacing back and forth, Face pointed his gun at Betho and said, "What the fuck do y'all want?"

Betho replied, laughing, "Are you fucking kidding me? We want your heads, asshole."

Face cocked his hand back, prepared to hit Betho with the butt of his gun.

"Wait! We need him in one piece. He might be our only chance at getting outta here alive," Banks said, calming him down.

"What about him?" Awol asked while pointing his gun at Mafi.

"We're taking him, too. This is his hood. Those soldiers take orders from him."

"You don't need me. You got the boss. I'm just the middleman—I ain't got no beef wit' y'all," Mafi said.

Hearing those treacherous words infuriated Betho, causing him to spit a loogie in Mafi's face.

"I'm going to cut your fucking throat, you fucking rat," Betho stated furiously.

Mafi replied, "Hey, I ain't no fucking rat, man. These idiotas are your fucking problem, not mine."

Banks yelled, "Both of y'all shut the fuck up. Both of y'all are coming with us. Face, get something to tie these fools up wit."

Face quickly grabbed more shoelaces and aggressively tied their hands behind their backs.

Mafi said, attempting to manipulate the situation, "Man, all this shit ain't even necessary. Just let me out there, and I'll tell my boys to let y'all through. This ain't our beef anyway."

"Fool, you think we're stupid? Keep talkin', and I'ma smoke yo bitch-ass. Now, what are them fools doing out there, Awol?"

"Shit, I don't know, I don't see nobody. They're gone," Awol replied.

Face said, "Them niggas probably trying some slick shit. Awol, look out the peephole and see what's goin' on."

Awol crept to the door and peeked through the peephole, hoping no one outside heard him move. With his beady eyes wide, he turned to Face and whispered, "They're outside."

"Boom!"

Suddenly, a bullet tore through the peephole, hitting Awol in his right cheek, sending him flying backward, holding his face.

"Aw shit!" Face exclaimed as he ran to Awol's aid.

Awol retreated from the front door, clutching his cheek, trying to stop the bleeding.

Banks yelled, "You muthafuckas shot my cousin?" while waving his gun between Betho and Mafi.

Ironically, Betho looked amused, grinning like he had just dodged a paternity test.

Face grabbed Awol's head and said, "Let me see that shit," like he had medical expertise.

Awol quickly turned his head sideways and let Face examine him.

"What's it lookin' like?" asked Banks.

Face replied, "He's gon' be a'ight. It's just a flesh wound. He do need a doctor, though."

Banks yelled, "Fuuuuck!" feeling the pressure from the walls closing in around him.

After regaining his composure, Awol stood over one of the sicarios tied up on the floor. He then shot him in his chest before shooting the other one in his face, killing him instantly.

"Now we're even," Awol muttered coldly.

Betho said, "Muthafucka! Javier is goin' to kill your whole fucking family for that shit."

Awol replied, "Not if I get to him first," while still grimacing in pain.

Banks grabbed Mafi's shirt collar and said, "If you plan on making it out of this shit alive, you'd better do exactly as I say. Or you'll be the first one I kill, ya hear me?"

"Yeah, man. I hear you," Mafi replied fearfully.

"Good, because you're gonna be the first one out that door. So I want you to tell your chickas to disperse. You better make it loud and clear—unless they want their boss with a hole in the back of his head, they had better let us pass. And don't be saying no slick shit in Spanish, either. If I hear one word I don't understand, you're dead, feel me?"

"Yeah, dog, I feel you."

"Good."

Banks then turned to Face and said, "You're going to be right behind me with your gun to Betho's head. Awol, you're going to flank us to prevent them from getting a kill shot on one of us. That means you'll be covering fire. We just gotta hurry up and make it to the whip so we can get the fuck out of here."

Face said, "Shit, I'm ready when you are. But what about the drugs and the money?"

Banks asked Awol, "Can you manage with them duffel bags draped over your shoulder?"

"Yup, I'll be straight," Awol replied, still wincing in pain.

"A'ight, cool."

"You sho, blood? 'Cause you are kinda soft," Face asked, unconvinced.

"Yeah, blood, I'm good," Awol replied, not in a joking mood.

Face then retrieved both duffel bags before slinging them over Awol's neck to see how he'd react. Surprisingly, the drugs and money weren't even a priority considering their current situation. However, having a reliable gunman was, especially if they weren't going to be alive long enough to spend it. Therefore, Face examined Awol subjectively. He was weighing whether he could be dependable with two heavy duffel bags and a bullet hole leaking from his cheek.

Awol said, "I told you I'm straight, bruh," fully aware of Face's discernment.

Banks said, "It sounds to me like the man knows what he's doing."

"It's your call," Face replied.

"Let's do this shit, then."

Betho said, "Ay, man, can you tie my leg up to stop the bleeding? Ain't no point in having no dead hostages, right?"

Banks thought about it briefly, then replied, "Face, get something to tie this fool leg up with."

Face walked into the nearest bedroom and returned with a torn T-shirt shortly afterward.

He said, "This is gonna have to do, lil' mama."

"Fine wit me," Banks replied.

Face then kneeled and tied the shirt above Betho's bullet wound as tight as he possibly could, causing him to cringe.

Face said, "Stop crying like a little bitch! Now get yo hoe ass up!"

Then Face yanked Betho up by his arm, damn near pulling his shoulder out of the socket.

Banks said, "You too, nigga. Let's go," before snatching Mafi up by his shirt.

Next, Banks walked Mafi to the front door with the barrel of his gun pressed against the back of his head.

You better let your boys know you're comin' out, before they accidentally shoot yo ass. Unless you plan on catching a stray bullet."

It only took Mafi a split second to make his presence known to his homies, especially after realizing he could've been the one who looked out of the peephole instead of Awol. So, in that case, he damn sure didn't wanna get shot by mistake.

Mafi shouted at the top of his lungs, "Yo, Flacco! It's me, Mafioso. Don't shoot! I'm comin' out!"

"Good boy," Banks mocked before opening the door.

The scene appeared to be exactly as they had expected. There was a trail of soldiers leading from the stairway all the way to the courtyard. Flacco and the two cowboys stood on the front line, and they were undoubtedly out for blood.

Mafi said, "Just one question. How did you know it was a setup?"

Banks replied, "Your boy Betho ran his mouth too much, that's how. When you do a hit, you're supposed to make sure your target is dead, especially after announcing why they're being murdered. Now tell your boys to back the fuck up and clear a pathway."

Mafi hollered, "You fools better back the fuck up! Can't you see this fool has a gun to my head? Don't try to be no fuckin' heroes and get me shot, putos."

Suddenly, Mafi's soldiers slowly began to back up, one after another.

"And stop pointing your fucking guns at me!" Mafi added.

Banks whispered into Mafi's ear, "That was a great speech. It just may've saved your life."

Banks waited for all of Mafi's homies to reach the base of the staircase before pushing him out of the apartment. Then, he slowly escorted him to the top of the handrail, where he could watch them closely. Meanwhile, Face followed them cautiously, gripping Betho by his Mongolian ponytail.

Banks said, "Tell them fools I said back the fuck up, dog. I ain't playin' witcha. I'll blow your shit out right here."

Mafi yelled, "Yo! Didn't I say back the fuck up! So back the fuck up!"

This time Mafi's soldiers retreated with urgency. They were reluctant to be the cause of either Mafi or Betho being executed.

"Cover us, Awol," said Banks.

Awol raised the barrel of his AK-47 over the guardrail, aiming it at the crowd to deter anyone from getting an angle on them.

He said, "Go ahead. I'll meet y'all at the bottom. If I catch them trying anything, I'ma air their asses out."

"A'ight, stay on point," Face replied.

"No doubt."

Banks said, "As a matter of fact, I'll take Betho down first."

Banks gripped Betho's shirt and dragged him down the steps, ignoring his cries of agony. Face followed closely, gripping Mafi by his ponytail. Once Banks hit the base of the steps, he could clearly see that they were outgunned and outmanned. Therefore, the best solution was to force them to increase their distance. Given their circumstances, it was their best tactical option.

Banks said, "Tell them fools to part like the Red Sea and make a pathway to the parking lot."

Betho nervously translated Banks' demands into Spanish—and then, WHAM!

Banks immediately whacked Betho across the back of his head with the butt of his gun, causing blood to trickle down the back of his neck.

"Didn't I tell you not to say shit in Spanish, muthafucka?" Banks asked rhetorically.

Betho snapped, "Man, fuck you!" he replied.

Seeing their boss get assaulted like that caused the sicarios' blood to boil. So naturally, they aimed their guns at Banks' head, hoping for a kill shot.

Using Betho as a shield, Banks pointed his gun back at them and said, "Don't even think about it." Then Banks yanked Betho by his collar and said, "Tell them fools to lower their weapons before they make me kill yo bitch-ass."

This time, Betho spoke immaculate English.

"Lower your fucking guns," he said.

Mafi shouted, "I said let these putos pass. Can't you see they have fucking guns to our heads?"

Suddenly, Awol rushed down the stairs, covering them as they maneuvered through the angry crowd.

After Banks decided they had given them enough space to navigate their way to their escape vehicle, he said, "Okay, let's go!"

Then, with those words, he ushered Betho through the hostile crowd, ignoring the threats and insults being hurled at them. Meanwhile, Face and Mafi were still following closely behind as Awol guarded their rear. He was backpedaling carefully while swinging his AK-47 from side to side. There was no doubt about it, Awol was fully prepared to unload the clip on anyone feeling froggish enough to make a move. As they made their way through the pathway, the divided soldiers quickly regrouped, forming a tight mob around them, following closely behind Awol. Banks was surprised to have made it back to the parking lot in one piece. He hadn't felt that much anxiety since he was in the middle of a prison riot, fighting for his life. He knew the cartel members were ruthless, so he expected at least one of them to make a calculated attempt to free Betho from his grasp. *But so far so good,* he thought.

Banks said, "Here, get the door, Awol," before pulling out his keys and handing them to him.

Banks and Face then backpedaled, using Betho and Mafi as shields in case their soldiers got trigger-happy. Awol then jogged to the truck and opened the driver's and rear side doors. Once they were opened entirely, he positioned himself to provide covering fire.

Awol yelled, "Let's go!"

Suddenly, Betho went limp, turning himself into dead weight. Therefore, Banks had no choice but to drag him backwards in a headlock as his shoes slid across the concrete. Face hurriedly pulled Mafi around to the rear passenger's side door, opened it, and forced him inside. Face knew there was no time to waste after witnessing Betho's pathetic escape attempt.

Face hopped inside the passenger seat and said, "Help Banks. I got this fool."

By then, Banks had already dragged Betho's upper torso into the truck, but his legs were still flailing wildly outside of the door. Therefore, Awol aimed his rifle at their soldiers while using his other hand to force Betho's legs into the back seat. Then after helping Banks secure Betho, Awol hurried into the driver's seat and started the engine.

Betho sneered, "You'll never get away with this. Every sicario in Cali will be hunting you stupid fucks."

"We'll see," Banks replied calmly.

Awol peeled out in reverse, disregarding any possibility of running over an innocent bystander. His only objective was getting the hell out of that apartment complex alive. Unfortunately, they could see that some of Mafi's soldiers had already started their cars, clearly preparing to give chase. Therefore, Awol skirted off, zooming through the parking lot with reckless abandon. He refused to slow down even as two unsuspecting pedestrians crossed the driveway. Instead, he gave them fair warning by honking his horn, giving them just enough time to dive out of the way before impact. Then, with screeching tires, he hit a quick right, causing him to swerve directly into traffic, barely dodging a head-on collision with a white Ford Mustang.

"Here they come," Banks announced.

Then he watched intently as a black Grand National zoomed out of the parking lot directly into two cars, causing a pile-up.

Banks watched the wreck and said, "'Well, that should buy us some time."

Afterward, Awol weaved through traffic, trying to get as far away from Mafi's soldiers as possible. He knew running a red light was out of the question because it would instantly trigger the stop light's camera, capturing a still shot of him. He also knew he couldn't underestimate the loyalty of Mafi's soldiers. Or the capability of the cartel's soldiers, who they had just recently discovered were sicarios. They couldn't afford to be pulled over by SFPD. If they were, the DA would stack so many charges on them that would be buried under the jail. Even under those unlikely circumstances, Betho and Mafi chose to keep it solid. The guns and drugs, combined with the bullet still lodged in Betho, would be more than enough to bury the driver—and Awol knew it. Getting caught wasn't an option. Not while he was behind the wheel.

Betho said, "I need some air, dog. I feel like I'm gonna pass out."

Face scoffed and replied, "Yeah, right. So you can scream for help? You a be a'ight, bitch."

Awol reached over and cut the air conditioner on because he didn't want to be pulled over with a dead cartel member in the back seat.

Banks said, "Just stay on the back streets, and we should be straight."

"Yeah, it looks like we lost them," said Awol.

After maneuvering through the back streets for what felt like an eternity, Banks said, "Make a left up here for the freeway."

Awol followed Banks' instruction and made a left at the corner heading straight toward the freeway. All that remained was a right onto the overpass, which he took without hesitation. Suddenly, as they entered the on-ramp, Banks saw a black Suburban run a red light behind them, speeding up the on-ramp. It came only inches away from scraping against the guardrail, causing sparks to emit from underneath the SUV. Awol immediately knew they had to distance themselves from the Suburban before they hit rush hour traffic.

Face said, "Let's go! Speed up, blood!"

Awol smashed on the gas, honking the horn like a madman as he weaved through traffic. He was dangerously tailgating cars until they created a passing lane for him to proceed. The Suburban attempted to weave through traffic in the same fashion, yet they weren't as successful due to irritated drivers refusing to let them pass. It turned out most big city commuters didn't like to be intimidated on the road. In fact, a Pakistani taxi driver purposely blocked a passing lane, simply to give the passenger of the Suburban the middle finger. Unfortunately, that was a grave mistake because the sicario rolled down his window, reached out his AR-15 assault rifle, and fired six rounds into the taxi. The rapid shots caused the taxi driver to crash into the back of a pickup truck as he keeled over.

Awol had maneuvered as much as he could without drawing any unnecessary attention. Unfortunately, now that they had reached rush hour on the bridge, it would only be a matter of time before they were in a full-on high-speed chase. The Suburban was close enough to be seen through the rearview mirror yet trailing just enough to give them a decent head start.

After sitting through bumper-to-bumper traffic, it eventually began to flow freely upon reaching Oakland's city limit. Thus, Awol didn't hesitate to take full advantage of his head start. He instantly smashed on the gas, accelerating to high speeds once he cleared the pile-up.

"Where to now?" asked Awol.

Face replied, "Get on Eight-Eighty. We're going to take them to Brookfield. I'ma have a surprise waiting for their asses."

Face then pulled his phone from the glove compartment and made a call.

"Nigga, why'd you slow down?" Banks asked nervously

Awol replied, "Because, fool, there be hella highway patrol around here. Besides them fools ain't gon' shoot at us. We got their bosses in here."

Mafi said, "Speaking of, that fool ain't lookin' too good."

Banks immediately turned to Betho, whose head was propped sideways against the window.

Banks yelled, "Aye, muthafucka!"

However, Betho didn't respond to his outburst. Instead, he remained so still that he appeared lifeless.

Banks said, "This muthafucka done passed out," before placing his finger under Betho's nose to see if he was still breathing.

"Aw, shit, blood. This nigga ain't breathing," Banks exclaimed.

"Well, tell that to his homies. Because they're right behind us," Awol replied.

Mafi said, "Y'all done fucked up now. Y'all just signed your own death warrants."

Face said, "Shut the fuck up before you be next, nigga."

"Alright, playa, it's cool."

Suddenly, the Suburban rammed their rear bumper, catching everyone off guard.

Awol said, "What the fuck! They're trying to make us crash with their own folks inside?"

Banks looked back and instantly noticed the passenger talking to someone on his cell phone.

Banks said, "Change of plans. They're receiving new orders from somebody. We have to get them off of our asses, ASAP. Get in the slow lane. I've got an idea."

Awol managed to dodge the Suburban and maneuver into the slow lane unscathed. He had no idea why Banks would order him to slow down during a high-speed chase. Though at the time, it didn't make sense to Face either.

Face asked, "What are you up to, blood? These niggas ain't playin'."

Banks replied, "Awol, just get ready to get off on Sixty-Sixth Ave. I'ma get them off us."

Suddenly, Banks opened the door and shoved out Betho's inanimate body, causing him to tumble along the road. The driver of the Suburban tried to swerve out of the way, but he reacted too late and ran over Betho's body. The tires screeched as he slammed on the brakes, hoping he hadn't just killed his boss's nephew. But little did he know, he was already dead. Meanwhile, Banks watched through the back window as the sicarios scrambled to recover Betho's mangled body.

Banks said, "I told you I was gon' get them off us."

Awol replied in a hostile tone, "Nigga, you could've warned me before throwing a dead body out of the car."

Face said, "Look, we're past that. Take San Leandro Boulevard all the way to Brookfield. There's never any police on the back streets."

Banks said, "And hurry up in case someone took down our license plate. We need to switch vehicles fast."

Mafi said, "First, y'all killed Javier's niece, and then you turned around and killed his nephew. Man, he's going to scorch the earth hunting for y'all muthafuckas. The Faction ain't gonna stop comin' until they've killed everyone you've ever loved. Even down to your fucking pets, dog."

Face replied, "Yeah? Well, this ain't Mexico, homeboy. They're in my backyard now. I run these streets. Now sit back and shut the fuck up!"

Mafi peeked over at Banks, tempted to test Face, but something told him it wasn't a wise decision. So he just sat back and tried to figure another way out. Soon after, Awol pulled up to a red light, and an opportunity arose when Mafi had least expected it. Surprisingly, a cop car pulled up right alongside the driver's side. Banks reacted swiftly and pressed the barrel of his gun against Mafi's ribs.

Banks said, "You bet not try nothin'. Unless you want to get all y'all killed."

Knowing a cry for help would surely get him shot, Mafi decided he would have a much better chance of talking his way out of danger later. He actually prayed the cops didn't pull them over because he liked his chances of survival better without their help. His game plan was to offer up a ransom they couldn't refuse, hoping in return they would spare his life. He knew they would need all the help they could get to prepare for the war with The Faction.

The K9 in the patrol car's back seat started barking at Banks like he sensed something was awry. He barked so aggressively at Banks that the officer looked at Awol to see what he was barking at. Though, of course, Awol played it cool and waved at the officer like he had nothing to hide. The officer waved back at Awol, pretending to be friendly.

"What is it, boy? What are you barking at?" the officer asked curiously.

His partner said, "He probably has to use the bathroom because I know I sure do. I'll pull over next to one of these warehouses and take him for a walk."

"So you can go? Or he can?" he asked jokingly.

"Both."

Then, with that being said, they were off. They turned the corner without a hint of suspicion regarding the illegal activity going on merely feet away.

Awol said, "We gotta hurry up and get off the streets 'cause that was too damn close, blood."

Face replied, "Don't trip. We'll be there in a minute," trying to ease the tension.

Awol crossed the intersection, feeling the perspiration from their close encounter with the law. It caused him to drive even more cautiously than he did before. Luckily, since the back streets were pretty empty, they didn't take long to reach Ninety-Eighth Avenue. He made a left on Ninety-Eighth, then cruised through a few intersections before finally reaching the residential area where traffic had picked up dramatically. Shortly after passing a gas station to Awol's left, a pearl white Cadillac pulled up alongside them. Then suddenly, the passenger lifted an M16 assault rifle and pointed it directly at Awol's head.

"What the fuck?" Awol asked, stunned.

"What?" Face asked, unable to see the gunman.

The gunman yelled, "Pull yo ass around the corner!"

With one glance, Banks instantly recognized the man in the back seat of the Cadillac.

He said, "Fuck! That's Mustafa."

Now, you see, Mustafa was Cell-Bo's older and much more sophisticated brother. It may be hard to believe this, but Mustafa somehow had a few more screws loose than his younger brother. He was once a decorated soldier until he flew off the hinges and put his commanding officer in the infirmary. All over an Iraqi insurgent they had both secretly been sleeping with during deployment. That incident earned him a life-changing stint following a court martial. Of course, once he was released, he didn't hesitate to exact his revenge on Uncle Sam. He contacted his loyalist brothers from his old unit and convinced them to start running military-grade firearms throughout the Southern Hemisphere. Oddly, that was the last time that they had seen or heard from him again. In several years, no one in the hood had even spoken of Mustafa's name.

Face said, "Pull over, Awol. So I can see what this nigga's trippin' on."

Banks said, "Really? Wit a fuckin' hostage in the car?"

Awol said, "Yeah, nigga! He's aiming a choppa at me."

Awol turned the corner and parked diagonally, blocking someone's driveway. He hoped the threat of multiple witnesses would prevent him from being shot. The Cadillac CTS then parked directly behind them, boxing them between a black Buick Regal parked in the driveway. Mustafa was the first one to bounce out of the car, clutching a high-capacity submachine gun—one they had never seen before. So, it only added to the fear of being shot by it. The man in the passenger seat was clutching an camouflage-patterned AR-15. He hopped out directly behind Mustafa since he was strategically taking up the rear. Mustafa then beelined straight toward the passenger side door, where Face calmly awaited him.

Mafi said, "Damn, man, everybody wanna kill y'all janky muthafuckas, huh?"

"Whack!"

Banks hit Mafi in the mouth with the butt of his gun and barked, "Shut the fuck up!"

Mafi coughed, then spit out a bloody tooth before laughing like a masochist, as if he enjoyed being assaulted. Awol suddenly locked eyes with the middle-aged black man occupying the property they were on. The man quickly closed his blinds to avoid being identified as a loose end. Afterward, Mustafa yanked Face's door open and pointed the barrel of his gun directly at his forehead.

"Where the fuck is my brother at?" asked Mustafa.

Face replied, "Look, bruh, all this gunplay ain't even necessary. I don't know where Cell-Bo is. I've been looking for him my damn self. Now, can you please get that gun outta my face?"

"Nah, nigga, that's some bullshit. I heard Sincere got smoked. And I also found out that Bo was last seen wit Reiko and Tyson. Reiko was found murdered in his own house. Now Tyson and my brother are missing. You better tell me somethin', nigga! Or I'll blow yo shit out right here!"

Face knew that Mustafa was actually crazy enough to smoke him right there in broad daylight and be content with the consequences. So, it was best to tell him exactly what he wanted to hear to vindicate himself.

Banks said, "Tell that nigga everything you know. And make it quick before the police show up. Because if they do, we're all fucked."

"You should listen to your brutha," said Mustafa.

Face said, "Look in the back seat, dog," while briefly rolling down the back window.

Mustafa then stared back at Mafi with sheer confusion.

"Who the hell is that? And what the fuck does he have to do with my brutha going missing?" asked Mustafa.

"As far as I know, everything. This fool just tried to line us up over an unsanctioned hit your brutha did. Neither Sincere nor I knew about it until just now. He was only ordered to kidnap Sav's sister. But instead, he detoured and accidentally killed the niece of a cartel boss."

Banks said, "That's why those punk muthafuckas shot up my mama's house. It was in retaliation to that shit. I'm lucky my kids weren't home."

Mustafa said, "So what you're saying is, you think these dudes killed my brutha?"

"I don't know, but I wanna live to find out," Face replied.

Mustafa asked, "Well, you think this fool in the back seat knows what happened to them?" as he lowered his weapon.

"I'm sure he knows something."

"Good. Then we've got work to do."

Mustafa told his point man to follow them, then hopped in the back seat, squishing Mafi between him and Banks.

"Drive," Mustafa demanded.

Twenty minutes later, they arrived at a mosque and drove up a dirt road, entering a private parking lot. Then, one of Mustafa's men bounced out of the Cadillac and opened the security gate so they could enter. Mustafa got out of the truck first before aggressively snatching Mafi out behind him. It was evident by the way Mustafa's crew operated, that particular mosque was used for criminal activity.

Mustafa said, "C'mon, so I can see what this nigga's really hiding. I still remember some of my old interrogation tactics."

"What, you gon' waterboard me?" Mafi asked sarcastically.

"Nah, bitch. I'ma put your muthafuckin' ass through electroshock therapy."

Suddenly, a quick dose of reality knocked the annoying smirk off Mafi's pretty little face.

Mafi screamed, "Help!" hoping someone would intervene.

Consequently, Mustafa slung his submachine gun over his shoulder, then bear-hugged Mafi, lifting him off of the ground. The amount of pressure he applied almost completely restricted Mafi's lungs. He then covered his mouth while aggressively applying the chokehold.

Mustafa stated calmly, "You better shut up before I snap your fuckin' neck."

Mustafa then looked back at Face, Banks, and Awol and decided they weren't moving as promptly as he expected. Therefore, he gave them a little nudge to speed them up.

"Man, y'all niggas hurry the fuck up!" he yelled.

Mustafa stood 6'7" and weighed a solid 280 pounds. He dragged Mafi up the walkway as effortlessly as dragging a tantrum-throwing child into a dentist's office. Meanwhile, Mustafa's three soldiers followed closely behind Banks, Awol, and Face, all heavily armed.

After entering the mosque, Mustafa handed Mafi off to Ahmed and said, "Y'all follow me," before heading toward an office.

Once inside, Mustafa walked over to a table in the center of the room and said, "Don't be shy. One of y'all grab the other end."

The trio looked back and forth at each other, waiting for a volunteer, until finally, Face stepped forward and grabbed the other end of the table.

Mustafa said, "Now move it backward toward that wall."

They moved the table back and set it down along the wall. Then Mustafa returned to the rug beneath the table and kneeled. After pulling back the rug, he revealed a pattern of staggered hardwood floorboards.

"What's this?" Face asked, perplexed.

Suddenly, Mustafa started removing the floorboards, exposing a full arsenal of weapons.

Mustafa said, "Are y'all going to help me or what? If we're about to go to war with the cartel, we're going to need some heavy artillery. If we need anything more than this, we have to hit my secondary stash spot in Chinatown."

"Chinatown?" asked Face.

"Yeah, nigga, Chinatown. How do you think I've been exporting my guns all these years? We have what you would call a symbiotic relationship."

"Shit, that's good, then. 'Cause I have a feeling we're gonna need their help."

"We? Nigga, you ain't French."

"You know what I mean. If you think me, my brutha, and these fake-ass Taliban wannabes are enough to take on the cartel, you're even crazier than I thought. We need as much assistance as they can provide."

Ahmed said, "He's right, Mustafa. If we're gonna avenge your brutha, and live to tell the tale, we gotta come correct."

Mustafa replied, "Yeah, a'ight. But it ain't gon' be cheap. I can get the soldiers, but you two niggas are footing the bill."

Face nodded and said, "Say no more."

CHAPTER TWENTY-NINE

Javier and Grandpa sat inside a VIP booth at Javier's five-star restaurant, El Estrella Fugaz—The Shooting Star. They were surrounded by sicarios, eating fine Mexican cuisine while discussing their rapid expansion into the East Coast. The restaurant was temporarily closed to ensure their meeting went undisturbed. They intended to avoid any ill-advised interruptions, creating a rare sense of solace. However, they were interrupted by loud banging at the restaurant's back entrance. It was where Javier usually conducted his illegal transactions to avoid being seen by any unwanted eyes. The cooks were the first to hear the banging, but they knew better than to answer the service door while Javier was in a private meeting. Naturally, one of them chose to alert one of Javier's sicarios to the disturbance instead.

After receiving the news from his sicario, Javier ordered him to investigate. The sicario then nodded to one of the other sicarios, signaling him to assist him in checking out the disturbance. As they entered the kitchen, they pushed past a cook, who was on his way to notify Javier of the unexpected visitor. Most of the cooks had already stopped what they were doing and were watching the two men as they drew their weapons. Fearful of a possible shootout, the cooks quickly scampered out of their way. When the first sicario reached the back entrance, he signaled his partner to prepare. Next, he slowly pushed the door open, his gun barrel aimed steadily at the narrow opening. He was shocked by what he saw next.

"Don't shoot. It's me, Poncho," said the blood-covered man.

"Poncho? What the hell are you doing here? And whose blood is that?" asked Jose.

"It's Betho's, man. He's dead."

Jose rushed out of the restaurant and saw Hector holding up Betho's limp body by his armpits.

Jose said, "What?! And you decided to bring him here? Are you insane?"

Poncho said, "I didn't know what else to do. We couldn't just leave his body on the side of the road."

Jose looked around nervously and said, "Hurry up and bring him inside."

Once they all got back inside the kitchen, Jose ordered Alex to inform Javier that his nephew's body was lying on the kitchen floor. Jose couldn't help noticing the overwhelming fear in Poncho's eyes as he paced back and forth. They all knew Javier would still need someone to blame, even though it wasn't Poncho's fault. Javier would surely need someone to punish, at least for his sister's sake, especially after she lost her only daughter less than a week prior in the same fashion. Naturally, Poncho considered running, but then they would murder his mother and sisters as consolation. They were easy targets, considering they were stuck in Mexico under the watchful eye of the cartel, which meant running was definitely out of the question. Even though he felt Betho was a dumbass who had it coming because he never followed the rules, Poncho knew his death would have serious consequences. It was probably because he was a spoiled little brat who never put in any real work. He just happened to be the nephew of the great Javier, which was the only reason his pompous ass had survived for as long as he did.

Javier and Grandpa both watched Alex as he frantically approached their table. They were curious who had the nerve to interrupt their private meeting with such disrespect. They were sure it wasn't a sting operation because they would've just busted through the front door with guns drawn, screaming, freeze. Yet Javier could tell by the look on Alex's face that something was extremely wrong, prompting him to jump up. Grandpa looked on suspiciously, peering at Alex as he whispered into Javier's ear.

Grandpa asked, "What is it?" at the sight of seeing Javier's jaw drop.

"Come with me," Javier replied.

Then, everyone in the room followed closely behind Alex, tense with anticipation. He subsequently led them through the kitchen to where the disgraced sicarios were idly standing over Betho's bloodied body.

Javier snatched Poncho up by his shirt and said, "What the hell happened to him?"

Poncho replied, "Jefe, it was those fucking mayates. They got the drop on us."

"What mayates?" Grandpa asked, completely unaware of what was going on.

Javier released Poncho's shirt and straightened it, as if calming him. That gave Poncho a chance to explain himself without the immediate threat of violence. Javier hoped his leniency would earn him a more detailed account of what happened.

Poncho said, "The ones who killed Maria. The bounty you put out worked. Those fuckers were attempting to make a drug deal with one of your distributors down in San Francisco. It was the wild one they call Mafioso. He and Betho devised a plan to set a trap for them inside Mafioso's barrio. But somehow, the mayates got the drop on them and took them both hostage. That's why we had to let them escape, but we chased them across the Bay Bridge, waiting for an opportunity to free Betho. And that's when they threw his dead body from their truck. We had no choice but to end our pursuit if we were to retrieve Betho's body. At the time, we thought he was still alive, but he had already bled out from a gunshot wound to his leg."

Grandpa looked at Javier and asked, "Did you know anything about this?"

Javier replied, "It was my idea to offer a bounty to everyone in our network, but I was unaware that Betho had already located the men responsible for Maria's murder. I instructed this imbecile to notify me the moment he got wind of their whereabouts. If only he would've listened—"

"He would still be alive. But you knew Betho, he didn't listen to anyone. We all have to choose our own paths, and he chose his."

"Now, what do you suppose we do?"

"Well, if they want a war, we'll give them a war. We simply have to put ourselves in a position to win. First off, we have to know our enemy."

Poncho said, "I think I can help with that," then pulled out five photos and showed them to Javier.

"How?" asked Javier.

Poncho replied, "These first two are brothers. Their names are Face and Banks. This one right here is Face. He's the one Sav informed us about. He was the right-hand man to Sincere, who we recently found out was executed inside of his home. Now that Sincere's dead, Face controls a major portion of the drug trade in Oakland. This one right here, is his brother Banks. He was recently paroled from prison for a drug beef but is also well-connected. The third guy is unknown, but he seemed to be their muscle. I believe if we eliminate them, the city will be yours for the taking."

"Is that all?"

"Yes, sir. I promise I can—"

"Boom!"

Poncho never saw it coming. Jose pressed the gun to the back of his head and fired, splattering brain matter across Javier's face. Javier calmly removed the handkerchief from his suit pocket and wiped his forehead.

Jose asked, "What about him?" referring to Hector.

"Oh, I almost forgot."

"Boom! Boom!"

Javier shot Hector through the chest and neck, sending him stumbling backward until he collapsed against the service door. Javier then crouched and gathered the scattered photos from the floor.

After briefly studying them, he told Jose, "Get Mr. Sauvage on the phone. It seems we'll be working together again."

To Be Continued.......

Prelude

• • •

Lincoln Falls

Chapter 1

Allison lay on her back emotionless, staring at the ceiling fan as the blades rotated in slow motion, creating a vexatious whirring sound. It was that time of day when her conscience defensibly permitted her to sever the connection to every microscopic nerve in her body. Over time, she gradually mastered the art of projecting her consciousness into another plane. It was a tactic she had developed to escape her calamitous reality, even if only for a short while. It was as though she watched herself from above as her poor excuse for a father repeatedly violated her twelve-year-old body. It was the routine every other night after work, just before he passed out from all the scotch he had consumed. When he would finish, he simply rolled over and passed out like most lushes do. He didn't even have the decency to remove the bloody condom that clung to his inner thigh. Allison felt a strange sense of relief when she noticed the jaundiced tint in John's eyes as he mounted her. It meant that one of the poisons had finally begun to take effect. Since she had been moderately poisoning him with various household cleaners, she had no idea which one was causing the damage. She had learned how to poison someone in moderation from an episode of Alfred Hitchcock.

Every time she prepared a meal for him, she slipped in just enough poison to seep into his bloodstream, but not enough for him to notice the taste. Besides, he was usually too intoxicated to notice the difference. Sometimes, she even took the risk of chasing his glass of scotch with a shot of bleach, which she kept hidden in the cabinet beneath his bar.

Allison was a scrawny, freckle-faced Caucasian girl with blonde hair that she always wore in two nappy pigtails. She couldn't afford the fancy shampoo and conditioner most girls her age used. Clearly, she wasn't winning any beauty pageants, and her father made sure she knew it. He always said that's why his friends called him Honest John, although he was as far from honest as any politician.

He was the sole reason she began cutting herself with broken razor blades, a ritual she used to cope. She relied on self-infliction as a neutralizer whenever her emotional pain became unbearable. She would make shallow incisions into her calloused skin, letting her pain drain freely.

She was trapped on the lower east side of Brighton, sharing a double-wide trailer with a pedophile and a helplessly senile Golden Retriever. Watching their dog, Buck, regress the way he did only added to the heartache and pain she had already endured. It wasn't as though she could express her innermost secrets to the mean girls at school. They had already mocked her relentlessly for her dingy clothes and smelly hair. She refused to give them any more ammunition that could be used to degrade her further.

The only somewhat normal human interaction she'd had in recent years was with a seventeen-year-old boy named Brandon, who lived two trailers down from hers. He was 5'9", with sandy blond hair, and for some reason, he always seemed to wear his flannel shirt unbuttoned, exposing his oddly shaped athletic physique. She undoubtedly thought he was nice, but she still avoided him because she couldn't understand why he took such an interest in her—especially since, from what she could tell, his family was just as messed up as hers. The last thing she needed was to open herself up to more physical or emotional pain.

Sometimes, she could hear yelling and screaming coming from his trailer late at night after his father had been drinking excessively. Most of the time, the pleas came from his mother, begging his father to stop beating him. The next day, both Brandon and his mother would often have scrapes and bruises, clear indicators of the abuse. But no one in Liberty Park dared to intervene in a family quarrel, no matter how bad things got.

Liberty Park was often called the bottom of the barrel because most people who lived there were headed nowhere, fast. It was a place junkies flocked to shoot up heroin, knowing the police didn't give two shits about what happened there. The only time law enforcement visited the park was to serve an arrest warrant or conduct a pop-up parole check. It was as though they had given up on the citizens living there, writing them off as lost causes. They felt the residents weren't even worth arresting since it would cost more money to house them than their lives were worth in the first place. The lack of due diligence from the Brighton County Sheriff's Department only led to an unabated increase in criminal activity. Everything from drug trafficking to underage prostitution transpired directly under their noses on a regular basis. Unfortunately, they showed no interest in enforcing even an ounce of law and order to address the crime-ridden environment.

There was no doubt in Allison's mind that her mother would still be alive if not for the negligence of the Brighton County Sheriff's Department, especially since one of their stray bullets had struck her through the right cheek during a shootout. The damage the bullet caused was so extensive that it exited through the back of her skull, carrying with it a chunk of brain matter. Since John couldn't afford a proper burial, cremation became his only option, making the decision a no-brainer.

Everyone in Liberty Park knew her as Mama because she treated everyone as though their lives most certainly came before hers. She was the one and only person Allison knew she could always depend on.

Sadly, her life was cut short simply because a crew of meth heads decided to rob a local pharmacy. Her mother never told her much about her grandparents—only that she had chosen John over them, and that John's parents were both dead.

Sometimes, while John raped her, he would call her by her mother's name, as if in his sick, twisted mind, he pretended she was her mother to justify his defilement. This only increased Allison's hatred toward him, as every time he mentioned her mother's name, it reminded her that she had a gaping hole where her heart used to be. Regretfully, nothing she tried was capable of filling the empty void her mother left behind.

One fateful night, she stared intently at John as he slept, hoping to finally witness him take his last breath. It was the moment she had patiently awaited since deciding his death was her only chance at liberation. The room became eerily quiet until John's eyes abruptly shot open, and he grabbed at his heart in a panic. Allison freaked out as he rolled over and locked eyes with her. It was as if he had suddenly realized she was the one who caused his heart attack.

"Call 9-1-1!" he moaned as he reached for her hand.

She immediately snatched her hand away from his grasp and slowly stood up, peering down at him mercilessly as he slid onto the floor in agony. She couldn't believe that piece of shit had the nerve to ask for help after all the pain he had caused her. The callousness he displayed when he violently deflowered her made her the last person on Earth who would ever save his life. She watched nervously as he crawled toward the door, uncertain of what he would do if he survived. She feared how he would respond after discovering her plot to kill him. When he suddenly changed direction, she realized he remembered the phone was on a dresser drawer and was making his way toward it.

"Oh, no you don't," she said as she ran across the bed and snatched it out the wall.

"Why?" he asked faintly before collapsing on the floor.

Allison couldn't believe that she had finally broken free from the web her tormenter had savagely woven. Even Buck stood cluelessly in the doorway, looking back and forth from Allison to John, trying to figure out what was happening.

She said, "C'mon, Buck," as she motioned him over with her hand.

By that time, she was so distraught that she casually sat down cross-legged, staring at John's lifeless body while affectionately caressing Buck's head. Then, suddenly, reality struck her like an enormous lightning bolt. Now that John was dead, Buck was the only remaining family she had left, and he was on his last breath. What would happen to her next? she wondered. She realized she hadn't thoroughly thought things through. However, for some reason, she was okay with that because, for now, she was essentially free, marking the beginning of her new life.

Two hours later, after crying herself to sleep, she was awakened by the generic ringtone emitting from their landline. Naturally, she looked over at the clock to see what time it was.

"Ten o'clock," she whispered before jumping up.

Then she frantically scanned the room, looking for John, and that's when she noticed Buck lying asleep on his corpse. Calmly, she stepped over John's body, walked into the living room, and grabbed the phone off the wall.

She thought, *who could this be?* as she looked down at the receiver, perplexed.

However, she was not surprised when she heard Sam's voice through the receiver, considering it was Friday night—the night they routinely went out drinking with cheap hookers. Now, she just hoped Sam wouldn't decide to stop by looking for John because she hadn't been able to reach him by phone. To avoid that possibility, she answered the phone and lied through her teeth.

She said, "My dad's not feeling good. He said he'll have to take a rain check."

Sam replied, "Okay. Tell him I called and to call me back as soon as he's up to it."

"Okay, will do—"

Click!

She thought, *there, that should buy me some time.*

Then she unplugged the phone before heading to the refrigerator to snag a beer.

I've always wanted one of these, she thought.

Brandon

By most standards, Brandon would have been considered a great kid—the type of kid any upstanding parent would be proud to boast about. However, neither of Brandon's parents had been upstanding at any point during his short life. Unfortunately, this wasn't an exaggeration because, as far back as Brandon could remember, his father had used his mother as a punching bag. As soon as Brandon became old enough to try and stop his father from beating his mother, he too became a victim of the brutal assaults.

Like most victims of abuse, his mother blamed Dillon's vicious attacks on the fact that he'd had a little too much to drink. But, to be honest, it didn't matter what excuse he used. Considering his dominating size and strength, there wasn't much they could've done to prevent the assaults anyway. As Brandon grew older, he was forced to stand by and watch helplessly as his father beat the nurturing glimmer of light from his mother's eyes. By the time he was thirteen, it was undeniable that his father had completely beaten all the motherly sustenance from the windows of her soul. It gradually reached a point where she no longer attempted to block the flurry of punches and kicks thrown at her. Sometimes, even after she was knocked unconscious, he would still stomp on her body to see if she was faking. He claimed she was just overreacting while aggressively yelling at her to get up. There was no doubt they were living in a constant state of terror without a conceivable escape plan.

Dillon was Lilly's first and only love. She was so infatuated with him that she allowed him to distance her from anything that could have been perceived as an escape route. He even forbade her from getting a basic education, forcing her to drop out of high school. He claimed he knew exactly what was in her best interest since he was older and much more experienced than her. He had manipulated her to the point where she eventually accepted his abuse as a conventional reaction to a man being unsatisfied with his wife. As for Brandon, he didn't know any better. He was born in Liberty Park, so Liberty Park was all he knew.

On the days when Brandon's physical appearance permitted him to attend school, his academics reflected his sentiment—he had an overwhelmingly passionate love for learning. Some of his teachers even expressed to his father how much potential they believed he had. Nevertheless, their assertions fell on deaf ears because Dillon had already decided that Brandon would work on the same factory line as him, just like his father before him. Dillon often reminded Brandon that, contrary to what his teachers believed, he wouldn't grow up to be anything—just like him. To prove him wrong, Brandon began secretly studying the mechanics of the broken-down cars throughout the trailer park by disassembling and reassembling parts. Over time, he started experimenting with the cars of neighbors who couldn't afford repairs. Before long, he became the go-to guy for minor car repairs. Strangely, his sudden rise to fame only increased his father's aggression toward him, leading to a catastrophic ending on one fateful night.

Brandon had been working nonstop on Mary-Beth's Volkswagen since eight in the morning. By the time he finished, all he wanted to do was take a hot shower and crash undisturbed. It was only a quarter moon, but the lunar brilliance illuminated the night sky. As he turned onto the roadway leading to his trailer, he immediately caught the distinct stench of a skunk. Although the smell didn't faze him much—since he had grown accustomed to living next to the creek—he lit a cigarette to mask it. Meanwhile, he mentally prepared himself to deal with the usual onslaught of physical and verbal assaults his father regularly hurled at him.

As he got within thirty feet of his trailer, he could hear the faint cries of his mother begging his father to stop beating her. Creeping closer, he heard the increasingly vivid sounds of dishes being thrashed around. Nervous, he took a deep breath, held it, and flicked his cigarette into the bushes, completely disregarding the fact that he could have started a serious fire. Like clockwork, his hands began sweating profusely, and his heart rate shot through the roof. He was sick and tired of his father beating his mother, and now, after years of mechanical work, he was finally strong enough to do something about it.

Fed up with the perpetual abuse he'd endured from his father, Brandon inserted his key and opened the door, intent on finally standing up to the bastard. He remembered witnessing a brawl that prior summer, where he had seen a biker named Gunner use his set of keys like a pair of Wolverine's claws. Similarly, he placed his keys between each finger on his right hand, gripping them as tightly as he could. Dillon was so preoccupied with smacking Lilly around that he didn't even notice Brandon had entered the room behind him. Pinned against the counter, Lilly peered over Dillon's shoulder and felt a sense of coldness emanating from Brandon as they locked eyes. It was as though, at that exact moment, they silently decided to stand up and fight back.

Dillon noticed something had caught Lilly's attention unexpectedly, causing him to whip his head around. The interruption only made matters worse since he hated being disturbed while chastising his wife.

Realizing it was only Brandon, he sneered, "Oh, it's just you. Close the damn door, or you'll be next."

Yet Brandon didn't budge. Instead, he just stood there, staring at his father and crying, like all the years of abuse had finally broken him, leaving him emotionless.

Dillon shouted, "I said close the damn door, you fucking idiot!" as he approached with clenched fists.

Once Dillon reached Brandon, he stretched out his arms, clearly with the intent to do him harm.

"I said close the fucking door," Dillon roared, wrapping his hands around Brandon's neck.

A rush of adrenaline surged through Brandon's body, fueling him with enough courage to finally fight back.

WHAM! Brandon punched Dillon in the throat as hard as he possibly could, utterly determined to put an end to his father's violent reign of terror. The shock hit Dillon like a ton of bricks, causing his eyeballs to bulge from their sockets. Staggering backward, he immediately extracted the keys from his neck, creating the excruciating sound of flesh ripping.

Ironically, in a desperate attempt to survive, Dillon turned to Lilly and gurgled, "Help me."

"I hate you!" Lilly screamed, whacking him across the head with a cast-iron skillet and sending him crashing to the floor.

Surprisingly, the blow didn't kill him. He was still alive, twitching on the floor like a fish out of water. Lilly knew she couldn't allow him to live another moment, so she stood directly over him and bashed his face in until he lay completely motionless. Stunned by the atrocity she had just committed, she sat frozen, straddling Dillon and staring down at his disfigured face. Brandon slowly walked up behind her and pulled the skillet from her bloodied hand.

"Come on, Ma, we've gotta get you cleaned up," Brandon said.

Suddenly, he heard a soft voice from behind say, "I can help you with that."

He immediately recognized the kiddie voice, prompting him to slyly tuck the bloody keys into his front pocket before turning to face her. It was Allison, standing in his doorway, holding Buck by his leash. She looked absolutely petrified.

"What are you doing here?" he asked frantically.

"I need your help!" Allison replied.

12 Years Later

Only twelve years had passed, yet the details of that dreadful night were but a distant memory. They were stored and locked away in the deepest, darkest recesses of Allison's mind, hidden in a secret cavern created by her subconscious solely to suppress her most painful memories.

Allison sat across the playground on a wooden bench, watching enviously as identical twins played happily with four other children. Their fire-red pigtails bounced wildly as they ran about, playing an innocent game of tag. Their braided pigtails reminded her of how her mother used to style her hair back when she was their age. It deeply saddened Allison to acknowledge that she would never be able to relate to the experiences of a normal childhood—primarily because her own childhood had been so twisted that the mere thought of her father's face made her stomach turn.

Monica and her five-year-old twins, Amy and Amanda, had been visiting the local park regularly on Saturdays for the past six months. It was a great opportunity for Monica to exercise since it was about a twenty-minute walk from her home. The twins were always full of energy, but after an exhausting day at the park followed by a hot bath, they would be out like a light. That gave Monica a chance to decompress with a tall glass of wine while reading the latest sizzling erotica. It was the only real alone time she could enjoy because she was stuck slaving back and forth between diners, barely staying afloat. Raising two children alone in a household built for two incomes was far more complicated than she had ever imagined.

Two years had passed since her husband vanished without a trace following a horrible boating accident in Liberty Lake. The accident had left her completely devastated. She felt all alone as she tried to single-handedly piece their lives back together. Adding insult to injury, the insurance company refused to release a payout without a death certificate, and the coroner's office refused to issue a death certificate without his body. Monica knew the insurance company was exploiting his disappearance as a technicality to create a loophole, justifying their refusal to pay. She couldn't fathom how any of the sleazeballs working on her claim could live with themselves—especially after being informed that releasing even a portion of the payout could have made a world of difference for her family. There was a special place in hell for people like them, and she knew it.

Over the years, Monica had occasionally heard the adage "time heals all wounds," but only recently did she begin to feel the pain subside. It was almost impossible to gain closure or move on without knowing what had truly happened to the love of her life. The vicious rumors circulating throughout their small town regarding the events leading up to his disappearance only made things worse. The cruelty was uncanny. She had even heard rumors that he had been spotted skipping town with the nanny, which she knew couldn't have been further from the truth. She figured it was a complete lie because, prior to his disappearance, she had been a stay-at-home mom.

However, those false accusations prompted her to investigate further, which ultimately led her to discover that he was, in fact, an adulterer. After reading the detailed love letters he had received, she almost wished they had been from a hot blonde half her age. Maybe then it wouldn't have been as painful. Instead, they were from the woman who had been her best friend and the godmother to her children. The betrayal, therefore, cut deeper than she had ever imagined.

Monica eventually gave up trying to find pleasure in others and decided to find happiness within the confines of her home. Her daughters became the inspiration for reentering the dating game. She wanted them to be raised in a two-parent home, as she believed God intended. Besides, she was tired of switching vibrators whenever it was time to add excitement to her life. That was why she felt her prayers had been answered the day Allan walked into her life holding a bouquet six months earlier.

Allan had been a regular customer at her diner, ordering the same meal just to see her beautiful smile. Finally, one day, he worked up the courage to ask her out. His invitation became the spark that launched her ascension out of a pit of self-loathing. Allan helped her realize there was nothing wrong with her and that she wasn't to blame for her husband's infidelity. He gave her the confidence she needed to move forward. She had come a long way from crying herself to sleep, wondering what she lacked that made her feel insufficient.

Things were becoming serious. Allan made it clear he was ready to commit. He was adamant about meeting her daughters, especially since she had already met both of his sons. Allan expressed his dream of blending their families, like a modern-day Brady Bunch, and even hinted at wanting to add a few more children to the mix. Monica suspected his unusual sense of urgency and excitement might mean he was secretly planning to propose. That suspicion grew stronger when he called her first thing in the morning, ecstatic about the special night he had planned for her and the twins. He explained how they were finally about to meet their future stepbrothers.

Monica had the whole day planned. She decided to let the girls play at the park for a couple of hours before taking them home for baths.

That way, they wouldn't be restless or embarrass her when it was time to sit down and behave. Nothing could ruin her special night. She believed it marked the beginning of their new lives together. It felt like a fairytale. She was so deep in thought, mesmerized by the mere idea of marriage, that she didn't notice Allison approach.

"Wow, today is such a beautiful day, isn't it?" said Allison.

Startled, Monica replied, "Oh, yes. It sure is."

"May I sit down?" Allison asked.

"Sure, why not?"

"My name is Sabrina, by the way. What about you?"

"My name is Monica. Nice to meet you, Sabrina."

"Nice to meet you too, Monica."

"Do you come here often? Because I've never seen you here before."

"Um, yes, actually. I come here quite often. I live about twenty minutes from here. Occasionally, I bring my little rug rats here to tire them out. They're the two carrot tops playing hide and seek. What about you? Do you come here often?"

Allison proudly lifted her Canon camera and said, "Not really. I just recently took up bird watching as a hobby. I'm still learning how to catalog the different species of birds, so I stop by here to get some practice every now and then. I live about fifteen minutes up the road."

"Wow, that's pretty cool. Your camera looks amazing. It looks like it costs a fortune."

"Yeah, it was pretty expensive."

"I sure wish I could afford something that nice, but raising two kids on a single income doesn't leave much room for self-indulgence, if you know what I mean."

"Yeah, I know what you mean. Here, give it a try."

Allison lifted the camera strap over her head before handing it to Monica.

"There! In those trees. Let's go get a close-up of those Blue Jays," said Allison.

"Um, okay. If you don't mind."

Allison then ushered Monica through the clearing to the edge of the woods to get a closer shot of the majestic birds. Monica took photo after photo, completely taken aback by the incredible display of imagery she captured. She had never experienced nature in its purest form before. Seeing the birds' vibrant colors filled her with an invigorating sense of joy. It gave her a glimpse through her late husband's eyes, allowing her to understand why he had loved the great outdoors so much.

"Wow, this is really cool," she said.

"I know. Don't you just love nature? Go ahead, take some more photos. I just bought some new rolls of film. I have plenty to share."

"Are you sure?"

"Yeah, don't worry about it."

"Okay. Well, if you insist."

It was Amy's turn to hide, and she thought she had found the perfect hiding spot. It was a place she was certain her sister Amanda would never find. She remembered her mommy had told them not to leave the playground, but she had to. She didn't like being 'it' all the time. So she hid behind the giant green garbage can next to the ladies restroom, where she could see Amanda coming from a mile away. That's why she jumped when she suddenly heard a deep voice behind her.

"Hi there, sweetheart. Are you lost?" the man asked.

"No. I'm playing hide and seek with my sister. Wanna play?" she replied.

"Of course. But first, I have something special for you. Do you like lollipops?"

"Ooh, yes! They're my favorite."

"Good, because I have one for you."

The man then reached into his jacket pocket, pulled out a red lollipop, and handed it to her.

"Can I have another one for my sister? She likes them, too," said Amy.

"Sure. But first, you have to eat yours quickly because we can't let your mommy know. She wouldn't want you to have too much sugar. So hurry up."

"Okay."

Amy quickly unwrapped her lollipop and bit off a chunk, trying to consume as much of it as possible before her mother could spoil her fun.

After swallowing most of the sucker, she whined, "This lollipop tastes weird. I don't feel good."

The man knelt, picked up the wrapper, and looked around suspiciously, making sure no one noticed him.

Amy groaned, "I want my mommy," and turned to walk away.

She tried to make her way back to her mother's loving arms. Unfortunately, she only managed to take a few steps before collapsing into the stranger's waiting arms.

Monica handed Allison back her camera and said, "Thanks a lot, but I should be heading back."

"Oh, okay. Maybe we could do this again sometime."

"Yeah, that would be nice. Do you have a phone number where I could reach you? I'll give you a call sometime."

"Yeah, I do, but could you give me yours instead? I'm kinda in between places right now. You know how it is."

"Oh yes, I know exactly what you mean. C'mon, I have a pen in my purse."

Allison unzipped her fanny pack and said, "No need. I have one right here."

Allison then handed Monica a pen and a Post-it note. After Monica returned the pen and paper, she said, "I really should be heading back."

"Okay, cool. I'll walk you back."

"Oh, look! Here come my angels now."

At first glance, Monica immediately noticed that Amanda was alone, causing her to speed up her pace.

Amanda whined, "Mommy, Mommy, I can't find Amy. She's cheating. You said we can't leave the playground."

"What do you mean you can't find your sister? Where is she?" asked Monica.

"I don't know, Mommy."

Monica snatched Amanda up without breaking stride and spun around frantically, scanning the entire park. "I don't see my daughter. I need you to help me find her," she said in a shuddering voice.

"Okay, what's her name?" Allison replied.

"Ammmmmmmy!" Monica shouted at the top of her lungs.

"Got it. Let's ask that couple over there if they've seen her. Those other kids are with them, right? They were there the whole time. I'm sure she's fine."

Monica jogged toward a unsuspecting teenage couple, who were clearly high out of their minds. They were shocked to see her approaching with such urgency, but the THC they had smoked caused them to react leisurely.

"Did either of you see my daughter? Her identical twin," Monica asked, pointing to Amanda. "She was playing over there with the other kids."

"No, ma'am. She's not here?" asked the John Lennon look-alike.

Monica mumbled, "Obviously not. Fucking hippies," before heading off to the playground.

"I'll go check the restroom," said Allison.

Monica asked all four children, one by one, if they had seen Amy, but each child said no. Then, it suddenly occurred to Monica that if Amy was somehow lost, the longer it took them to find her, the more danger she was in.

She shouted at the couple, "Well, don't just stand there! Help me find my baby!"

The two potheads scrambled to gather the kids to help Monica look for Amy. The last thing Ashley wanted was for the police to discover that she had been smoking marijuana with her boyfriend instead of monitoring the children. Monica made her way toward the bathroom, screaming Amy's name, hoping for a response. Even a cry for help would've eased her mind at that point.

"This isn't funny anymore, Amy!" Monica yelled. "Stop hiding from Mommy. You're scaring me! It's time to go! Now!"

Monica began to sweat as she realized she had practically searched the entire park. The only place she hadn't yet checked was the bathrooms, and that was only because Allison had already opted to do so. However, although she believed Allison had no ill intentions, Monica felt obligated to check it out herself. She couldn't possibly leave any stone unturned—not in a situation as dire as one of her children going missing.

She entered the bathroom, shielding Amanda from its walls while calling for Amy. After realizing Amy was nowhere to be found, she checked stall after stall, praying her daughter was playing a foolish joke on her.

"No, no, no," she cried.

"What's wrong, Mommy? Why are you crying?" asked Amanda.

"I can't find your sister."

Monica then sat Amanda down and gently held her face. "Baby, I need you to tell me exactly where you saw her last," she said.

"Umm... It was my turn to be it, so I went by the slide and closed my eyes to count. When I was looking for her, I couldn't find her. I don't know, Mommy, I'm sorry."

Amanda started sobbing because she understood something was wrong and felt she was to blame.

"It's okay, babygirl. C'mon, let's go!"

Monica exited the bathroom, determined to do whatever it took to find her missing child. She circled the bathroom, desperately calling out for Amy. Then it suddenly dawned on her—Allison was nowhere to be found. Things were now becoming stranger by the second.

Ashley jogged over to Monica and said, "I'll go check up the street. Maybe she just wandered off or something."

Monica replied, "Okay. Oh wait, did you see what happened to the lady I was with? The one with the expensive camera."

"Umm, no, ma'am. I'm sorry, I didn't."

"Okay, well, do you have a car? Because we can cover more ground if you do."

"Umm, yes, but—"

"But what? My baby is missing."

"Uh, nothing, ma'am. My boyfriend, he has a car. He can take you. I'll stay here with the kids in case she shows up." She yelled, "Hey, babe! Give this nice lady a ride to find her missing daughter!"

He replied, "Okay, cool. I'm Zack, by the way," as he walked up.

"I'm Monica. Where's your car parked, Zack?"

Zack pointed and said, "Over there. Follow me."

"You look stoned, Zack. You don't mind if I drive, do you?"

He said, "No, ma'am, I don't mind," and handed her his keys.

Meanwhile, Allison casually walked toward an off-yellow Volkswagen Beetle and opened the passenger side door. She grabbed Brandon's face and gave him a sloppy kiss before climbing inside and closing the door.

"We did it, babe," she said, snatching off her brunette wig and throwing it on the floor.

"You know I'd do anything for you, pumpkin," Brandon replied.

Allison stared intently at Amy in the back seat with admiration. She was captivated by how precious the child looked as she slept peacefully. Finally, she was about to have the family she had always deserved. Now they could be a complete household—picnics, birthday parties, PTA meetings, and the whole works. She knew it was all part of God's divine plan. He was restoring the damage her father had inflicted upon her. It was her father's fault she couldn't have children of her own, thanks to the severe damage he caused to her cervix from repeatedly raping her at such a young age.

Allison rubbed Brandon's head and said, "Let's go, baby. This place will be swarming with police soon."

"Away we go!" he replied, starting up the engine.

"I can't wait to show Kimberly her new home. I'm going to be such a great mom."

"I know you are, pumpkin. You're going to be the best mother in the world."

About The Author

• • •

William Travis III is a highly talented writer. He has been writing poetry and rap lyrics since the age of eleven. However, his passion for writing gradually grew, and so did his aspirations. He desired to reach a broader audience so his words could be more impactful to the world. Therefore, he began writing novels, children's books, and screenplays.

Also Available

* 9 7 8 9 6 9 5 8 9 2 3 7 4 *